Happy reading —

Becki Willis

TANGIBLE
SPIRITS

Becki Willis

ISBN: 0998790206
ISBN 13: 9780998790206

BOOKS BY BECKI WILLIS

He Kills Me, He Kills Me Not
Forgotten Boxes
Tangible Spirits
<u>Mirrors Don't Lie Series</u>
 The Girl from Her Mirror, Book 1
 Mirror, Mirror on Her Wall, Book 2
 Light from Her Mirror, Book 3

<u>The Sisters, Texas Mystery Series</u>
 Chicken Scratch, Book 1
 When the Stars Fall, Book 2
 Stipulations and Complications, Book 3
 Home Again: Starting Over, Book 4
 Genny's Ballad, Book 5

SPECIAL NOTE FROM THE AUTHOR

The following story is set in the very real town of Jerome, Arizona and, to the best of my knowledge, the historical anecdotes are true. However, I've taken the liberty of blending bits of truth, bits of fancy, to craft this story. While the landmarks—including the *Sliding Jail, Cuban Queen Bordello,* and the old *Bartlett Hotel*—are real, all businesses and characters exist only in my imagination. The blasts, Spanish Expeditions, and Executive Order 6102 are all a matter of record.

My husband and I first visited Jerome in May, where the unique architecture of the town and the ghost legends immediately intrigued me. In September, my daughter and I returned to do in-depth research. We stayed in a "haunted" hotel, engaged in ghost tours, and soaked up as much lore, legend, and history as possible. Thank you, Winter, for helping me research and for making it a fun and productive mother/daughter trip!

I also want to thank Jane Goddard for her invaluable information, dienel96 for a wonderful cover, and *you* for reading.

1

Dead was dead. Gera didn't believe in ghosts.

That was why this assignment rankled her so. Why was she, of all people, assigned to a story about ghosts? The magazine might as well have sent her to the North Pole to interview Santa Claus himself.

It was bad enough being surrounded by desert. Miles and miles of barren terrain, the flat Arizona landscape broken only by scattered saguaro cacti and shrubs. No real trees to speak of. Plenty of bushy, thorny shrubs and desert plants. The most interesting thing she had seen so far was the odd warning sign for a wild donkey crossing.

With rays of heat beaming down from the cloudless azure sky, today promised to be a scorcher, but she could handle the heat. The dry, blustery wind was a nuisance, sweeping across her skin like sandpaper and playing havoc with her hair. Why had she even bothered with a comb this morning? She could simply add gel to the spikes and go for that edgy, badass look so many reporters favored.

Lord knew she needed all the edge she could get.

The further north she traveled, away from the armed cacti that stood like sentries along the roadside, the elevation climbed. The famed saguaros of the Sonora desert gave way to a multitude of prickly pear, intermingled with bushy shrubs and a few more trees. The Black Hills of Yavapai County rose in the distance, teasing the eye with variety, beckoning travelers onward.

Pulling Gera closer to her assignment.

"There are ghosts in them thar hills," she drawled aloud. Her voice dripped with sarcasm.

"Your first big story with the rag, and it may be your last." Gera gave voice to the pessimistic thought as she sped down the highway, racing toward the faraway mountains. She grumbled to an empty audience in her rented sedan, giving free reign to her frustrations. "I don't know what Jillian was thinking, sending me in for this one. I wanted to cover the story on the new cancer hospital opening in Dallas. Seniority shouldn't be the only deciding factor on who gets what story, should it? Enthusiasm should count for something. *Believability* should count for something! How am I supposed to give a fair and unbiased report on something I don't even believe exists?"

Some people, such as her Aunt Geraldine, believed that lives were recycled. How else, her aunt insisted, did one explain déjà vu, that sense of walking into a building one had never been in before, and knowing its exact layout and feel, right down to the rear exit? The obvious answer, according to her aunt, was that one had been there before, in another life.

And how, her namesake wanted to know, did she explain love at first sight, if not for the fact that souls were already acquainted from another time, another life? How did she explain pets that were as smart as human beings, if not for reincarnation? Life was simply too precious to discard with the cessation of breath. Aunt Geraldine believed that when one host body died, the soul found another body in which to reside.

Other people, such as her grandmother, believed that upon death, souls were sent either to Heaven or to Hell, depending on one's time here on Earth. The good, pious souls were granted eternal life. The disobedient were banished to the devil.

Gera liked the thought of eternal life, but she still had her doubts. Grams dragged her along to Sunday school when she was a little girl. Taught her about the Bible and the perils of good and evil. Yet her grandmother was also the one to tell her about the Easter Bunny and the magical Tooth Fairy, not to mention a jolly old elf that drove a team of miniature reindeer upon people's rooftops. Grams—who never lied—had a theory about how one man could deliver presents to good little boys and girls around the world at seemingly the same time. Something about wind currents and the flux in temperatures worldwide, compounded by time zones and language barriers. The strange phenomenon caused some clocks to stall inexplicably, while others raced forward, bringing time to a virtual standstill for the course of one evening. Much to young Gera's dismay, none of those fanciful notions panned out. Would the concept of Heaven be any different?

Still others believed in a third option. Some—though certainly not Gera Stapleton—believed that a person's spirit could linger on Earth before crossing over to the other side. Something to do with unfinished business in life.

But did anyone ever have their lives pulled together and neatly tied with a bow? Didn't everyone leave behind unfinished business? While Gera liked the thought of one last opportunity to right the wrongs she had done in life, even from the grave, the idea sounded no more plausible than streets paved in gold.

Her co-worker Ramon was one such believer. During a séance last fall, the seasoned reporter insisted he had spoken with a beloved relative who was taken from life too soon. Ramon volunteered as a ghost-walk tour guide in downtown Notre Dame. He refused to accept money for his time, saying it was an honor to walk among the spirits and share their stories. Her co-worker was sincere in his belief, as certain about ghostly spirits as Grams was about the Holy Spirit and Aunt Geraldine was about reincarnation.

In Gera's mind, *dead* was just that—dead. No afterlife, no recycled spirits, no caught between worlds. Just dead.

She stewed for a while, railing against the injustice of it all. Ramon was the obvious choice for this story. His '08 Corolla had bumper stickers that said, 'I see dead people' and 'I'd rather be ghost hunting.' He watched the full array of television programs devoted to spirit sightings and haunted places. Ramon would've done this story better justice than she could. Even Gera knew that.

Ghost stories were all the rage these days. A few years ago, just the rumor of being haunted was a stigma hotels could little afford. These days, an in-house ghost meant instant fame and fortune.

The town of Jerome, Arizona was a perfect example. According to locals, ghosts freely roamed through the small town of less than five hundred people. Instead of scaring visitors away, tourists flocked to the mountainside community, hoping to see the visions for themselves. Television shows and ghost hunters alike joined the melee, eager to capture the spirits on film or meter. Not so long ago, the historic mining town was destined for extinction. Now it enjoyed new life through old spirits, and gave fresh meaning to the term 'Arizona ghost town.'

The town even had its very own resident ghost, a friendly apparition named Mac. Residents spoke of him as if he were an old friend. However, a recent string of mischief and petty crimes had taken place in the small town, and rumor had it that Mac was to blame. *When It Happens Magazine* thought it was worth investigating, so they sent in their newest reporter, Gera Stapleton. They even booked her in one of the town's more notoriously known haunted hotels.

"I just hope the ghosts don't rattle their chains and moan all night long. I need all the beauty rest I can get." She glanced into the visor mirror. "Especially with this hair."

Half an hour later, Gera turned off the interstate. The terrain here was higher and dotted with green. Not nearly as high as the San Francisco Peaks in the distance, but at least the dirt swelled with hills and valleys, many of them congested with actual green, leafy trees.

Until now, Gera hadn't realized how fond she was of the willowy giants. Trees reminded her of a simpler, gentler time, when she and her cousins climbed in the trees at their grandmother's farm. They would hang upside down from the sturdy limbs, studying the clouds as they rolled across the sky on a lazy summer afternoon. Robbed a snack from crab apple and pear trees heavy with fruit. Built a fort in a favorite old oak, where they spent long hours slaying dragons and fighting off pirates, hiding from Indian attacks and enemy soldiers. And on rare occasions, when her male cousins agreed, they played house, where she stirred up dishes of mud, leaves, and pecans, and served them in salvaged bits of pottery and metal scavenged from the burn pile.

A smile lingered on Gera's face as she recalled the fun they had over those long summer visits. The farm was gone now, sold to a developer who turned the orchards into a strip mall and the goat meadow into an apartment building. One of those upscale ones, with a coffee shop and deli on the ground floor, and boutiques that sold trendy clothing, scented soaps, and fake tans. Progress, they called it.

The further north Gera traveled, the more impressed she became.

"Oh, wow. Now this is gorgeous!" Gera wiggled excitedly in her seat, thrilled to see the impressive red rock formations looming ahead. She thought of all those old westerns her father liked to watch on Saturday afternoons, the ones with bigger-than-life heroes cast against backdrops just like these.

After stopping for a bite to eat in the picturesque town of Sedona, she hit the road with more enthusiasm. Iconic formations gave way to clustered canyons and foothills. As the elevation rose, so did her spirits. She passed through an idyllic canyon canopied by trees. Drove alongside a gurgling river stream. Gazed up at impressive rocky ledges on either side of the road. Hugged mountain curves and prayed no one crossed the yellow line that separated her lane from the oncoming traffic.

She hoped to reach Jerome before dusk. She needed daylight as she traversed the squiggled blacktop road weaving its way up Mingus Mountain. A series of switchbacks and sharp curves sharpened her awareness and set her nerves on edge. Going up wasn't so bad. It was coming down that already worried her.

Signs along the roadway tracked her progress. Two more miles to Jerome. Another sharp curve, another incline. Another sign, this one announcing the altitude of five thousand feet. A few more twists, and she had just one mile to go.

The first glimpse of the town came into view. A few rooftops jutted through the trees, perched along a ledge on the side of Cleopatra Hill. The structures at the top of the mountain's peak beckoned her, but after a half dozen switchbacks and yet another mile, she still hadn't reached them. She passed a sign welcoming her to Jerome, Arizona, Elevation 5246, Founded 1876.

More buildings came into view, stacked one upon the other in layers against the mountain. Gera stared in amazement at the many tiers of the town. She had read somewhere that the town was propped against a thirty-degree slope, two thousand feet above the Verde Valley floor. Until now, she hadn't realized how precarious thirty degrees would look. There had to be at least fifteen hundred vertical feet between the top and bottom tiers of the town.

"This could be interesting, in a slide-off-the-mountain kind of way," she decided aloud. She peered through the windshield, trying to get a better look at the mountaintop ahead. "Maybe this gig won't be so bad, after all."

She made another curve and followed the one-way street up yet another hill. Hull Street led past a tiny string of old buildings, through parking spaces on either side of the street, past an oddly leaning stone structure, and to another small collection of buildings at the top of the hill. The town's main street was one block over.

The one marked with all the crime scene tape and the coroner's van.

2

Emergency vehicles lined the streets, their red and blue strobe lights casting an unnatural glow into the fading light of day. It had taken longer to wind up the mountain than she anticipated.

The journalist inside her demanded that she stop, even before she saw the police officer. He waved her down, stepping up to the side of her vehicle with his yellow flashing wand.

"Sorry, but I need to ask you to wait for a few minutes while crews work the scene."

"What happened, Officer?"

"Tending to a bit of business, Miss," he said evasively.

Working a hunch, Gera flashed her press badge. "I'm with the press."

The officer looked surprised. "How did you guys already get wind of this? We just found the body, not twenty minutes ago." He waved his wand to the car behind her, halting their progress. "Only reason the coroner is here is 'cause he was already on the mountain. This is Tuesday night poker with the boys."

He didn't question which media she was affiliated with, so Gera took it as a sign. Here was her chance to work a real story, not some fluff piece about a ghost. "Where do I park?" she asked quickly, taking advantage of the moment.

"Uh, just pull down there in the parking lot and walk up the hill," he decided. "Show them your badge and tell them Royce cleared you."

"Thanks, Royce!"

Gera whipped the car into the empty parking area to her left. Grabbing her camera and her recorder, she looped her badge lanyard over her head as she made her way up the hillside. Emergency vehicles blocked off the street directly in front of her, leaving her pathway clear.

The building facing her was but a skeleton. At least two stories of brick, stone, and metal railings. Intriguing arches and empty chambers. Gera could only see the side profile of the gutted structure. The front of the building faced Main Street, parallel to the one she arrived upon. A growing crowd assembled there, cast in the strobing shadows of blue and red.

A uniformed man stepped from the gathering shadows and blocked her progress. "Sorry, Miss, this entire block is quarantined."

"It's okay, I'm with the press." She flashed her badge with breezy confidence. "Royce already cleared me." She turned and waved down the hill, pretending the other man could see.

The officer squinted his eyes, studying her as if he noticed vines sprouting from her ears. "Who called you?" he demanded. "I've never seen you before."

Gera countered with, "Does it really matter?" She looked beyond him, to the stretcher lifted from the lower levels of the ruins. "What happened?"

The officer turned to watch the progress of his fellow first responders. "Looks like Abe Cunningham fell to his death."

Gera eyed the ornate iron railings across the front of the missing wall, thinking they were reminiscent of a jail cell. Too tall to go over, too narrow to slip between, the bars created an effective barrier between the sidewalk and the exposed stone floor below. She edged closer, trying to judge the distance of the fall. From the sidewalk, it would be an easy fifteen feet. Her eyes scanned the brick walls on two sides of the skeletal structure, imagining how a person might scale the excessive height in order to plummet to their death. The buildings were from another era, when twelve and fifteen-foot ceilings were standard. At one time, this had been a two-story building with a sub-level, even though the sky was now its only ceiling.

"How did he get through?" She had the recorder whirring, awaiting his reply.

"Best as we can tell, Mac pushed him."

Gera tried, but she couldn't temper the astonishment that bled into her voice. "Mac? You're blaming a ghost for this death?"

The officer pushed the hat up from his forehead and scratched at the crease it left behind. "Folks reported seeing ole Mac right here on the corner, minutes before Abe came along. No one else was on the sidewalk. Seems to be the only explanation so far."

"Assuming I believed the ghost was responsible—and that is a huge assumption, by the way—how do you explain Abe getting from this sidewalk to that lower level?" Gera gestured with her hands to mark each spot. "Even if this 'ghost' could slip between the bars, how do you explain a full-grown man getting past them?"

She raised a valid argument, but the officer wasn't impressed. Instead, he looked her over again. His gaze was skeptical. "Who did you say you were?"

She thrust out her hand for a firm handshake. "Gera Stapleton, *When It Happens Magazine*. And you are?"

"Officer Mike Cooper."

"So, Officer Cooper, who discovered Mr. Cunningham's body?"

"That would be Grant Young," he said. He nodded to the man speaking to another officer in low, confidential tones. "He noticed Abe lying on the floor below and immediately called for help, but it was too late. Abe was already gone."

"Do you have any idea how long he had been down there?"

"Witnesses saw him pass along the street less than an hour ago, so not long."

"And you don't think it was a suicide?"

The policeman gave her a sharp look. "Why would Abe want to kill himself?"

"I have no idea. You tell me."

"Now, look. If you're talking about that misunderstanding with the bank, he got all that cleared up..."

Using an old reporter trick, Gera looked non-convinced, even as she shrugged. "If you say so."

On the defensive for his late friend, the officer unwittingly stepped into her trap. "What? You think there really was something to him owing all that money in back taxes?"

"I never said that."

"But you insinuated it," he accused. His lips curled in derision. "All you reporters are the same. You get one whiff of controversy, and you blow it all out of proportion. So Abe got a little behind in his taxes. So what? He paid them in full before the state started proceedings. There's no way he would've offed himself over that, so don't even go there."

Somewhat amused at the officer's angry retort to her fishing expedition, Gera made nice and backed off. "You know what? I think you're right. But tell me. Why would your friendly ghost Mac want to kill Abe?"

"Because lately, Mac hasn't been so friendly."

"Why do you think that is?" She cocked her head to one side, pretending not to be asking about the personality quirks of a ghost, of all things. Had her journalism degree come down to this?

She worked long and hard to get that degree. She started college later in life than most of her classmates, at least six years older than the incoming freshman class. Even after working two jobs all that time to pay tuition, she only had enough saved up for one year. During her eighteen-month hiatus from school, she worked four part-time jobs. There had been times when she met herself coming and going, juggling the different schedules as she worked herself to a frazzle and enrolled in online classes. The grueling pace almost landed her in the hospital. When she scored a position at the newspaper, doing grunge work for the assistant editor's assistant, she allowed herself the luxury of quitting one of her jobs. Her stint as a night janitor was the first to go, even though it paid slightly more than her gig at Crispy Chicken Delight. If she ever saw a mop bucket or a deep fryer again in this lifetime, it would be too soon for her. It took her longer than expected, but last year, at the ripe old age of thirty-one, Gera trotted across the stage and accepted her diploma.

It was the single greatest accomplishment in her life.

And here she squandered that degree, inquiring about a ghost who supposedly killed a man.

Officer Cooper never knew how difficult it was for Gera to ask that question, how hard it was for her to keep the look of interest upon her face. He thought it perfectly normal to discuss a ghost.

He actually looked worried. "We haven't figured that out yet. For almost eighty years, ole Mac has been roaming this town, friendly as can be. Been known to help out more than a few times, stepping in to guide someone out of the way of traffic, finding lost items, keeping watch over the town when times were hard. One time, back when I was just a kid, little Dewey Miles fell down in one of the old mine shafts. Mac was the one to lead searchers right to the boy. So, you can see why we're all stumped, wondering what the heck has gotten into him after all this time. I hate to say it, but Mac has been downright ornery these past few months." He looked over his shoulder, to the closing doors on the coroner's vehicle. "And now this."

No, Gera didn't see. She didn't see how an entire town could be so naive. An abandoned mineshaft was the obvious place to look for a missing child. Lost items turned up every day, even without the benefit of a ghost. Why did they credit a dead man for these everyday deeds? And why did they blame him now for a death?

Jillian briefed her on the town's history—brief being the operative word—before Gera boarded the plane, but the details were still sparse. Perhaps Officer Cooper could fill in some of the gaps.

"So, Mac has been roaming these streets for almost eighty years, huh?" She tried her best to sound conversational. In her wildest imaginations, this was never a conversation she saw herself in.

The policeman nodded. "That's right. Jerome was a big mining town, back in the day. Pulled over thirty-three million tons of copper, gold, silver, and more from the depths of these mountains; over a billion dollars' worth, even way back then. Old Horace McGruder—Mac to his friends—was killed in a blasting accident back in '38, the same one that sent our jail over there sliding down the hill." He nodded toward the oddly slanted structure Gera noticed on the way into town. "He's been seen roaming around town ever since. When they pulled his body from the blast site, he was missing an ear. Some folks say he's been searching for it all these years, not willing to cross over until he was a whole man again."

Not just a ghost, but a one-eared ghost. Now that was a new one.

"Hey, Mike!"

The officer turned to see who called his name. Gera knew her time was slipping away.

"Just one more thing before you go," she pressed. "Does Abe Cunningham have a family?"

His face was suitably mournful. "He did," he said, sadly emphasizing the past tense. "He and Ruth have been married forever. They must have at least a dozen grandchildren. This will hit them hard."

"Where did Mr. Cunningham live?"

Irritation crossed the policeman's face. "Now look, don't you go snooping around Ruth, stirring up troubles where none exist."

Gera shook her head in denial. "For identification pur- poses," she was quick to assure him.

An odd look replaced the irritation. His nose flared, as if he had gotten wind of a foul smell. "Do you feel that?" His voice was lower than before.

A slight breeze stirred the evening air. After the heat of the day, it was a welcomed respite. "The breeze? Yes, it's nice."

He shook his head. "Not the breeze. The chill. One of them is here."

Gera looked around. "One of whom? One of Abe's family?"

"No. One of the ghosts."

With that very odd statement, the officer turned away to see to his duties, leaving Gera there alone on the sidewalk.

Just her and the ghost.

She scoffed at the idea and moved back to the hollowed-out building, the one where Abe Cunningham's body had been found. Try as she might, she still couldn't imagine how a grown man, no matter how thin or how tall, could possibly penetrate the bars surrounding the entire structure. Not even a child could press between the narrowly spaced spindles. A cat, yes. A person, impossible.

She snapped off several photographs before a different lawman approached her.

"This is a crime scene. I'll have to ask you to leave."

"It's okay, Officer. I'm a—" The words died on her lips as she turned and saw the man who spoke.

He was a western character straight from the movies, come to life from those old movies her father liked so well. Rawboned features and a tough attitude, with a thick shock of rusty brown hair, drooping handlebar mustache, and sharp, piercing eyes.

A smirk lifted one side of his mouth. "You were saying?"

Snapping out of her trance, Gera grabbed her press badge and wiggled it in front of his face. "I'm a reporter."

His lips thinned into a narrow ribbon of disapproval. "I'm the chief of police. And we didn't call the press."

Gera offered a bright smile. Her father always insisted it was her best feature. She had a smile like her mother, he said. Then his eyes would grow troubled, and he would fall into one of his strange moods. More often than not, he would shuffle off to the den and plop down in his easy chair, losing his cares in the dependable plot of a shoot-em-up western and a can of beer.

"A happy coincidence, I suppose," Gera said now, flashing her mother's smile. "I'm booked at *The Dove Hotel* for the entire week."

"In that case, you can come back tomorrow and take all the pictures you like. Right now, you're standing in my crime scene." His tone brooked no argument. Neither did his steady glare.

"Two questions before I go." Gera ignored the steely look in his eyes and barged ahead. "One, do you have any suspects or persons of interest? And a ghost doesn't count."

Something flashed in his gaze. She thought it was most likely surprise. "No comment."

She had expected as much. "Okay, question two. Where is *The Dove?*"

He pointed to the mountain behind them. "Up there. Follow this road, turn beside the church, and watch for signs. You can't miss it."

"Thanks, Officer—" She stopped abruptly, realizing they had foregone introductions. "I'm sorry, I didn't catch your name."

"Miles Anderson."

She thrust her hand forward. "Gera Stapleton, *When It Happens Magazine.*"

He shook her hand, the automatic action terse and forced. "Thanks for the directions. And I will see you tomorrow morning."

He made no reply, but as he turned away, she thought she heard him mutter, "Not if I see you first."

Gera was slow to move away. She took more photos, documenting the milling crowd and the street beyond. She snapped candid shots of the people's faces, tight with shock and wrung with worry. Some of their faces were filled with revulsion. These people's eyes skittered away from the crime scene, not yet willing to accept that one of their own had been murdered. Other faces held horrified fascination, their eyes shimmering with unadulterated greed. No matter how appalling or how close to home this death hit, some of the townspeople were hungry for more. They craved a glimpse of horror.

Without a word, Gera slipped quietly among the people, listening to snatches of conversation and the murmur of low, shocked voices.

"—couldn't see a face, but it looked like Abe Cunningham's red shirt and boots."

"Poor Ruth. This might be the straw that breaks the camel's back. I don't know how much more that poor woman can take."

"Things like this just don't happen here."

"…Ever since Mac turned on us, strange things have been happening. Haven't you noticed?"

"Mac's always been so friendly. Why would he turn on us now?"

"Leroy says it's the moon. A black moon, he called it."

"…did a body get down there and through those bars?"

"I heard Mac picked him up and threw him over the top. Came crashing down like a sack of potatoes."

"…Someone said it was Abe. Tell me it wasn't. He finally got all that settled with the bank and now this! Poor Ruth."

"…Terri Perkins saw Mac, plain as day. Came floating down the street, not minutes before Abe sauntered by. Next thing we knew, Grant Young was calling for help. He was the one to find Abe, you know."

"…over at the hardware store just this morning. He was buying paint for their new fence."

"A shame, that's what this is. No matter who they just loaded into the wagon, it's a pure shame."

Officer Cooper tried to corral the crowd's attention. "Folks, there's nothing more to see here. You might as well go on home."

"What happened, Mike?" someone called from the back. "Who was it?"

"We can't release the details just yet, Bobby. You know that. Now you go on home, and see what Ginger cooked you for supper."

"Hell, Mike, Ginger don't cook. You know that."

A chuckle passed through the crowd and a few of the onlookers began to disperse. Tourists lost interest in the scene and drifted on, unconcerned with matters that didn't involve them. Gera attempted to question a few of the first responders, but they brushed her aside as they tended their duties of securing and surveying the scene.

With nothing more to see tonight, Gera soon gave up and headed toward the hotel.

3

A narrow, patched blacktop road squiggled up the hill, twisting and turning at odd angles to navigate the steep mountainside. Gera stared at her destination with trepidation. She had seen trails in the woods that looked more promising than this.

The Dove perched precariously on a rocky bit of earth, wedged between the road out front and the mountain behind it. With no room for a walkway, not even a curb, one corner of the columned front porch planted itself mere inches from the pavement.

To its credit, the structure rose straight and tall, with no inclination to lean away from the rocks. Gera counted three stories, all laced with a long porch across the front. The side view revealed yet another level, much of it submerged deep into the mountain.

As dusk gathered thick and murky for the evening to come, floodlights illuminated the hotel. Twinkling party lights gave the somber structure a merry feel and trailed their way to a small garden out back, hinting at hidden pleasures nestled into the rock.

Gera spotted a driveway tucked amid the spindly trees. It opened into a parking area just large enough for a dozen or less vehicles. Parking was no problem; only two other cars were in sight.

As she swung her rental into the very first space, her unease spiked. What kind of hotel had Jillian booked for her? Gera didn't expect luxury, but there were a few necessities she was particular about, running water and electricity being two of them. What if she was the only guest booked in the rambling old structure? Gera thought of a movie she had seen once, about a demented innkeeper who lured innocent victims into his lair and locked them away.

So maybe she would just peek inside, before she brought in her suitcase...

With no room for a front entrance, access to the porch came from either side. LED ground lights, twinkling like a thousand midnight stars, guided her path as Gera ascended the stone steps. Everything not bricked was painted an appropriate dove gray, save for the trim. The trim was the color of bright, freshly flowing blood.

Gera pretended not to notice how the boards creaked beneath her feet, or how the door moaned in sorrow as she pushed it open. She concentrated on the cheerful jingle of the overhead bell.

The interior was better than she hoped. It could use an update, but Gera admitted it possessed an antiquated sort of charm. An impressive staircase spindled its way through the very center of the old hotel, stringing all four stories together in a single stairwell. A chilling thought crossed

Gera's mind—a fall from either of the top two floors would be deadly.

"Good evening. Welcome to *The Dove Hotel.*"

The pleasant voice drew her attention away from the staircase and to the check-in desk on the left. With its intricate carvings made of gleaming mahogany and polished copper, the vintage counter was from another era, as were the ancient switchboard system and old-fashioned mail grid behind it. Both pre-dated digital messaging and bar-coded plastic by the better part of a century.

A man stood behind the counter with a friendly and expectant smile. "May I help you?" he offered.

She couldn't very well admit the truth. *Yes, thank you, I came in to see if the coast was clear from psychotic innkeepers and murderers.*

Gera hoped her smile looked more confident than it felt. "Yes, I have a reservation."

His smile broadened. "You must be Gera Stapleton. We've been expecting you."

Odd, how a single statement could, at once, be both pleasing yet disconcerting. The personal recognition was nice, and in stark contrast to hotel chains, where faces and patrons changed as often as the bedsheets. Yet a disturbing thought nibbled at the edge of her mind. *They were waiting for her.*

Step into my parlor, said the spider to the fly.

Her smile somewhat stilted, Gera shoved the crazy thought aside and pushed herself toward the counter. "Yes, that would be me," she confirmed.

"We have you booked for a third-floor suite. The view is exceptional." Behind black-rimmed glasses, the man's blue eyes twinkled as if he knew a secret.

"That sounds fine," she murmured.

"If you'll just fill this form out, I'll get your key."

Gera tried to keep her expectations high, even when he handed her an old-fashioned metal key dangling from a wooden fob. No high-tech electronic keypads here, meaning high-speed internet was probably out of the question.

"We serve a full complimentary breakfast every morning from six to nine in the dining room downstairs. The restaurant closes tonight at nine, so you still have time to grab a bite to eat. Instructions to connect to our free internet are in your room."

She visibly brightened. "So, you do have internet."

His eyes twinkled again. "Don't let the elevator fool you. We do have modern conveniences, running water included."

His playful smile was disarming.

It was an odd reference to make. "The elevator?" Gera questioned with a frown.

He peered over the counter at her feet, noting the absence of any luggage. "If you need help bringing in your luggage, I will be happy to assist you."

"No, I can manage, but thank you."

"I'll show you up to your room whenever you're ready."

Again, the personalized attention could be charming, could be creepy. She decided to go with the former as she returned to the car for her suitcase. Surely, she could endure one night here. If she was too uncomfortable, she could always check out in the morning and relocate.

As she made her way across the darkening path, Gera saw movement in the shadows near the rear of the house. She was encouraged to see a woman lift her hand in greeting. At least there was someone else on the property.

The man from the front desk met her on the porch and offered to take her luggage and camera case. "I'll show you how to operate the elevator," he said.

Where did he think she came from, a cave? "I'm familiar with elevators."

He ignored her smug retort with an amused grin. "Not with this one, you're not."

A young woman had taken his place at the check-in desk. She offered a friendly smile as her colleague led Gera to the rear of the staircase.

"We still use the elevator original to the property, installed sometime in the thirties," the man explained as they rounded the staircase. His eyes twinkled again as he said, "This was high tech in its day."

Gera eyed the ancient contraption skeptically. A birdcage-style gate covered the front of the car.

Pushing the gate open, the man offered, "After you."

"This still works?" Gera asked dubiously.

"Like a charm."

She moved inside and watched as he pulled the gate closed first, and then a door made of burnished copper. "You'll need to remember to close the gate each time you exit," he advised. "Otherwise, the elevator won't come when you call for it. Do you have your room key? You'll need it to operate the elevator."

"Seriously?"

He nodded. "Seriously. Without a room key, the elevator will only access the dining room and the lobby. You'll insert your key here." He took her key from her to demonstrate. "Turn it like so, and press your floor number. And, voila." With the slightest lurch, the elevator cranked into action. Gera heard the gears churning as they slowly moved upward.

"The stairs would be quicker," she murmured.

"True. And you're more than welcome to use them. But I feel there is something quaint and charming about using the original old car. A piece of the past still with us, and all that." The man had a very nice smile. His glasses accentuated a strong jawline and bright blue eyes set into an arresting face. His hair was thick and dark, with a bit of a cowlick in the front. He seemed the friendly, helpful, all-American type. Very attractive, Gera belatedly realized, if one liked that in a man.

She had no time for charming men. She had a rendezvous with a ghost.

Gera glanced around the boxy car, taking in the intricate ironwork and the pressed copper tiles. "I take it this hotel dates back a few years."

"Built in 1907," the man confirmed, "but as a private home."

Her eyes snapped back to his. "Wow. How big was their family?" With a house this size, she imagined at least a dozen children.

"The couple was childless, but dozens of babies grew up here."

"This was a foster home?" she guessed. "Impressive."

The man shrugged, but his blue eyes twinkled. "I never said it was a foster home."

Gera frowned. "Then what was it? A private orphanage or something?"

"Promise not to judge."

Gera rolled her eyes. The guy had an irritating sort of charm about him. "Promise."

The elevator chugged to a stop. Reaching past her to open the double layer of doors, the man grinned as he motioned for her to exit the car. "Back in the day, *The Dove* was home to unwed women who found themselves in the family way. With so many brothels in town, let's just say few of the rooms ever stood empty."

His smile was infectious, but Gera tried to resist. She struggled for an appropriate scowl. "I'm staying in a half-way house for prostitutes."

"Actually, you'll be staying in the nursery." He closed the elevator grill and started down the long hallway with her luggage.

"The nursery?" She hurried to keep up with his long-legged pace.

"This was the labor and delivery ward. There was a private doctor and two nurses who lived on the premises."

"So, the name derives from soiled doves?"

"Exactly." He stopped at a door marked '405' in gleaming copper letters. "This is your suite. I hope you'll find everything to your liking. The balcony opens from two sides, but please make sure the doors are securely latched at night. Sometimes the wind will force them open."

"The wind? Or one of your famed ghosts?" Gera scoffed.

When his only reply was to arch his brows, Gera felt a pang of regret. She knew the guy was too good to be true. He obviously believed this whole ghost nonsense. He probably bought into the hype about the town's once-friendly ghost wreaking havoc upon the townspeople and murdering one of their own.

"If you need anything, lift the receiver. It will automatically connect you to the front desk. Someone will be available all night." He turned the key into the lock and held the door open for her. "Do you need help getting your suitcase inside?"

"No, no, I've got it from here." Realizing she should tip him, Gera scrounged around in her purse for a few bills.

He motioned her efforts away. "No, please. It has been my pleasure. By the way, my name is Jake if you should need anything further."

"Thanks, Jake, but I'm good."

"Remember, the dining room is open until nine tonight, and reopens in the morning at six."

"Got it."

He backed away with a slight bow. "Have a good evening."

As Gera watched him retrace his steps down the hall, she recognized the muted tune filtering through the hall. "Hey, is that a lullaby playing?"

He shot her a charming grin. "Gotta put all those babies to sleep," he claimed as he stepped into the elevator.

Even at this distance, she had no trouble hearing the clank of metal against metal as he closed the doors and engaged the ancient gears.

"Let's hope it works for me, too. Those ghosts may not rattle their chains and keep me awake, but that elevator just might," she grumbled.

With a rueful shake of her head, she dragged the suitcase behind her into the room.

First impressions of the hotel aside, the third-floor suite was a pleasant surprise. If nothing else, the space itself was more than generous.

A plump loveseat covered in flowered chintz beckoned her into the room. Gera had recently interviewed a designer who claimed the popular fabric was making a comeback. If the rest of the furnishings were any indication, she suspected this particular piece was more a holdover from the past than a trendsetter for the future. Still, something was oddly comforting in the eclectic mix of styles and eras. Gera liked how a funky art deco lamp reigned atop a Victorian side table, the one whose delicately turned legs were a study in understated elegance. She could already picture herself at the Queen Anne writing desk, fingers flying over her laptop. The accompanying chair gave off a mid-century Oriental vibe, but it looked comfortable enough. So did the armchair, strategically placed in direct view of a very sleek, modern, flat-screen television set.

The entire space vibrated with warmth. Not the kind that kicked up the thermometer, but rather toasted from the inside out, reminding Gera of childhood memories sweetened with hot cocoa and hand-knitted mittens.

"Definitely no ghosts here, not if temperature is any indication," she scoffed aloud. "This room is as cozy as one of Grams' flannel nightgowns. A bit dated, sure, but nicely done." She looked around again, nodding with satisfaction. "Nicely done," she repeated.

She wandered through the efficiency kitchen, fully stocked with the essentials should she be struck with the whim to cook. Gera knew she was more likely to be struck by lightning, but it never hurt to have a back-up plan. She doubted a town this small could have many dining options available to visitors. The adjacent bedroom had a queen-sized bed, its own flat-screen television, and a small loveseat tucked into one corner. By the time she reached the luxurious bathroom, Gera had to admit that not even her own apartment was this nice.

The outburst of voices startled her. Gera had poked her head into the marble shower, examining its dimensions as if she were a hotel critic writing her review. Her forehead banged against the stall door. Her heels slipped on the tile underfoot and she did a precarious balancing act, narrowly escaping a nasty fall. Her pulse ticked up a notch as she stumbled from the bathroom. Had someone entered her room? Or were the walls really so thin she could hear her neighbors?

She saw the culprit the moment she entered the sitting room. Moments ago, the television had been black. Now a western movie blared from its display.

"Jeez, could it be any louder?" she grumbled, covering her ears as she searched for the remote. She located the set beneath the cushions of the couch, only to discover it had no batteries.

She groped along the sides and back of the television frame until she felt the ridge of tiny buttons, lined up in a row like a spiked spine. She pressed the top button. A kaleidoscope of color flashed across the screen. The next button distorted the picture into a long, thin line. She fumbled around for another button. Cowboys shouted at her in Spanish. By the time she found the *Off* button, Gera predicted a hearing aid in her near future.

She unlatched the balcony doors and flung them outward, hoping to release the noise still echoing within her ears.

One step, and she came up short. The air escaped her lungs in a single rush.

Stepping onto the balcony was like stepping into the night sky. The earth fell away and only the stars surrounded her. Surely, she could reach her hand out and catch a bit of stardust on her fingertips.

Gera followed the curve of the balcony as it wrapped around to the front of the hotel, where she discovered that Jake was right. The view was impressive. Lights twinkled in every direction, fading into the vast openness of the valley beyond. She detected tiny clusters of light that shimmered in the distance, isolated homes and small towns scattered far, far away.

So, there is life beyond this mountain, she mused with a smile. It would be easy to imagine otherwise. Tucked against the mountainside, practically standing among the stars, it felt as if she were alone in the universe. Just her, the stars above, and the twinkling lights below.

And a ghost, she reminded herself. She couldn't forget about Mac, the one-eared ghost.

Notebook in hand, Gera took the ancient elevator down to the dining room. She planned to jot down thoughts and plot her next course of action as she ate.

A handful of diners were scattered around the rambling space, but she tried not to let the sparse population alarm her. At least she wasn't the only person here.

Gera overhead the conversation from the nearby table and knew the patrons were local citizens, celebrating a birthday. Ignoring the unease that skittered along her nerves—they weren't guests of the hotel—she picked up enough of the conversation to know they were discussing Abe Cunningham. To her amazement, the consensus among them was that Mac had committed the crime.

Was everyone in this town brainwashed into believing in ghosts?

Two men sat at another table, dissecting graphs and charts as they ate their meal; traveling businessmen, no doubt, and probably staying here at *The Dove*. She could include the starry-eyed couple at the far table into the count, as well, if the chunky key fob she spotted was any indication.

Gera relaxed enough to enjoy her meal. To her delight, the restaurant employed a five-star chef and the meal was delicious. A nice glass of wine soothed her tense muscles. A second glass numbed the sting of a hopeless assignment.

After indulging in a slice of cheesecake for dessert, Gera opted to take the stairs up to the lobby, where she stopped by the front desk.

The young woman she had seen earlier was behind the counter, scrolling through the internet. She looked up and greeted Gera with a smile.

"Good evening, Miss Stapleton. What can we do for you?"

"I need some batteries for the remote control."

"Certainly. I'm so sorry about that." The girl rummaged beneath the counter with a series of bumps and knocks before presenting her with a small box of AA batteries. "I trust the room is to your liking?"

"Other than a rogue television set that comes on at full volume, it's lovely."

The young woman's smile faded into a perturbed frown. "I swear, half of our ghosts must've been the children that were born here. Some of their antics are so elementary."

Not at all the reply Gera would've expected, but she decided to play along. "Oh? What do you mean?"

"The ghosts are bad about pulling childish pranks, like the one you experienced. They might turn on a television, or water faucets, or lights in the middle of the night. Sometimes they leave little gifts, like rubber balls and paper airplanes. More often they hide things… remote controls, bars of soap, wash clothes, keys, that sort of thing."

Gera had a more reasonable explanation. The television set had been on all along, displaying a blank screen when she arrived. Once the station worked out their technical glitch, the screen roared to life. Simple as that.

She kept her opinions to herself, opting to go with a conversational reply. "Have you ever seen one of these ghosts?"

"Not as clearly as I would like," the woman admitted in a wistful tone. "I've seen orbs, and sensation of light and shadow. Once, I saw the reflection of a woman standing behind me, but when I turned around, no one was there. And once I caught a glimpse of a vision in white as it disappeared into thin air. But that's as close as I've come." Her voice sagged with disappointment.

"But you still believe there are ghosts present." She made it a statement, not a question.

"Oh, absolutely. Just because I can't see something doesn't mean I think it doesn't exist. I can usually sense when they're in the room, even though I can't actually see them. And of course, I've seen what the ghosts do."

"Besides turning on televisions and hiding soap, what else can they do?"

"Open and slam doors. Erase phone messages. Shuffle the papers here on the desk. Turn the clocks back an hour, then forward two. Throw all the pamphlets off the racks."

Again, Gera had a reasonable explanation—local kids, bored and looking for a cheap thrill. "Don't you think that sounds more like a bunch of kids?" she suggested.

The young woman nodded vigorously, missing the note of doubt in Gera's voice. "Exactly. That's why I think most of the ghosts are children."

The conversation was ridiculous, on so many levels. For the second time in one evening, Gera ignored the voice of logic playing in her head and engaged in a deliberate conversation about ghosts.

"You said they must be children who were born here. But wouldn't it be more like children who *died* here? We're talking ghosts." *As ridiculous as that is.*

A strange expression crossed the other woman's face. Worry lines burrowed into her forehead and echoed around the corners of her mouth. "Well, that would sort of be the same thing."

It was an odd statement to make. "I don't understand," Gera said with a frown.

The woman—whose nametag identified her as Leah—nibbled on the pad of her thumb. Her eyes darted around the lobby. When she spoke, her words started out hesitantly, and then gained momentum to end in a rush. "Well, you see... there was an incident that happened here in the thirties. Almost a dozen children died. I believe their ghosts haunt *The Dove.*"

"What—What sort of incident?"

"Some of the blasting at the mines ruptured a gas line. Eleven children and three adults died in their sleep."

"That's horrible!"

"I know. It was truly tragic. They say Mrs. Luna was never the same after that. Eventually, she closed the home and became a bit of a recluse. She let the staff go except for one maid. She was the only person allowed near her."

"How sad. When did this become a hotel?"

"I'm not sure. It was a bakery before it was a hotel. Mrs. Luna died a few years after the accident and left everything to her maid. With a house this size, there wasn't much else she could do with it," Leah said with a shrug. "It has been in the Cody family ever since."

"And when did it become 'haunted?'" Gera tried to keep the skepticism from her voice.

"I'm not really sure. You could ask Jake, though. He knows all the history."

"I'll do that. And thanks for the batteries." Gera started to turn away, but a last thought occurred to her. "I, uh, I'm staying on the third floor. I don't suppose those children..."

Leah saw her unease and offered a reassuring smile. "Their ward was on the second floor at the time. So you're good."

Gera gave a sheepish smile. "Okay, just wondering. Thanks. And good night."

"Good night, Miss Stapleton. I hope you sleep well."

4

D espite the ancient elevator and the twinkling tunes in the hallway, Gera had an uneventful and peaceful night of slumber.

She awakened refreshed and ready to start the day. If she thought the nighttime view from her room was impressive, it dimmed in comparison to the same vista by light of day. Bright sunshine danced upon rooftops and shimmered across the panoramic scene below. Mountains rose up from the valley floor, ridge after ridge, visible for miles in every direction. Gera knew some of the peaks were mighty, many of the canyons steep and ragged, yet the formations looked small in comparison to her position on Cleopatra Hill. Perspective was everything.

Gera felt a glimmer of optimism push its way into her soul. That was exactly what she needed—a new perspective. She needed to view this assignment with fresh eyes and a positive attitude. What started as an improbable ghost story was now a murder case. It was her job to turn the fluff assignment into a serious investigative piece, one with substance.

Her mind was already churning with ideas as she went down for breakfast. She ordered an omelet and opted to eat outside on the patio, where the fresh air and sunshine could stir her creative juices.

Like most everything else in this curious town, the patio was stacked in layers against the mountain. Three distinct tiers sandwiched between the hotel and its stony backdrop, staggered at random heights and all abloom with surprising bursts of color. Flowers and plants edged each of the tiny spaces and left little room for seating. Gera spotted a table on the middle terrace and followed the stone path up, picking her way between rose moss and petunias.

She jotted down notes while eating. For starters, she needed to view the crime scene in daylight, talk with the chief of police, interview possible witnesses, and get an overall feel for the town.

"Good morning to you. Fine day, now isn't it?"

Gera's head whipped around in surprise. An older woman sat behind her, resting on a bench beneath the arbor.

"Oh!" Gera peeped in surprise. "I didn't see you there."

It was true. Even now, it was difficult to detect the small figure tucked amid the lush garden scene. The woman's floral dress all but blended into her surroundings. Morning sunlight filtered through the overhead vines, casting her with alternating shafts of shadows and light.

Yet the woman's smile was infectious, reminding Gera of a warm hearth on a cold, winter day. She felt a smile tug at her own lips. "And yes, it is a lovely day," she agreed.

"The sunshine is good for the soul. I sit out here every day, soaking the morning rays into my weary old bones," the woman confided.

"Oh, do you work here?"

"Not anymore, my dear." She flashed an impish smile and Gera was reminded of a toddler, caught with her hand in the cookie jar. The old woman leaned slightly forward and whispered aloud, as if her words were a well-kept secret. "I'm a bit past that, you know."

Gera bit back a laugh. The woman was near eighty if she was a day, and definitely old enough for retirement. Half-hidden in the shadow of the arbor, her body was bent as surely as a weeping willow, and seemed as unsteady as its billowing branches on a summer breeze. The dress she wore—a front-button sheath scattered with flowers and vines—was faded and worn, and at least two decades out of vogue. Despite the warmth of a sunny Arizona morning, a crocheted shawl crisscrossed her shoulders, as if attempting to bind her small frame together. Gera noticed that the threads were frayed and the color a few shades away from white, a telltale sign of countless washings.

She idly wondered if the woman was poor, or just frugal. Grams was like that, never parting with anything that still had an ounce of life left within it. *Thriftiness is next to Godliness*, she often claimed. More than once, Gera suspected her grandmother would use coupons to get into Heaven, if it meant a discounted ticket.

A thin ray of sunlight beamed down through the tangled vines and shone directly upon the old woman's head, accentuating her mop of white curls like a halo around her head. Her skin was puffy and paper thin and, with the light hitting it just so, practically glowed translucent. *Maybe she's an angel*, Gera mused. But she had no wings, and Gera was fairly certain that angels didn't wear support hose and orthopedic shoes.

Her hands were folded in her lap, sparking Gera's suspicion that her fingers were stiff and brittle. They curled inward like those crazy fries offered by street vendors and food trucks. Gera also noticed the band of gold circling the woman's left ring finger, winking in the spotlight like a shiny new penny. It sparkled as brightly as the blue depths of the old woman's eyes.

"You're a local, I take it," Gera surmised.

"Oh, yes. I've spent my entire life on this mountain. More years than I care to claim, if the truth be known." Her smile begged indulgence.

Gera shifted in her seat, finding a more comfortable position as she faced her companion. "So, you could tell me about the town, couldn't you?" she asked hopefully.

"What would you like to know, my dear?"

"Everything!"

The elderly woman chuckled. "That would take awhile, now wouldn't it? Perhaps you should be more specific."

"I suppose you're right. My name is Gera, by the way."

"My friends call me Minnie. So tell me, Gera, what is it you would like to know about our fair town?"

It would be rude to come out and ask why so many people here believed in the silly notion of ghosts. Perhaps she should take a different tactic and work her way to the tough questions. She settled on a neutral introduction.

"We could start with *The Dove*. What can you tell me about this hotel?"

Minnie's entire countenance changed. As she leaned forward from the bench, the light touched her face and Gera could see how her blue eyes glowed, like bits of sapphire in a jeweler's case. "Oh, she's a lovely thing, now isn't she?" the older woman gushed. "So grand and majestic, yet so warm and welcoming."

None were words Gera would use to describe the hotel, but she couldn't be rude. She went with evasive. "I understand it was originally a private home?"

"Yes, that is correct. Raymond Luna was one of the bigwigs at the copper mine, and built the house for his new bride. The location alone tells you just how well-to-do the couple was." She gave a smart nod, as if that explained it all.

Gera tried to imagine the neighborhood in its prime, before potholes and flora edged out the road, reducing it to a ribbon of neglect. Perhaps back in the day there were grand houses around it, not worn and weary structures best suited for demolition, like the one she glimpsed next door.

"I suppose this was a popular neighborhood?" she guessed.

Minnie merely shrugged. "I wasn't referring so much to the neighborhood, as to the height."

Gera frowned. "Way back when, I would think the higher up the mountain you went, the more difficult the travel would be. Wouldn't a lower location be more favorable?"

A smile lifted the corners of Minnie's mouth and pushed a sea of wrinkles across her face. "You must remember, back when Jerome was settled and the first homes were built, there was no indoor plumbing or sewer system. Waste was simply tossed out the window." Her blue eyes took on a new sparkle. "There was a distinct advantage to living at the top of the mountain, and a luxury few could afford. Because it is true, you know. Certain things do, indeed, run downhill."

Gera burst out in laughter, amused by the older woman's genteel manner of explanation. "I see your point," she grinned.

"Raymond spared no expense for his bride. She was from New York, you know, and was accustomed to a fine home. He wanted her to be happy here, even though it was a far cry from the life she knew."

"I understand they couldn't have children."

Minnie's face turned mournful. "Miss Cordelia wanted children so badly. They planned for at least a half dozen. But a few years went by, and still they had no baby. She went to the finest doctors in San Francisco, but no one could help her. She came back home and accepted her fate, but she never gave up the notion of filling her home with babies."

"Is that why she opened her home to unwed mothers?"

"Yes. Mind you, in most towns it would've been a truly scandalous thing to do, but in a town where prostitution was so prominent, it was grudgingly accepted. Some here, of course, were outraged with the notion, but her husband was a rich and powerful man. And so, Miss Cordelia finally filled her house with babies. And when her husband died at an early age, those very babies saw her through the grief and despair of being widowed before she even turned thirty-five."

"That's not much older than I am," Gera murmured. "How sad. Did she ever re-marry?"

"No, she devoted her life to taking care of her babies, as she called them."

Gera cocked her head. Doing a bit of quick math in her head, the numbers didn't make sense. The house was built over a hundred years ago. The tragic gas incident happened in the thirties. Did Minnie even know the woman she spoke of with such familiarity?

Her curiosity got the better of her. "You sound as if you knew her, but how could that be?"

"Oh, it's local legend, my dear. Everyone knows the story of Miss Cordelia and her home for soiled doves."

"It was a very commendable act on her part. Most people would never do such a thing."

"No, indeed. But I understand she befriended one of the young prostitutes, quite by chance. When the girl found herself with child, Miss Cordelia couldn't abide the notion of getting rid of the baby. Back then, abortions were vile and dangerous things. As many times as not, the mother died along with the baby. I heard Miss Cordelia brought the girl home with her, and within a month's time, two more doves asked for her help."

"And, what? She raised the children as her own?"

"Some, yes. Sometimes the mothers moved away and took the children with them, starting over in a new town. Sometimes other childless couples were willing to give the children a home. A few of the luckier ones spent their childhood here, raised by Miss Cordelia and her staff."

"I heard she even had a doctor for them?"

When Minnie nodded, her white curls bounced up and down. "Yes," she confirmed, "and two nurses. You remember, money was no object, and she could hardly care for all her young wards by herself."

"And then tragedy struck."

Minnie seemed to shrink before her eyes. She leaned back into the shadows and her body sagged like a deflated balloon. Her voice was heavy, weighed down by the grief of fourteen lost souls.

"It was devastating. A ruptured gas line, caused by the blasting. Eleven children were asleep in their beds. A nurse, a wet nurse, and a mother who was sitting with her sick child were also in the ward. Not a single one awoke the next morning. They say Miss Cordelia was never the same after that. She slowly went half mad and kept to herself, shutting herself into this big old house." Minnie wearily shook her head. "Some say she grieved herself to death."

"That is so sad." Gera's heart went out to the kind woman who had given so much to others and asked for so little in return.

"Our town has a lot of sad history, I'm afraid."

"Yes, I understand it has burned on several occasions." Best to turn the conversation, if the overwhelming sadness in Minnie's blue eyes was any indication.

Perhaps she chose the wrong topic. Minnie still looked mournful. "Yes, in the late nineties the town burned three times. Within eighteen months, mind you. One fire alone took out twenty-five saloons, fourteen Chinese restaurants, and much of the gambling and red-light district." She stared into the cloudless sky beyond the mountain, as if seeing a pattern in the endless expanse of blue. "But the folks around here are resilient. Or maybe they're just stubborn. At any rate, they didn't let something like fire and ash stop them. They simply rebuilt."

Gera gasped. "This happened in the 1990s?"

"Oh, no, dear, the 1890s," Minnie clarified.

Gera bit into her lip as she processed the previous statement. "Twenty-five saloons? It sounds like Jerome was a rough town."

Minnie chuckled. "It was known as the wickedest city in the west. Back in the day, Jerome had a population of some fifteen thousand residents."

"You're kidding!"

"Absolutely not. What is it you do nowadays? Ogle it? Go ahead, ogle it and you'll see."

"You mean google it?"

"Yes, yes, whatever you call it," Minnie nodded. "You can read all about it. Ours were some of the richest copper mines in the world. A billion dollars' worth of ore came out of these hills. And it wasn't just copper they found. It was gold and silver, too, and zinc. Jerome was a very rich town."

Gera turned to look down the hillside. Much of the town lay in ruins. Many buildings were nothing more than skeletal remains; others were crumbled and inhabitable. Even more were empty. Nothing about the present-day town hinted at '*rich*.' She thought '*scraping by*' seemed a more suitable term.

At the risk of sounding rude, she asked, "What happened?"

"After World War II was said and done, the ore deposits were all but depleted. When the mines closed for good in '53, Jerome was little more than a ghost town. Population fell to less than a hundred people."

"And you lived here then?"

"Like I said, I've spent my entire life here."

"I realize it's still no metropolis, but it appears to have come back to life." She glanced back over the small town and amended her statement. "Somewhat."

Minnie gave a smart nod. "No matter what some people say, the hippies have been good for Jerome."

"The hippies?"

"Back in the heyday of free love, Jerome became a sort of refuge city for the flower children. When the mines closed, many people just walked away from their homes. They left behind anything they couldn't carry. Maybe they planned to return one day. Maybe they hoped the mines would one day reopen and they could pick up their lives right where they left off. At any rate, when folks vacated the mountain, most left their pantries full, their gardens bearing fruit, their furniture just as it was. Then the hippies came along, and they found the homes fully intact, like forgotten toys left behind."

Gera stared at the older woman in disbelief. "So, what? They just moved in?"

"More or less. There were no utilities, of course, but the hippie lifestyle could function without things like running water and electricity, so it was a perfect fit for them. After a few years, some of them drifted on. But many of them stayed and became permanent citizens of our town. Productive citizens, I might add. Have you visited the shops downtown, dear? We have an array of art galleries and glass-blowing studios, potters, and poets, musicians, and chefs. The hippies brought arts and crafts into our town, and the money soon followed."

"That's very interesting."

"We have a lot of interesting history here, too."

Gera hesitated only a moment before testing the waters. "And of course, I've heard some of that history. From what I understand, Jerome gives a different meaning to the moniker of 'ghost town.'"

Minnie's pale, puffy cheeks sagged into a frown, deflating like a fallen soufflé. "You're a non-believer, I fear."

Gera countered with, "You're not?"

For a long moment, the older woman stared out at the sprawled scene below. Her eyes traced the ribbon of asphalt that wound up the mountain in an impossible chevron pattern. Landmarks crowded around the ribbon, desperately clinging to the side of the cliff. Cars and people shuffled below.

When Minnie finally answered, her voice was faint. A note of melancholy mingled with inflection, and just for a moment, it sounded something like hope. Then Gera felt the old woman's soul fairly sigh with resignation.

"There are things in life that are beyond explanation. The smell of the mountain air after a spring rain. The beauty of a sunset beyond those hills yonder. The translucent prisms of a rainbow across the clear Arizona sky." She turned her vivid gaze toward Gera. "And the eternal and often tangible spirit of life."

Minnie made a valid argument, but Gera's analytical mind sprang into action, spinning scientific explanations to all but one of the natural phenomena mentioned. The last example stumped her.

Gera made an effort to understand. Minnie seemed like a nice lady, and she seemed sincere in her belief of the spirit world. Perhaps she could explain her beliefs in a way that could make sense to a nonbeliever such as Gera.

"So how does it work? This spirit thing, I mean."

"For some, I think they have a mission they must complete, before they can accept their own death. Until they find the closure they're looking for, they're often caught between worlds."

"But doesn't everyone have unfinished business?" Gera reasoned.

"I'm sure that most people do. And I have no ready explanation as to why some people cross over without incident, and why some get stuck. I suppose it is the same reason that some truly good people die young, while other mean and evil folks live long and prosperous lives. Some things in life cannot be questioned. They just are."

"Have you ever seen a ghost?"

"Would you believe me if I said yes?" Minnie countered softly.

Instead of answering, Gera tried another line of thought. "What can you tell me about Mac?"

The morning sun crawled higher into the sky and no longer illuminated the woman upon the garden bench. Without the sparkle of sunlight, Minnie looked tired and drained. Her already pale skin appeared washed out and drawn. Gera wondered about her health.

"Plenty, but I think that subject is best left for another day," Minnie said. Her voice sounded strained now, and weary. "You'll be here tomorrow?"

"Yes. As a matter of fact, I'm staying all week," Gera volunteered.

"Then we shall visit again in the morning."

Gera sensed she had been dismissed. She was uncertain of garden etiquette, but she had a busy day planned and was happy to take her leave.

She stood from the table. "Thank you for talking with me, Minnie. I enjoyed our visit." It surprised her to realize how very true her words were. Background information for her article aside, she had sincerely enjoyed talking with the older woman.

"I enjoyed it immensely, my dear," Minnie replied. "I often get lonely, sitting here alone each day."

"You live nearby?"

"Oh, yes," Minnie assured her with a nod. "Have a nice day, dear," she smiled.

Gera gathered her notebook and dishes and picked her way back down the stony path. At the entrance to the building, she stopped and waved to her new friend. Once again, she could've easily overlooked the slight figure in the garden. Minnie all but blended into the shadows beneath the arbor, alone with the flowers and her belief in ghosts and lingering spirits. Gera felt a pang of pity for the old woman and wondered if she had any family.

When Minnie lifted a frail hand and returned the wave, Gera smiled. At least she had one friendly contact in the town.

Now to win over the chief of police.

5

Yellow and black police tape flapped in the air like a drove of buzzing bees, swarming around the skeletal building that stood on the corner of Main and First. Gera wasn't afraid of being stung. She slipped beneath the flimsy barrier and walked right up to the railings, eager to view the crime scene in the light of day.

The structure looked different by day. Starker. There was really no other way to describe the old building than to say it was gutted, stripped of all but its outer frame and the inner support walls. Staring at the far wall of century-old masonry, Gera still recognized the raw beauty in the building's architecture. Perhaps that beauty had spared the ruins from final destruction.

That, Gera conceded, and the historical significance. She stepped back to read the plaque that identified the building as the old *Bartlett Hotel*. It was built in 1901, after its wooden predecessor—the first two-story building in Jerome—burned to the ground three years earlier. The *Bartlett* featured five rooms for stores along First Street, explaining the series of inner chambers stretching along the far side of the building. Those, too, were gutted, most of them now filled with grass, weeds, and rubbish. According to the plaque, the interior of the hotel was quite lavish, with each room decorated in a different color. Before the building was deemed unstable in the slides of the thirties, and before the second floor was completely dismantled and sold for salvage in the fifties, the *Bartlett* housed a variety of shops and businesses, including a pharmacy, newspaper, and a bank.

That explained the monstrosity on the left.

By today's standards, the vault was tiny, not much more than a dozen feet in either direction. Gera thought of a story she had covered last month, about a man in Indiana who was preparing for the fall of Wall Street and the world economy as we know it. He had installed a vault twice this size in his own private home. This ancient commercial model, she noted, was constructed from a massive chunk of concrete that sat two floors deep and accessed by a single doorway. Without a sub-floor, that doorway was now some fifteen feet in the air. Not that it mattered; she could see into the cement vault and knew that it, too, was completely gutted.

The only money left in the one-time bank was now scattered across the floor below. Tens of thousands of coins littered the sub-level, resembling a giant wishing well gone dry. Collection vessels—urns, a rusty bucket, and, of all things, a disembodied commode—snaked throughout the space, encouraging bystanders to perfect their aim. All it cost was the change in their pockets.

Tossed coins were where the similarities between a wishing well and the old hotel-turned-bank ended. Few wishing wells featured crime scene markers. Here, a parade of the tented white markers marched in a crooked line through the coins, vaunting the shape of a sprawled body.

Like much of the town, the old *Bartlett* stood on a grade. What was sub-level along Main Street became street level around the corner. Gera followed the sidewalk down First Street, acknowledging the operate word was definitely *down*. The sidewalk fell with the steep angle of the hill. By the time she reached the first inner support wall, she stood directly in front of the crime scene.

As luck would have it—hers, not poor Abe's—the site was clearly visible by a huge arched opening within the brick, the first of three along this side of the building. Gera suspected this had never been an actual doorway. Most likely, it was a plate-glass window, a sneak peek into the wonders that lay beyond.

If the masonry was any indication, *The Bartlett* was quite fancy for its day. In her mind's eye, Gera pictured tables set with white starched linens and gleaming silver candlesticks, glimpsed from street level through the grand window. Had commoners peered through the glass, wishing they were a part of the finery? Did they look down at their calloused hands and thrice-mended clothes and find themselves lacking? Did they turn away from the glitter of sparkling wines and crystal chandeliers to drudge their way down the hill, toward their own small and dingy homes on the lower level of town? When the hotel tossed out their excess and rubbish, was it their own rooftops it landed upon?

Gera edged closer. Ornate ironwork now filled the arch, some creative artisan's answer to stained glass. The result was as artistic as any intricate panel of colorful bits, but this barrier was stronger. Gera could see through the iron bars, but there was no penetrating them.

Abe's body was found just a few feet inside, near the interior brick wall. She angled her camera through the fancy railing and snapped off a dozen photos.

Three sweeping steps, at least six feet wide and gracefully curved for a more dramatic feel, accessed whatever lay beyond that wall. Had it been a stage of some kind? Gera could imagine operas and vaudeville acts, brought in to appeal to the finer senses of *The Bartlett's* elite clientele. But no, there wasn't enough room to serve as a stage.

Gera stepped back to study the side view of the building. The other two arches, she noted, had subtle gates set within the intricate rails. Both securely locked, but they offered a means of entry she hadn't noticed the night before.

She saw now that both housed recessed entrances, each with double doors for two distinct entries. No doubt, both had been magnificent in their day, a far cry from the weathered, dilapidated panels that now let in more of the elements than they kept out. Most of the crown molding was still intact, a product from a by-gone era, hand carved with fleur de lis and intricate markings. A hint of pale green clung stubbornly to the wood, perhaps protected from the harsh weather in some small measure by the barest of ceiling still stretched over the stoop. It wasn't much of a covering, with daylight clearly visible through the matchstick-thin laths, but it was more than existed elsewhere. The only wood left in the entire building was behind these two arches.

The main entrance to the hotel had probably been in the last of the archways, if the doors were any indication. They once swung inward, inviting guests to step inside, beckoning them toward the staircase beyond. Gera imagined the rusted hinges no longer obliged such movement. The brass push plates were long gone, as were the full panels of glass from both doors and from the massive arched space above them. No doubt, that had once been stained glass. Now they were but gaping holes, showcasing a crumbling staircase that arose amid a swatch of grass and saplings, and led to nowhere.

The double doors in the first archway stood slightly ajar. Gera wondered if it were from recent use or warped wood. They, too, were missing the glass from their oval insets. The doors led to the area she first believed was a stage. Now she wondered if it weren't the front desk area. A few partial walls still existed down the narrow galley, not much more solid than the spotty ceiling overhead. None of the structure had a roof.

So perhaps, she surmised, the curved steps had been part of the entryway. Just three steps, but enough to make a grand entrance.

Gera imagined ladies dressed in their evening finery, sequins and feathers and heels, stepping off the grand steps like a model steps off a runway. With their frivolous hats and long, side-slit skirts, they would step daintily into the room, offering a modest peek at their stocking-clad legs and shockingly bare ankles, all in the guise of elegantly maneuvering the steps. The display would be subtle, and nothing as distasteful and brazen as shown by the fallen doves just a few streets over. When the lights were out and the wives were soundly sleeping in their beds, Gera imagined many of the same men from these very rooms slipped away, traversing the dark and crooked streets to visit those doves. She idly wondered if the results of any such late-night rendezvouses had been born at the hotel she now occupied. The babies might have well been born in the very room she slept in last night.

Shaking the images from her head, Gera focused on the crime scene. Last night, the locals had been content to believe that a ghost tossed—or carried—Abe Cunningham over the impossibly tall railings, causing his death. She saw a more likely scenario in broad day.

Abe, or someone he met there, had a key that unlocked the gates and allowed them access to these doors. Perhaps that was why the panels now hung slightly askew. Keeping to the semi-privacy of the inner chambers, the two had a discussion that ended in an argument. A shuffle pursued and Abe was pushed down the steps. At the right angle and with the right force, he could've hit his head or broken his neck. His death may or may not have been an accident, but one thing Gera was certain of—it hadn't come at the hands of a ghost.

"You again. You're standing in my crime scene."

The snarled words came from behind her. Gera whipped around, dismayed to see the chief of police behind her. With the glare of the mid-morning sun behind him, he looked more menacing than she remembered.

She flashed her mother's smile, hoping it had half the charisma her father claimed it did. It hadn't seemed to impress the lawman last night, but maybe the daylight would change his perspective, as well.

No such luck. The corners of his mouth drooped alongside his mustache. He stood with his feet planted apart, hands propped upon his belt. Gera half-expected to see a six-shooter strapped to his side, not the sleek Glock nestled in its holster. He may not have worn chaps and a rawhide vest, but the khaki uniform wearing his rugged form did nothing to diminish his old West demeanor.

She couldn't resist the smile that teased her lips. "Seriously? You're going to draw on me?"

For one solid second, he stared at her in confusion. "What?" Then he glanced down, at the stance of his own legs and the implied placement of his hands. He immediately dropped his hand and pulled his feet closer together, making his tall form that much taller. "No, of course not. But I need to ask that you move."

"It's morning," Gera reminded him. "You said I could take all the photos I wanted."

Again, her smile was lost on him. He lifted the ribbon of tape and replied calmly, if not sternly. "You can. From this side of the tape."

"But I can't see as well from back there."

His voice remained even. "I never mentioned how close you could get, just that you could click away to your heart's content."

She mumbled under her breath as she ducked beneath the tape. Some dark comment about him not having a heart of his own.

Popping upright on the other side, Gera fired off her first question. "Chief Anderson, what can you tell me so far about the investigation?"

"Nothing."

"Nothing? Surely you have a few leads."

"Didn't say I had no leads. Said I had nothing to tell you."

Biting back her frustration, Gera kept that smile plastered on her face. "Have you ruled Mr. Cunningham's death as accidental, or as a homicide?"

"We're still investigating."

"If it is ruled a homicide, do you have any suspects?"

"Too soon to say."

"Were there any witnesses?"

"None have come forward so far."

"When was the last time there was a murder in town, Chief?"

His bushy brows puckered at the sudden change in topic. He looked as if he suspected a trap of some kind, so he stepped carefully with his words. "Jerome is a peaceful town. Murder is rare around here."

"But it does happen."

He grudgingly agreed. "Of course. But it's been three years since it's happened in this town."

"Until last night."

"As I said, Miss Stapleton, we're still investigating."

"I understand Mr. Cunningham had some previous troubles with the bank and a matter of back taxes."

Miles Anderson eyed her with cool reserve. "Understand this. I have nothing to say about the current investigation. Or the deceased."

His high-handed manner rankled Gera's nerves. She couldn't resist goading him, just a bit. She cocked her head to one side and flashed a smile as manufactured as molded plastic. "Not even to assure the townspeople they're in no danger from a killer?"

"I have no reason to believe the residents are in any more danger today than they were this time last week, Miss Stapleton." His tone almost sounded bored.

"Very well, Chief. You won't talk about Abe Cunningham or his death. Will you at least talk to me about the recent troubles you've had in town?"

"You'll need to be more specific than that, Miss Stapleton. Like all towns, we have our fair share of troubles from time to time. For example, we're currently having trouble with our local internet provider here on the mountain. Bandwidths and download speeds have fallen off drastically within the last few weeks. For most residents and particularly our businesses, that classifies as major trouble."

She glanced down at her notes and nodded. "Actually, I did hear about that. I also heard about a string of petty thefts, two assault cases, one breaking and entering, attempted arson, and three cases of robbery or attempted robbery. I'd like to talk with you about all of these, Chief Anderson."

His face tightened into a pinch and his mustache drooped south. "With most of those cases still under investigation, I'm not at liberty to discuss them."

"But these are all a matter of public record, Chief. I have no intentions of revealing classified information, but I would like the opportunity to ask you a few questions." She detected the slightest of cracks in his stony demeanor. Her next words were hasty. "Could I buy you a cup of coffee?"

The length of time it took him to answer was an insult within itself. Gera felt her face grow warm. One would think she asked to pull his eye teeth. With no anesthesia.

"One cup," he finally ground out.

Gera tried not to be offended when he took her elbow and led her across the busy street. She told herself he did if for her own safety, not to treat her like a child. He thrust his arm out to stop the one-way traffic, placing his large body between her and the oncoming cars. *Just like a parent would do*, Gera thought irritably. She resisted the urge to drag her feet.

Once inside the café, he released her arm. A harried wait-ress threw a smile their way and waved in the general direc-tion of the crowded dining room. "Find a seat and I'll be right over."

They settled around a tiny table shoved against the front window. Knowing the clock was already ticking, Gera wasted no time in beginning her interview.

"Let's start with the recent rash of thefts. Have any of the cases been solved so far?"

Miles Anderson studied her for a long moment before blowing out a deep breath. Gera thought she heard a note of defeat in the weary tune. "I can say one thing for you, Miss Stapleton. You don't give up." An odd light of appreciation wormed into his sharp gaze. "I like that in a person, so I'll answer your questions."

Gera thought that was already a given, since he had ac-cepted her invitation for coffee, but she wisely kept her mouth shut and waited for him to continue.

"As of yet, none of the cases you mentioned have been solved. It is very unusual for us to have a crime spree here in Jerome, particularly one that doesn't involve out-of-town-ers. Most of our complaints revolve around fender-benders, scratched car doors, speed control, that sort of thing. From time to time, we get a few strangers here on the mountain, the ones that think we're either too lazy or too ignorant to solve a case of shoplifting or outright theft. We'll hear a string of complaints up and down the streets, but the complaints go away the moment the troublemakers roll out of town."

It was the most Gera had ever heard the man say. Before she could reply, the waitress popped up by their side. "What can I get started for you two?"

Chief Anderson was quick to answer, "Just coffee, Loretta."

"Could you make a fresh pot, please?" Gera smiled prettily, ignoring the scowl her comment earned from her companion.

"You betcha."

The waitress had barely turned away before Gera pelted the officer with more questions. "Are you saying you suspect a local resident is responsible for the crimes?"

"We haven't ruled out the possibility—or probability—of that being the case." His shaggy mustache turned downward. "I can tell you this. If it is a stranger, they aren't registered in any of the hotels or rental properties around town. It could be someone coming and going in and out of town, but a hasty getaway off this mountain isn't an option. Which leaves us with the very real possibility of our culprit being one of our own citizens."

Gera heard the unmistakable sorrow in Miles Anderson's voice. It was obvious how much he cared about the town and its residents. The thought of one of their own being guilty of the crimes wasn't only disappointing, but disheartening.

Gera tread softly with her next question. "From what I understand—and, to be quite honest, the reason I was sent here to cover this story—many of the townspeople are accusing Horace McGruder of committing the crimes. How do you respond to that theory, Chief Anderson?"

He all but snorted. "Horace McGruder died in the blast of '38."

"I'm aware of that. But local legend says he still roams the streets of Jerome, and that up until recently, he was a friendly ghost."

"Do you believe in ghosts, Miss Stapleton?"

"Honestly? No. Do you?"

Instead of offering a direct answer, Chief Anderson looked out the plate-glass window to the town beyond. In one sweeping glance, he saw at least five references to ghosts. Many of the local merchants built their businesses—and staked their success—around the legend and exploitation of ghostly spirits.

His sigh was heavy. "Doesn't matter what I believe. What matters is that half of our town *does* believe in ghosts. The other half makes their living off them. Tourism revived our town when it would've died and withered away. And ghosts bring in the tourists."

It wasn't the answer Gera was hoping for. His cryptic reply did little to answer her original query. "People actually believe Mac still roams these streets, including one of your own officers. Don't you find it a bit… odd… that so many people not only believe in Mac's ghost, but also believe that he is somehow responsible for the string of recent crimes?"

Loretta returned with two cups of coffee. Steam wafted up from the hot liquid, momentarily fogging the eyeglasses that slipped down her nose as she leaned over to deposit the fresh brew. She scrunched up her face, realigning the foggy lenses so she could stab Gera with a pointed gaze. "Don't mean to eavesdrop, but I overheard you mention Mac. Being an outsider and all, I can see where you might be skeptical. But I can assure you, Mac still walks these streets. I've seen him myself, on more than one occasion."

Okay, she could play along. "How do you know it's him?" Gera asked.

"Not many men are as long and thin as Mac. And they say ole Mac had quite the fashion sense, even for a miner. He always wore a dark wool jacket, white placket shirt, even an old stovepipe hat. Looked a bit like Abraham Lincoln, folks always said. Not too many men dress like that nowadays."

"Is that how people identify him, simply by his clothes?"

"That, and the fact that his hat sits sideways now. Only one ear, you know," she offered in explanation.

Miles Anderson was already sipping his coffee, meaning Gera's time with the man was limited. "Loretta, I'd love to hear more about your experiences with Mac, but I hate to take up the chief's valuable time. Could we talk later?"

"Sure thing, hon." She turned away, tossing back the words, "I'll be here till three."

Gera studied the man across from her. His face was impassive as he sipped the hot liquid. Apparently, discussing a ghost was nothing out of the ordinary. "No comment?" she asked dryly.

"I think Loretta's comment speaks for itself. You can see that people do, indeed, believe that Mac's ghost exists."

Gera put up her hands, waving her palms in lieu of a white flag. "So for the sake of argument, let's assume that Mac's ghost is alive and well." It galled her to say the words, but she forced them out. "According to your own Officer Cooper, Mac has suddenly gone from watching over the town and finding lost children to stirring up trouble and now, possibly even killing a man. How do you explain that, Chief Anderson? Isn't that odd behavior, even for a ghost?"

"Mike Cooper talks too much," he muttered into his coffee. Setting the cup down with enough force to send a bit of dark liquid splashing over the rim, the policeman looked Gera in the eye. "I agreed to talk with you about matters of public record. I can assure you, you won't find mention of a killer ghost in any of my reports, Miss Stapleton."

Gera was duly chastised. "Fair enough. So, getting back to public record, I understand this newest crime wave began about two months ago?"

His nod was terse. "We didn't recognize a pattern at first, until about the third or fourth incident."

"Is there any one thing that ties these incidents together and leads you to believe they were all committed by the same perpetrator?"

"Other than the fact that crimes like these don't happen here on the mountain and it would be highly unlikely for a half dozen or more people to suddenly engage in criminal activity, all at the same time? No, not particularly," he admitted.

Gera shrugged and threw out a few suggestions. "It could be gang related," she offered. "A rite of passage, of sorts. Or some misguided initiation into a fraternity or club."

He nodded, but looked unimpressed. "Could be," he agreed dubiously.

"But you don't think so."

"All of your scenarios would be highly unlikely. Not impossible," he granted, "but unlikely."

"Were the victims and/or the witnesses able to give you a description?"

"They did."

Something in his resigned tone prompted her to say, "And let me guess. They all reported seeing a tall, thin man dressed like Abraham Lincoln. Right?"

He was slow to answer. When he did, his voice was tight. "Something like that."

Gera looked down at her notes. Jillian had e-mailed her an update this morning. "What can you tell me about accusations of corruption at the County Clerk's office?"

"Only what you'll find in the record. I believe there was a public investigation into that over in Prescott, the county seat."

"But I understand that one of Jerome's own citizens," she glanced down at her notes, "one Frieda White lost her job because of allegations of misconduct?"

"Did you find that in the public record?"

"Not exactly."

"Then no comment."

"What about Abe Cunningham? I understand he had some trouble with the bank recently."

Beneath shaggy brows, the chief of police gave her a reproachful look. "You know I'm not at liberty to discuss a victim's financial affairs."

"Even if they're a matter of public record? I see the state put a lien on his property for non-payment of taxes."

"You would need to discuss that with someone at the Department of Revenue, not with me."

"Your officers served him papers."

"If you found that in the public record, why are you asking me about it now?"

"I thought you might have something further to say about it."

"I don't." The policeman grabbed his cup, chugged back the remainder of the coffee, and set it down again with a final thud. "Thank you for the coffee, Miss Stapleton. I'm afraid I must get back to my duties now."

Gera bit back her frustrations. *You can catch more flies with honey than you can with vinegar,* her Grams always said.

But, a voice inside her mind argued, *I'm not trying to catch flies. I'm trying to catch a break!*

She pasted on a smile and extended her hand. "Thank you, Chief Anderson, for agreeing to answer a few of my questions."

He almost looked sincere. "You had more?"

Breaking out in a rueful grin, Gera shook her head in weary resignation. "Yes, Chief, I had more."

Something in his gaze flickered. It wasn't until he stuffed his hat onto his head and breezed out the door that she realized the source of the flicker.

He had finally responded to her smile.

6

Loretta suggested Gera return late morning, before the lunch crowd arrived. That gave her roughly an hour or so to wander around town and talk with other residents.

She turned to her right, following the sidewalk as it sloped downward. She admired the colorful pottery displayed in the window of the first store, but the door handle wouldn't budge. She belatedly noticed the small cardboard sign wedged against the glass and the words scribbled in a hasty hand.

Sorry. No internet, no cash register. No register, no sales. No sales, no reason to be here. As if an afterthought, the last line was large and scrawled. *Tell Mac to turn the 'net back on.*

"Oh, great," Gera grumbled aloud. "They're even blaming that on the poor guy. Like a ghost from the thirties even knows what the internet is."

She wandered past an empty storefront, thinking it was a shame such a large space would go to waste. She echoed that thought moments later, as she stepped into one of the narrowest stores she had ever seen. There was hardly room enough to turn around, much less display the many t-shirts the proprietor had to offer.

Slightly claustrophobic, Gera stayed near the front of the building, where the plate-glass windows gave the illusion of more space. She pretended to study the rows of t-shirts on display. They literally climbed the wall, reaching all the way to the twelve-foot ceiling, suspended from neatly draped clotheslines. If she stalled long enough, she was certain the saleswoman would come to her.

"Can I help you?" a bored voice called from somewhere beyond the first rack of Jerome-themed jersey knits.

"Uhm, I was looking for a shirt."

At the possibility of a sale, interest percolated in the woman's voice. "Anything in particular?"

"Something with a ghost, maybe?"

The sales clerk laughed. "We have plenty of those!" She pointed to the wall of shirts. "Third row up. Those are our bestsellers, but we have more on these racks. Something like this, perhaps?" She pulled a purple shirt from the rack and dangled it before her. Against the wispy image of a ghost, the words 'Keep Jerome Boo-tiful' were scripted in glittery hot pink letters.

Gera tried not to wince. "I was looking for something less…" She motioned with her hands, but could think of no hand gesture for gaudy. She finished with a lame, "Less. Just less."

Stuffing the shirt back among the rest, the saleswoman laughed. "I understand. You don't look like the pink glitter type."

"I'll take that as a compliment."

The woman tried sifting through the crowded rack, walking in a circle as she peeked at first one shirt, then another. The rack was so full, it was impossible to see the fronts of the shirts without pulling them free. "Do you have a preference on color?"

"Blue, maybe, or black." She bit back the urge to add, *something businesslike.* It was a t-shirt, after all, sporting the image of a ghost. Hardly her usual attire.

"Oh, I have just the thing! They came in this morning. We haven't even put them on display yet." She squeezed past the checkout counter and bent down, coming up with a dark gray shirt in her hands. "Ta-da. Our latest and greatest."

With a flourish, the woman turned the shirt around for Gera's inspection. It featured the wispy image of a tall, thin ghost wearing a top hat. *Jerome, Arizona* was stenciled in neat red letters, with a smaller caption beneath it in white. *Home of Mac the Ghost, circa 1938.*

"Aren't these great?" the saleswoman gushed.

I doubt Abe Cunningham's family will think so, Gera thought to herself. Aloud, she feigned ignorance and asked, "Who's Mac?"

The salesclerk stared at her in surprise. "You don't know who Mac is?"

"Judging from the shirt, I'd say he's a ghost."

The woman bobbed her head. "He's our local ghost around town. We have several, you know, but Mac is a town favorite. He's been roaming these streets since the big explosion of '38."

"Ah, so that's what the circa stands for." Gera pretended to hear about Mac for the first time. "He's a friendly ghost, I assume?"

"Some think of him as more of a guardian angel than a ghost. He's been watching over this town for as long as most anyone can remember."

"That sounds pretty cool. What does he do, exactly, that's so helpful?"

"Oh, lots of things. He helped my mom find a lost ring one time. She knew she lost it while gardening, but she could never find it, no matter where she dug. Then one day, out of the blue, it was there, right on top of the soil. She knew she had Mac to thank."

Gera struggled to look convinced.

"That's not all, of course. He saved a little boy who fell down the old mine shaft, and he guided a group of children to safety when their bus stop was hit by a drunk driver."

"You know, now that I think about it, I think I heard someone mention him this morning. But I got the impression he had done something bad. I think they mentioned that he pushed somebody?" She tried to look vaguely confused, even shaking her head for emphasis. "I didn't know what they were talking about, so I didn't pay much attention."

The saleswoman frowned. "Well, don't. Don't listen to such nonsense. There are some people around town who have turned on ole Mac, and decided he can no longer be trusted. They think he's the one behind all the mischief in town and that he somehow had something to do with Abe Cunningham's death. Isn't that the most ridiculous thing you've ever heard?"

No more ridiculous than believing in the ghost to begin with, Gera thought, but she kept her opinion to herself.

The door opened behind them and three women stepped inside, filling the small shop to capacity. The claustrophobic feeling returned.

"I'll come back tomorrow for the shirt," Gera said hastily. She hurried out into the wide-open space of the sidewalk. No more alley-sized stores for her today, thank you.

Gera wandered further down the street. No one was interested in talking with her in the first store, but in the second, the proprietor was more than willing to share his opinion about Mac.

It was all a bunch of hullabaloo, he insisted. There were no such things as ghosts, and certainly none that roamed the town wearing stovepipe hats. The storeowner claimed it was all a gimmick to attract tourists. He, of course, didn't need such nonsense to sell his wares; the quality of his merchandise spoke for itself.

If price tags were indicative of quality, Gera decided his merchandise was some of the finest.

By the time Gera retraced her steps uphill, she found Loretta seated at a back booth of the café, wrapping silverware. The waitress smiled and signaled for Gera to join her. "Perfect timing," she chirped.

"Okay, great." Gera slid into the seat across from her. "Because I'd love to hear more about your experiences with Mac."

"A ghost hunter, are you?" Loretta asked with a toothy smile.

"Something like that."

"Then you need to see my friend Anise. She runs the best ghost tour in town. Her office is two doors up the street."

A ghost tour actually sounded like a good idea. "I think I might just do that," Gera nodded thoughtfully.

"Make sure you ask for Anise by name. And tell her I sent you."

"I will, thanks. But back to Mac…"

"Like I told you earlier, some folks don't believe he exists, but I've seen Mac myself, at least a dozen times or more."

"So where do you see him? What's he usually doing?"

Loretta's nimble fingers flew over the silverware, sorting it into sets and wrapping each one in a paper cocoon. She answered without looking up. "I see him most often over at the *Cactus Bar*. I work the breakfast shift and have to be here at the crack of dawn, before most of the town is even awake. Sometimes when I pass by *The Cactus* and look inside, I'll see ole Mac, leaning against the fireplace mantel at the back. Usually he's just standing there, doing nothing." She shrugged her bony shoulders. "One time I saw him walking down Hull Street, over near Spook Hall. Another time, he was slipping off into the shadows beside the *Cuban Queen*."

Gera made a mental note to familiarize herself with the landmarks mentioned.

"The last time I saw him," the waitress continued, "was about a month ago. Come to think of it, I saw him talking to Abe Cunningham."

"*Talking* to?"

Loretta offered a self-conscious laugh. "Okay, maybe not talking. But he was standing there with Abe. It was late one night, close to midnight. I was coming in from a movie down in Cottonwood, that new Sandra Bullock film. I just love her, don't you?"

"Yes, she's one of my favorites," Gera agreed, but her mind was spinning. What connection was there between Abe Cunningham and this supposed ghost? "So, what were they doing, Abe and this ghost? Just standing there?"

Loretta scrunched her face in thought. "It seems like they were looking at something. Abe had some sort of paper in his hands, and I remember he was frowning. Mac was just standing there, looking on. His back was to me, but I knew it was him."

"Because of the lop-sided hat and all," Gera surmised.

"Yeah." She nodded her head, but her eyes looked thoughtful. Something in her tone sounded doubtful. "You know, I don't recall the hat being lopsided that night. But that's silly, right? Of course, it was leaning to one side."

"Maybe... he got a better-fitting hat?" Gera offered.

Still looking troubled, Loretta shook her head. "I must be remembering wrong. But I could've sworn..." Her voice trailed off and she shook her head a final time. With a sigh, she turned her attention back to the silverware.

"What can you tell me about Abe Cunningham?" Gera asked.

"Salt of the earth. A hard worker, and honest to a fault." Loretta's brow puckered with intensity. "Salt of the earth."

"I heard there was some issue with unpaid property taxes?"

Loretta's head jerked up. Her eyes narrowed and filled with suspicion. "Where did you hear that?"

"I happened to drive into town last night, just as they were removing the body." Which was true. "I overheard people on the street talking."

"You were a witness?" Loretta gasped. "Is that why Miles Anderson was questioning you?"

"No, no, I wasn't a witness. I just happened to be there. And I heard some people talking about past troubles with the bank, something about property taxes."

"Yes, but he got that all cleared up. Paid Grant Young off in full."

"Grant Young?" Gera questioned. "Isn't that the man who found the body?"

"I don't know about that, but Grant Young is the banker here in town. He's the one Abe had to get square with. For a while, it looked like Abe and Ruth might lose their house. A shame that would've been, seeing that it's one of the oldest houses in town and been in the Cunningham family since the early days."

Gera idly wondered about the condition of the house. Was it still in decent shape, or was it one of the many crumbling structures sliding down the mountainside?

Her wandering mind missed the rest of Loretta's short story, until she summed it up with a favorable nod. "...on speaking terms again, so it ended well." The waitress stopped suddenly and frowned. "Until last night, that is. I guess it didn't end so well, after all, huh?"

It was a rhetorical question, one she didn't expect an answer to. Flashing a toothy smile to her companion, Loretta shook the somber mood from her thin shoulders and changed the subject. "Where are you staying in town?"

"*The Dove.*"

"Oh, my, you're making a clean sweep of meeting the town's most eligible bachelors," the waitress teased.

Gera frowned and looked suitably confused. "Uhm..."

"You've met Jake, over at the hotel?"

"Yes, last night."

"Quite a cutie, huh?" Loretta teased.

"I suppose."

"Girl, if I was twenty years younger, I'd be all over that man like white on rice!" Loretta grinned, enjoying Gera's sudden discomfort. "And of course, you noticed how handsome Chief Anderson is."

"Well, I—"

"Those two are the most handsome and eligible men in town. Add Grant Young to the mix, and you've seen the best we have to offer. And quite the assortment. Sweet, sour, and salty."

"I didn't come to town to find a man," Gera assured her.

"No, but a little added bonus can never hurt, now can it?" Loretta beamed, eyes twinkling behind her wire-rimmed glasses.

"Hey, Loretta!" A voice floated out from the kitchen. "You going to sit back there on your tush all day, or get in here and work like the rest of us?"

Loretta rolled her eyes and her smile disintegrated into a sigh. She pushed away the silverware and lumbered to her feet. "Sorry, hon, but duty calls."

"I appreciate you talking to me. Thanks." Gera thrust out her hand for a quick shake.

"No problem. And don't forget to give my friend Anise a call and go on that ghost tour. Say, they have one over at *The Dove*, too. You should check it out. I hear Leo does a fantastic job."

"I'll do that."

The mischief returned to her eyes. "Might want to ask Jake to go along and keep you safe," she advised playfully.

Gera laughed off the suggestion.

It wasn't until she was out on the street that she wondered which man was sweet, which was sour, and which of the three was salty.

7

The moment Gera stepped into her room, she knew someone had been there.

Every light in her suite was burning. Every overhead fixture, every lamp, every night light. Even the light inside the microwave was on.

Nothing of hers was disturbed, nothing was out of place. Everything was just as she had left it, including the limited but scattered cosmetics on the vanity. Other than the glowing lights, fresh towels, and the neatly made bed, there was only one other indication that someone had entered the suite.

A small red ball and a set of jacks rested in the middle of her mattress.

Gera picked up the telephone to ring the front desk, but she hung up before anyone answered. This was just a publicity stunt, she was certain of it. A gimmick to make her believe in ghosts.

It would take more than a few lights and a toy to sway her.

Determined not to give the stunt any more attention than warranted, she stalked to the bathroom. After a day spent roaming the town, she needed a quick shower and a change of clothes. She had plans for the evening. Those plans included a delicious meal, a nice glass of wine, and plenty of time to scour her notes and reflect on all she had learned today.

Which, she admitted as she turned on the shower, wasn't much.

She was ready within thirty minutes. Her short haircut made styling a breeze, and a solitary dinner required minimal makeup.

Gera heard the voices before she stepped off the elevator, a half dozen or so chattering with excitement. To her surprise, a small group of people gathered in the lobby, the most she had seen so far at the hotel. Leah stood among them, holding a clipboard and trying to be heard above their noisy din.

"Okay, guys, the tour is about to get started. This is your last chance to back out. Speak now, or forever hold your peace."

"Are you kidding?" a young man said, drawing a giggle from the girl draped across his arm. Both sported purple streaks in their hair. "Bring on the ghosts, baby!"

Leah spotted Gera as she exited the elevator car. "Miss Stapleton? There's room for one more if you'd like to join us. We're about to do a ghost tour of the hotel."

Gera hesitated for only a moment. She had booked a tour with Anise for tomorrow night, but Loretta had recommended this hotel tour, too. "Uh, yeah, sure. Why not?"

"That's the spirit!" purple-haired guy said, pumping his fist into the air.

"Spirit," his girlfriend echoed with a giggle. "Get it?"

Biting back a groan, Gera forced herself forward. She hoped she didn't regret her hasty decision.

"Your host will be with you in just a moment," Leah assured them, working her way from their midst. As she passed Gera, she said, "I'll put the tour on your tab. You get a discount for being a guest of the hotel."

"Thanks," Gera murmured.

She watched as an older gentleman appeared from out of seemingly nowhere. Tall and gaunt, his back was crooked into a permanent arc, reminding Gera of a life-sized question mark. The top of his head was completely bald, fringed by a band of unruly white fuzz. Swimming in waves of wrinkles, even the pigment of his skin had faded away. His features suggested he was, in part, of African descent, but his skin was now pale and thin.

"Good evening to you," he said, his voice surprisingly strong. "Welcome to *The Dove Hotel*. We're about to embark on a journey into the spirit world. What you may see or hear isn't for the faint of heart. If you have any doubts, any fears, please say so now."

A low murmur rippled through the crowd, but no one moved aside.

"Very well. My name is Leo, and I will be your spirit guide this evening. Please, follow me."

There was something compelling about his voice. The way it reverberated within his chest drew people to him, made them listen. The weight of that rumble settled deep, giving him an inexplicable air of credibility.

Gera fell into line behind the others. It crossed her mind that they all followed him blindly, like lambs to slaughter, but she shook the unwanted thought away. They weren't headed to slaughter. They were headed to a steep, narrow stairway, shuttered away at the back of the great room.

"Watch your step," Leo cautioned as he led the way. "The stairs are steep and the lighting dim. We'll begin our tour in the basement."

They trudged down the stairs, single file, which emptied into a small storeroom of sorts. A dozen folding chairs were set into a semi-circle. With bare concrete beneath their feet and thick walls made of clay, the dimly lit room was cool. Sounds echoed.

Leo encouraged the small group to find a seat and get comfortable. He turned away to fidget with an array of gadgets scattered across a small table in the corner. The small group murmured amongst themselves, speaking in low tones and nervous giggles. No one knew what to expect.

Leo gave them time enough to settle, then dawdled long enough to give them time to squirm. He was a master at building suspense, Gera realized. By the time he turned and spoke in a quiet voice, the room fell silent and his audience hung upon every word.

"Tonight, we will explore the world of spirits and the possibility that ghosts do, indeed, walk among us. That life doesn't always end with death. That perhaps there is more to life than the naked eye can see." His weak eyes traveled around the room, settling upon on each of his guests. "Again, I say to you, if you have any doubts, now is the time to leave."

One man shifted in his seat, but his wife stabbed him in the ribs with her elbow. His grunt was the only sound in the room.

"Very well then," Leo continued, taking a chair of his own. "First, I wish to tell you a bit about *The Dove,* and how the hotel came to be."

He launched into the story of Raymond and Cordelia Luna, echoing much of the same tale Minnie relayed in the garden. Having heard the details before, Gera listened with half an ear and used the time to study her companions.

The young couple, the ones she secretly dubbed Purple One and Purple Two, grinned throughout the story. For them, the tour was one big adventure, and the perfect excuse for Purple Two to curl herself around her boyfriend. *Get a room*, Gera wanted to say, although she suspected they were too young to rent one.

She dubbed the other couple Mr. Grump and Mrs. Gullible. While the wife looked captivated with each word that fell from Leo's lips, her husband sat with his arms crossed over his massive chest and a skeptical smirk upon his face. He bore an odd resemblance to a bulldog, Gera noted.

The remaining members of their group were a trio of women. They appeared to have come directly from the beauty salon, via way of an open bar. A cloud of perfume and hair spray hovered in the air around them, as surely as any spiritual entity. One of the women seemed unsteady in her high-heeled shoes and Gera detected alcohol on their exhaled breaths. The blond among them blinked in rapid secession, obviously nervous at the thought of encountering ghosts. The tallest of the three bobbed her head a lot and murmured tiny words of agreement with everything Leo said. The third woman looked torn between fascination and tears. Gera called the trio Wynken, Blynken, and Nod.

She tuned back in as Leo continued his tale.

"When Miss Cordelia passed, she left the house to her one true friend and faithful employee, Minerva Cody. Minerva was her personal maid and confidant. The year was 1947, and production at the mines was beginning to slow. The war had exhausted ore deposits. A house this large was more of a burden than a blessing, and with only one son and a dozen bedrooms, Minerva and J.T. Cody opened the house to the public. It became a boarding house. And when the population fell away and less than a hundred residents remained in the town, it was Minerva's fine cooking that kept the house afloat. Not many folks came to Jerome in those days, but the ones that were here still had to eat, and they were willing to pay. I can tell you from personal experience, Minerva Cody was an excellent cook and a fine baker. She started the restaurant here on the other side of this wall." His voice fell with reverence, and the group leaned forward, eager to hear his words. "At night, when the house is quiet and the ovens are cold, I swear I can still hear the metal clang of her bread pans and inhale the sweet, heady aroma of her yeast rolls. Miss Minerva was a fine cook, indeed."

The old man let his words settle among them, pressing a pleasant mental image into their minds, causing their mouths to water. Then, just as quietly, he spoke his next unsettling words.

"And later, when the clocks slow to a crawl and the wind lays low, some swear that if you listen closely, you can hear the screams. The screams of women in labor without benefit of anesthesia, of secret abortions performed in the dead of night, of mothers who never wanted their child to begin with, only to be heartbroken when that child was born without air in its lungs."

His words shocked the group, but he continued in his purposeful voice, a master at his craft. "Some guests swear they still hear the children, crying softly in the night. They see the ghosts of children running in the hall. Mothers with swollen bellies and haunted eyes who pace the floors as they await their time, and the day they can return to the cribs and once again offer their bodies for pay. These cribs, mind you, aren't the kind where babies lay, but where all too often, babies were made. If you take one of the tours in town, you can see the old red light district, where the majority of the soiled doves once lived and thrived. It was only the lucky few, you see, who came here to live with Miss Cordelia. Lucky ones, like my very own mother."

Heads snapped up at that snippet of personal information. Mrs. Gullible gasped. "You mean, your mother was a—" She snapped her mouth shut, stopping just short of insulting their host.

However, old Leo wasn't insulted. His eyes shone with pride. "Yes. My mother was a soiled dove. And I was the very last baby to be born in this house, on a hot summer day in 1939. I spent the first five years of my life here, until Miss Cordelia could no longer care for her babies, as she called us." His old eyes misted over, but his voice remained steady. "I returned here when Miss Minerva opened her café and needed my help. Stayed on when they turned it into a hotel in the eighties. And when she passed on a few years after her husband, I took over and ran the hotel for the Cody family. They still own it to this day, and a finer family you will never know. I'm just the concierge now. The Cody family indulges me, allows me to play host now and then, and on tours such as these. Because no one knows this house better than I do," he boasted. "I know its secrets, its strengths, and its weaknesses."

Again his voice fell, causing an ominous air to stir about the room. A nervous rustle ran through his audience. A chill settled in, spiking the skin on their arms and ruffling the fine hairs on the backs of their necks.

"And believe me when I say," the old man said softly, "this house has more than its share of secrets."

He stood suddenly, moving his crooked body with more finesse than Gera thought possible. He shuffled toward the table of gadgets.

"Ghosts and spiritual beings are nothing new, but the science surrounding them has improved vastly over the years. A variety of gadgets can now detect when a ghost is in the room. I would like to introduce you to some of these electronic wonders, and encourage you to take one or more along with you on our journey tonight. We will start with this. Does anyone know what this is?"

Blynken, the nervous blonde, snapped off a series of rapid blinks and ventured a guess. "An EMF meter?"

"Yes, that is correct. An electromagnetic frequency detector. When a spirit is present, it projects energy. That energy, that electromagnetic field, can be measured by this device, and is indicated by the lights. No energy, no light." Leo waved the gadget in the air, turning it toward them to demonstrate the '0' reading. He then pulled out his cell phone and passed the meter over it. The lights blinked wildly and the number on the display suddenly spiked. "The current from my cell phone gives off electronic energy, as you can see here. To best detect the presence of energy in the room, you'll want to use an EMF."

He demonstrated some of his other tools. The handheld infrared thermometers measured temperature change. A sudden drop of ten or more degrees, Leo informed the group, was a good indication that a ghost was present. The radiation monitor evaluated gamma and beta particles in the air, much as a Geiger counter would do. Some might like to carry a UV flashlight to distinguish airborne particles from orb phenomena. However, perhaps the most useful of all the tools were the digital cameras with built-in flash photography. Orb activity was often spotted on digital film, even when undetectable by the human eye.

"Please, stay together. At times, the lights may be dim. Use your flashlight if necessary for safe passage. We have guests in some of the rooms, so our tour will flow around them. There will be plenty to see, plenty to explore. And we will begin in the hallway that leads to the kitchen, where a murder once took place."

A collective gasp went up from the trio of Wynken, Blynken, and Nod. Purple Two moved into Purple One's embrace. Mr. Grump frowned, while Mrs. Gullible visibly paled. Gera marveled at Leo's ability to tell such a riveting tale, and to sound so authoritative while doing so.

With tools in hand, the small group followed Leo from the room. They crowded close upon his heels, as if his nearness alone could keep them safe.

"Careful now, the way is dim," he cautioned, leading them into the corridor. At the far end of the hallway, bright light spilled from the commercial kitchen, but the lighting here was controlled, casting off shadows and the sense of isolation. The sounds of a busy kitchen—clattering dishes and hissing kettles, punctuated here and there by a bark of laughter or a surprised curse—mingled with muted sounds from the dining room, where guests already gathered for supper. Their voices were muffled, floating into the dimly lit space as if from a great distance, and therefore adding to the aura of secrecy.

"Right about here, in this very spot, one of the doves met her untimely death." Leo's distinctive voice held just the right note of mystique, just the right hint of danger. "Her name was Penelope, and it is said she was quite the beauty, with long dark hair and a creamy complexion. She was quite popular among the men, and, as you might guess, quite the thorn in many a wife's side. The story is that she caught the eye of Peter Scot, one of the higher-ups at the copper mine. He and his wife were part of the elite here in Jerome. But it was no secret that after the fancy parties and the elegant dinners, Peter would slip down to the cribs to be with Penelope."

They stopped in the hallway, and Leo's theatrical voice filled the small space. "When she discovered she was with child, she asked for Miss Cordelia's protection. She feared for her unborn child's life, for Peter's wife Deidre had heard of the pregnancy, and vowed no child of her husband would bear mulatto blood. Pen—"

Purple Two broke into his story. "What is mulatto blood?" the young woman asked.

Leo raised his withered brows, but answered patiently. "Mixed blood, much as my own. Like my mother, Penelope was the child of a black mother and a white father. There were still anti-miscegenation laws at the time, so such relations were illegal. Penelope feared Deidre would go to any length to keep such a union secret."

"That's a stupid law," the girl insisted, pulling a face.

"Like so much in life," Leo informed her sagely, "a law doesn't have to make sense to exist."

When he dropped his voice to a hushed whisper, his audience waited on bated breath.

"So one night, during a new moon that left the sky dark and no one the wiser, Deidre followed her husband, and found the two together, here in the hallway. They were discussing plans to go away together, once the baby was born. In a fit of rage, Deidre pulled a knife and plunged it deep into Penelope's belly." Leo's voice shook with quiet intensity, drawing another gasp from the tour group. "The baby died, and Penelope soon after. Bled to death, right here on this very floor. Peter sent Deidre away, to a mental institution in California. Not long after, Peter was found dead in their home, hung by his own night sheets." The group listened in stunned silence. Even the Purples were no longer smiling.

"It was the first of a long series of death and sadness here in the house. Just one of the many secrets here in *The Dove*," Leo said solemnly. "If you turn on your instruments, you might find a trace of Penelope's spirit. Often people say they see Peter's ghost here, roaming the halls where he last held his true love in his arms."

Even Mr. Grump was moved by the story. His arms fell to his sides, and he helped his wife adjust her EMF as she waved it through the air. When someone's meter went off, a murmur of excitement moved through the crowd.

Gera stood back and studied them, wondering why no one else saw the theatrical aspect of Leo's performance. The man was good. Very good.

But she still didn't believe in ghosts.

8

For the next hour and forty-five minutes, the aging concierge led the small group through the hotel, stringing them along on a spine-tingling, breathtaking adventure. Gera was certain the man had missed his calling. He should be on Broadway, she determined. Or in Hollywood. The man was a master at storytelling, weaving such a believable and heart-wrenching tale that even she almost succumbed to the notion that ghosts roamed among them.

Almost, but still not quite.

The tour ran over schedule. What the group lacked in numbers, it made up for in enthusiasm. Judging from the faces of her companions and the way they gathered around their guide for any last tidbit of information, even after the tour officially ended, Gera was the only holdout of the bunch.

When Gera quietly left the group, no one noticed her departure. Leo was telling another of his tales, this one about his life here as a child. His one true regret, he told them, was that he never knew Miss Cordelia in her prime. He was born months after the tragedy of '38. She was never the same after that, folks said, withering slowly away into a shell of her former self.

Gera consulted her watch and picked up the pace, hurrying downstairs to the restaurant. She hoped they would seat her, even though the clock showed straight up nine o'clock.

The lights were already dim. Only one couple remained at a table. Gera's stomach protested with a loud grumble as she turned away. Hopefully there was something in town still open.

When she heard someone call her name, she looked back and saw Jake, the night clerk, seated near the windows. He motioned her forward.

"Were you hoping to eat?" he asked.

"Yes, but it appears I'm too late. The kitchen is obviously closed." She looked around in disappointment, at the wait staff resetting tables for breakfast.

"Not necessarily. Have a seat." His smile was cryptic as he motioned to the chair beside him. "Is there anything you can't or won't eat?" he asked.

"Uh, I don't do liver. Or English peas." A ripple of revulsion shimmied through her. "And I'm a little iffy on most Chinese food."

He handed her a basket of assorted breads as he stood. "Here, nibble on these while I go sweet talk the chef. I'll see if we can still rustle you up a meal."

"Are you sure? I hate to be a bother..." She tried to sound humble, but her eyes lit with anticipation. Her stomach chose that moment to give another rumble.

Jake laughed aloud, a very pleasant sound. "Seriously, have a roll. I'll be right back."

Gera stole a glance at her reflection in the mirror and finger-combed her hair, smoothing down the wayward spikes.

After years of wearing her hair at or below the shoulder, she was still getting accustomed to the shorter style. The new cut emphasized her wide-spaced gray eyes, but she didn't like the way it often left her ears exposed. She picked at the ends now, tugging them over the tips of her ears.

She saw Jake's reflection behind her as he made his way back from the kitchen. He carried himself with ease, obviously comfortable in his own skin. She liked that in a man.

"One chef specialty, coming up," he reported as he took his seat.

"I'd say it wasn't necessary, but my stomach demands otherwise," Gera grinned. "Sorry to be such a bother. The tour took longer than I imagined."

"The ghost tour?" Jake asked in surprise.

"Yes. I've just returned from the *Leo the Performer Grand Puppet Show*." She used a flourishing hand movement to embellish her tone.

Amusement danced in Jake's blue eyes. "Ah, he must've changed up the act. I don't recall any puppets last time I tagged along."

"His entourage," Gera clarified. "I must say, that man is quite the performer. One tug and everyone danced like puppets on a string."

"Everyone but you," Jake noted shrewdly.

She lifted one shoulder. "In my opinion, he laid it on a bit too thick. But the others seemed to lap it up, so I guess it evened out quite well."

A waiter brought water and a chilled bottle of wine, compliments of the chef. Jake was clearly impatient as the man poured each of them a glass, but Gera noted that he remained polite. She liked that in a man, too.

The moment the waiter was gone, Jake returned to their conversation. He was eager to hear her opinion, another huge plus in Gera's book. Not, of course, that she was keeping score on his best qualities. Like she told Loretta, she wasn't looking for a man.

"What was it about the tour you didn't like?" he asked.

"Nothing. Honestly, the tour was fine. Very informative. I learned a lot about the hotel and the town as a whole. I just thought the whole thing was a bit… theatrical. There was one point when a woman on the tour almost broke out in tears. She's a guest in the hotel, and her room 'tested positive' for ghosts. The poor woman was almost hysterical."

A frown marred Jake's handsome face. "That is unfortunate," he agreed.

Gera continued with a nod. "I wouldn't doubt it if she checked out this evening or, at the very least, requested another room. She looked petrified."

"What happened?"

"Leo was telling us a tale about a young woman who fell to her death from the second floor. It shouldn't have killed her, except that she landed on a pointed rock that—well, you know the story, I'm sure." She broke off, realizing impalement wasn't a suitable topic for dinner conversation. "Supposedly her spirit roams the halls at night, looking for the person who pushed her. So when the EMF meters went off and someone caught what they called an orb on their digital camera, Mrs. Gullible almost lost it."

"Mrs. who?"

Seeing his confused scowl, Gera was quick to explain, "Sorry, it's a silly habit I have, assigning nicknames to people in my mind."

A teasing light sparkled in her companion's eyes. "Oh? And what would my nickname be?"

Without thinking it through, a name popped from her mouth. "Clark Kent."

Jake was clearly amused. He cocked his brow and said with mock indignation, "Not Superman?"

Gera hated the color that bloomed within her cheeks. So she found him attractive. And maybe he did remind her a bit of the caped hero's alter ego. She suspected there was much more to the man than his easy smile and friendly demeanor.

She tried for a casual shrug. "They're one and the same, aren't they?"

"I don't know, are they?" Behind his glasses, his blue eyes danced with merriment.

Gera fanned her flaming cheeks. "No need for an infrared thermometer in here," she muttered. "Definitely too warm for ghosts."

Jake threw back his dark head and laughed, but he was gracious enough to let her off the hook. "Was that the only spirit you encountered tonight?" he asked.

She happily changed the subject. "According to Leo, we may have also rubbed elbows with the murdered Penelope, a lovesick prostitute named Angie who mourned herself to death when her baby was stillborn, and a fellow named Samson. I forget what happened to him..."

"He was a worker who somehow managed to get trapped next to the furnace," Jake readily supplied. "He didn't actually burn to death, but from heat and dehydration."

"Is it just me, or is that more deaths than normal for one house to bear?"

With a shrug, Jake took a sip of wine before answering. "Not just any house, mind you. A century-old house. One with many occupants and a long, unique history."

She recalled Leah's words from the previous evening. "Yes, I understand you know all about the history of the house."

"I admit, I'm a bit of a history buff."

"So is it common, even here in Jerome, that one house has seen so many deaths?"

"I suppose we're a bit over our quota," Jake conceded.

"A nice bonus if you're running a haunted hotel," Gera said, studying Jake over the rim of her wineglass.

A look of irritation crossed his face. "Are you saying we exploit their deaths?"

"I'm saying it never hurts having such a tragic past, if you're trying to sell the concept of ghosts."

"Is that what you think we're doing?"

"Perhaps not you personally, but the owners are making a killing off the ghost angle."

"You say this because…"

"Oh, I noticed that Leo was quite careful with his wording. He did an excellent job of never coming out and making a direct claim that the hotel was haunted. He made a point of saying 'some folks say' or 'guests tell us.' He asked us to explore the *possibility* that ghosts exist, rather than claiming they were real. But the man is a master at his craft. His stories were suspenseful, his delivery impeccable. He didn't have to say there were ghosts present. Everyone else said it for him."

"Everyone but you."

"I don't believe in ghosts." It had become her mantra.

Before Jake could respond, the waiter delivered their meals. Jake's was a thick cut of steak, piled high with mushrooms, tomatoes, peppers, and thinly sliced potatoes. Gera's had many of the same vegetables, swirled into a creamy sauce over pasta and chicken.

"I have no idea what this is, but it is delicious," she breathed after just one bite.

"I'll be certain to tell the chef," Jake said. "Sometimes these conglomerations end up on the menu."

"This one should," she insisted. She closed her eyes as she took another bite. "Delicious."

Always a great moderator, the food worked its magic, chipping away at the sharp edges of their previous words. The mood shifted, mellowing with each click of their forks against their plates. By the time the waiter appeared with a tray of decadent desserts, they were chattering away and laughing like two old friends.

Gera eyed the sweet, delicate creations offered. "I can't decide," she admitted. "They all look divine."

"We'll take them all," Jake said, drawing a gasp from Gera. "Leave the tray."

"Absolutely, Mr. Cody."

"The whole tray?" Gera cried as the waiter slid the tray between them and promised to return with coffee. "Do you have any idea how many calories that is, not to mention the c…" Her words trailed off as she interrupted herself. "Wait a minute. He called you Mr. Cody."

"Yes, that is correct. My name is Jake Cody."

"Then that means you—you're—"

A light of amusement flickered in his eyes. He nodded and confirmed, "That's right. I'm one of the owners who is making a 'killing,' so you claim, off the 'ghost angle' of this hotel."

Gera opened her mouth to say something, then shut it. Words came out on the second try. "I do apologize. I had no idea…"

"No need to apologize. You gave me your honest opinion, something you wouldn't have done, had you known my true identity. I appreciate your candor."

"It would've been nice," she grumbled, "if you had kept me from inserting my entire foot into my mouth."

Jake pushed a piece of cake toward her. "If there's any room left in there around your foot, try this. It's a house specialty."

Jake pulled a bowl of bread pudding from the tray and set it between them, followed by a slice of cheesecake. One by one, he lined the treats along the table and encouraged her to sample them all, just as he intended to do.

As Gera dipped into one of the offerings, she asked, "So Minerva and J.T. Cody were your… what? Grandparents? Great-grandparents? Aunt and uncle?"

"Grandparents. And that apple dumpling you're eating is from her very own recipe book. My grandmother was an excellent cook."

"Mmm, it's divine." She had a second bite. "I understand she opened a bakery here, before it was a hotel."

"Yes, and continued to make breads and desserts for her guests, right up until her death."

"And when was that?"

His blue eyes clouded, as surely as the sky on a stormy day. His voice was quiet. Reverent. "Eight years ago. Leo didn't mention her death, I'm sure, but the truth is, my grandmother was the last and most recent person to die here at *The Dove*."

"I'm so sorry," Gera murmured. "If you don't mind me asking, how did she die?"

Jake studied the raspberry torte beneath his fork. He pushed it around the plate, poking it a time or two with no real conviction. "She fell from the third-floor landing," he said quietly. He sighed and set his fork aside, suddenly done with dessert.

"That's horrible. I'm so sorry."

"She was old and frail. Logic tells me she could've simply fallen." He shoved his fingers through his dark hair, leaving it in disarray. Even with his hair at odd angles, he was still decidedly handsome. What woman didn't like that in a man? "But my gut says differently."

"You—You think she was *pushed*?"

He looked miserable. "I can't prove it. The police ruled it an accident. The coroner refused to do an autopsy. But somehow, I *know* that she didn't just fall."

"I don't suppose there were any witnesses?"

"None."

It was Gera's turn to play with her fork. She peeled away the layers of cake, separating each of the four tiers from the cream frosting that held it together. "Leo spoke very highly of your family," she began softly. "He obviously adored your grandmother."

"He and Lucy were very close to my grandmother. When she died, they stepped up and ran the hotel. Did a great job of it, too. But then Leo's bursitis set in, and the day-to-day business got to be too much for him. Lucy is still over Housekeeping, but her mind is fading. If you meet her and she starts talking about my grandmother in the present tense, just agree with her. It brings her comfort to think she visits with 'Nerva, as she called my grandmother." A sad smile hovered at the corner of his mouth.

"Leo said he had never known a finer family. So—So why would anyone… I mean, who would—"

"Want to kill her?" Jake supplied.

"Yes."

He pulled in a deep breath, releasing it with an air of defeat. "I don't know," he admitted. "I just don't know."

When the waiter brought coffee, Jake retrieved his fork and finished off the apple dumpling. Gera divided her attention between the mutilated cake and the bread pudding.

"That," she proclaimed with a very satisfied smile, "was absolutely, positively, unequivocally, delicious."

Her mother's smile didn't go unnoticed by her dinner companion. The blue of his eyes deepened.

Gera noticed that he noticed. Between the wine, the decadent desserts, and the fascinating twinkle in his eyes, she felt warm all over. *Not now, Gera,* she reminded herself sternly. *No matter how much you like about the man—and let's face it, it's just about everything—now isn't the time for this. You're here to work.*

Another thought occurred to her and she visibly brightened. "Hey, if you're a history buff, you probably know the town's history, too."

"I can give you a fairly accurate account," he replied. "What is it you would like to know?"

"Mac," she said without hesitation. "Tell me about Mac, your one-eared ghost."

Jake looked over her shoulder, to the staff hovering politely in the distance. "We're keeping the staff," he murmured regretfully.

Gera was reluctant to have their evening end. *Only because he's a source of information,* she assured herself. *Strictly work related.*

"It's a nice evening for a stroll," she blurted out.

His eyes warmed with a smile. "A stroll it is, then."

Jake left a generous tip before guiding her out of the dining room, his hand light upon her back. As they stepped out into the evening, a gust of air greeted them, stirring in Gera's hair.

"Some would say," Jake informed her, "that was a ghost, saying hello."

She reached up to straighten her tousled strands. "Must've been a real swell fellow, back in the day," she grumbled.

They wandered off the long porch, turning away from the twinkling ground lights to find the ruffled edge of pavement.

"Watch your step," Jake warned, keeping his hand upon her back. *A safety precaution*, they each told themselves. "If we keep to the middle of the road, there's less potholes," he advised.

"How far up the mountain does this road go?" Gera asked as they trudged uphill.

"The pavement ends just past these houses, but a dirt road winds all the way around Cleopatra Hill to the other side."

The first house was dark, but the last of the houses was fully lit, with lights gleaming in most every window. A cluster of cars gathered out front and spilled onto the road.

"Looks like they're having a party up there," Gera commented.

Jake shook his head. "Not a party. More like a wake. That's Abe Cunningham's house."

"Abe Cunningham? The man who was killed yesterday?"

"Yes. It's one of the oldest houses still standing in Jerome. It was his parent's home until he and Ruth married. They gave the house to them as a wedding present."

"I understand he almost lost the property, because of un-paid taxes."

Jake sent her a sharp look. "You've been in town for twen-ty-four hours, and you already know about that? You must be good." Over dinner, she had revealed her profession as a re-porter and the reason for her visit to Jerome.

She gave a short laugh. "It didn't require much skill on my part. You know how people like to gossip."

"Ah, the universal language of small towns everywhere."

"I also heard about the hierarchy of the hillside." A smile hovered around her mouth. "The way I heard it, things do, indeed, run downhill. So, I take it the Cunningham family must've been well off?"

Amused by her statement, Jake's eyes twinkled behind his glasses. "Abe's father was a bigwig at the mine," he confirmed. "You can't see it now, but there is a huge ornate sign out front with their name on it, made of copper."

She studied the illuminated house up ahead. It was a rambling craftsman from another era, but hardly a mansion. From this distance, and silhouetted against the night sky, she could see only a faint golden luster amid the brighter lights.

"That must've been the popular thing of the day. I noticed a lot of copper accents at the hotel. That piece in the lobby is very intricate."

"Richard Luna had it commissioned in 1933, not long be-fore he died. It originally hung on the wall, before my grand-parents had it built into the counter."

"Wow. That was one large wall piece," Gera murmured.

"And too gaudy for my grandmother's tastes. But her own father was the metalsmith responsible for creating it and the other pieces, so of course they kept it. I learned from an early age that some things in *The Dove* can never be discarded. They're part of the hotel's legacy, my grandparents said. And besides, I think it looks good at the check-in."

"Yes, it was one of the first things I noticed when I arrived." *When I was on the lookout for a demented innkeeper,* she recalled.

"Let's walk this way," Jake suggested.

For the briefest of moments, when he guided her off the pavement and into the overgrown tangle edging the far side of the roadway, she thought again of that demented innkeeper from the movie. He, too, had been handsome.

"Where are we—Oh!" There was no need to continue her sentence. She saw where they were going. And the view was breathtaking.

Beyond the shaggy border of trees and bushes, there was just enough earth to qualify as a ledge. The ground fell away at their feet, making way for a fantastic view of the town below.

"Here," he offered. "This crooked tree makes a pretty good chair." Not surprisingly, given the staggered town below, the tree grew at an angle, offering the perfect spot to rest upon its bent and twisted trunk. Jake wedged his shoulders between two nearby trees and turned just so, lowering himself onto another bent trunk. He leaned back into the chair provided by nature and grinned over at her. "Pretty cool, huh?"

"Very cool," she agreed.

"I like to watch the cars coming into town," Jake admitted. "Look, there comes one now. It's making the first curve, down past the old high school." He offered a running commentary, noting when the vehicle passed different landmarks. As it maneuvered the series of twists and turns along Route 89A, Jake gave a play by play of the car's progress, based solely on the angle of the headlights and the repeated application of its brakes. The car would disappear from time to time, hidden behind the buildings and houses it passed, but Jake knew precisely when it traveled along Hull Avenue, noted it was turning right onto Jerome Avenue, then left onto Main, and now climbing its way up the steep incline of Clark Street. Would it turn up toward them? Take Hill Street to another hotel? Or meander out of town, via the continuing Route 89?

"Ah, looks like it's taking Hill Street," he decided. "There are some historic buildings up there, you know, including the last of the company hospitals. It's the big building you see when you come into town. They've turned it into a hotel now, and the former surgeon's house into a bed and breakfast."

"Is that the hotel that's been featured on one of those ghost shows?"

"A couple of times, I think. Quite honestly, I'm surprised your editor didn't book you over there. Don't get me wrong, I'm glad she didn't, but they're well known for their ghost sightings. I would've thought she would choose them over us."

"Yeah, well, I would've thought she would choose Ramon over me to cover the story, so there you go."

"Ramon?"

"One of our other reporters." She didn't mean to sound so accusatory, but the censor bled into her voice. "He actually believes in all this ghost stuff."

"And you don't."

"No, I don't." She hated the hint of apology she heard in her own voice. Why should she apologize for being the only sane person in this brainwashed town?

With Jake's sigh, she detected an air of resignation. Was it because he, himself, was a believer? Did her skepticism toward ghosts create too wide a chasm between them for…? *For what, Gera?* she chided herself. *This is an interview, not a date.*

As if he heard her arguing with herself, Jake asked, "What is it you want to know about Mac?"

"Okay, so we both know I'm a non-believer." Might as well lay it all out there, naked and ugly for all the world to see. "But I'm trying. I'm trying to wrap my head around how this works, for those who do believe. So, *if* I believed in ghosts, and *if* I thought such a thing was possible, I could understand how having Mac hanging around all these years, looking out for the town, would be a comforting notion. In that scenario, there's not a lot of difference between a ghost and a guardian angel."

"Which, I assume, you also don't believe in."

Her sharp look was confirmation enough.

"I'm trying to keep an open mind here," she insisted. "I know many people believe in angels, my own grandmother being one of them. So, for the sake of argument, let's say I did believe Mac's ghost was alive and well, and roaming the streets of Jerome." She resisted the urge to roll her eyes at the absurdity. "What I can't get is how these people—the ones who thought Mac was this good and decent ghostly guy, always looking out for the best interest of the town—can suddenly turn on him, and decide he is behind all the thefts and mischief in town, and now, as of last night, capable of murder. No matter how hard I try, I cannot make a logical leap from good ghost to bad ghost, just like that. It doesn't make sense."

As if any of this makes sense, Gera groaned inwardly. *Here I go again, discussing ghosts as if they actually exist.*

"What can I say?" Jake shrugged. "It's human nature to believe the worst in people."

"If Mac were real," she cracked dryly, "I might actually feel sorry for him. Seems to me the town has turned out to be somewhat of a fair-weather friend."

Jake was quiet for a moment, looking at the streets below. It wasn't even eleven o'clock, but the sidewalks were all but rolled up. The bars were the only businesses still open in town, and from here, none appeared to be busy. The streets were quiet. Being a weeknight, most of the houses were dark, as well.

"It's a small town," he told her needlessly. "We don't have a lot of crime here. Everyone knows everyone. So, I guess when something bad does happen, it is easier to blame a ghost, than to think one of our own may be guilty."

"I get that, but yet… I don't." She may as well come clean. "I'm sorry, Jake, but I really don't get it. How can an entire town be so gullible, as to believe a *ghost* murdered a man? We're talking a flesh and blood man—your own neighbor, in fact—" she flung her arm out to indicate the house behind them, "murdered in the middle of town, and people are content to blame it on a ghost!"

"Maybe it's different where you come from, Gera, but crime is rare around here. People are jumpy. And now there's been a murder. No one knows what to think."

"Apparently, no one is *thinking* at all," she retorted. "Someone started the idea that Mac was to blame, and it seems everyone else is all too willing to jump on the bandwagon, regardless of how ridiculous it is."

"You know what they say. Ignorance feeds on fear."

Gera threw him a sharp look. "You want to talk about fear? Do you know the scariest thing I see in all this?"

"What would that be?"

"While the town is content to blame Abe Cunningham's death on a ghost, his real killer is still out there, roaming free."

As if on cue, the night wind stirred, blowing a burst of cool air that seemingly pushed the moon behind a cloud. The night went dark.

Gera's voice fell to little more than a whisper.

"Now *that's* a scary thought."

9

She had no time clock to punch, but Gera was aggravated when she overslept the next morning. She had planned to get an early start on her day, before the Arizona sun teased the mercury, drawing it to a spike.

Nine fifteen wasn't an early start. With her luck, she would be too late for breakfast. She doubted the kitchen would be as gracious this morning as it had been last night.

Throwing on jeans and a t-shirt, Gera flew down to the restaurant. The buffet was still out and offered a decent selection, so Gera grabbed a plate. She skipped the breads and opted for fresh fruit, scrambled eggs, and ham. Coffee cup in hand, she headed out to the patio.

To her delight, Minnie was sitting under the arbor, apparently waiting for her to arrive. The white-haired woman greeted Gera with a wave and a warm smile.

"Hello," Gera smiled as she took the nearest table. "I overslept and was afraid I would miss you."

"Oh, I don't adhere to a clock these days," Minnie said, clearly dismissing the notion of a schedule of any sort. "And

I really don't have much else to do, other than sit here in the garden and admire the flowers."

"Have you eaten? I could get you a plate, if you like."

"No, dear, I'm fine." As Gera sipped her coffee, Minnie asked, "Did you get a chance to explore the town yesterday? Visit some of the shops?"

"A few. Many of them were closed."

"There will be more open over the weekend. We get a lot of tourists up here on the weekends, not to mention people from Phoenix, trying to escape the heat."

They chatted for a few minutes as Gera ate her breakfast, general topics that took no particular direction. As she pushed her empty plate away, Gera broached the subject foremost on her mind.

"I was hoping you could tell me more about the town. You seem to know it better than anyone I've met so far."

"As I told you, I spent my entire life here, and I'm hardly a spring chicken anymore. So, yes, I'd say I know our town quite well."

"Tell me what you can about Mac McGruder."

"I believe he came here after the Great Depression, when the mines re-opened in '35. He was some sort of specialist I remember them saying, something to do with dynamite and charges and things that go boom." She made a motion with her hands, her curled fingers mimicking a mushroom effect. "There had been a lot of blasting in the twenties, which damaged the fault lines and ultimately caused much of the town to slide. There was talk that this McGruder fellow knew a different technique, one that would be gentler on the faults. I remember my Papa said it was all a bunch of nonsense, that a blast was a blast, but the bigwigs at the mine believed in him, and brought him here from back East."

Minnie paused in her story. Gera drained the last of her coffee and wiped her hands, waiting for the older woman to continue. When Minnie said nothing more, Gera glanced over at her. Minnie sat staring into space, an odd expression frozen upon her wrinkled face.

"Minnie?" Gera asked in alarm. She sensed something was terribly wrong with her new friend. "Are you all right?"

The old woman was slow to respond. After spacing out for a decided moment of time, Minnie slowly came back to the present. Her movements were jerky—robotic, even—as she blinked and continued with her story. It was as if she had never paused, but Gera kept a close eye on her after that, concerned with her wellbeing.

"Everyone liked Horace, or Mac, as many called him. He was friendly and easy to get along with, and always eager to help with the community. Or so I've heard. At any rate, the townspeople were saddened when he died in the blast, but they knew they owed him a debt of gratitude. You see, he knew right away that something had gone wrong with the charges. It was said he stayed behind, knowing what the outcome would be, but he tried to save as many of the men as he could. He rushed them out, insisting they leave, particularly the ones with family."

"What about Mac? Did he have a wife?"

"No. I heard he was sweet on one of the doves. Promised to marry her and take her out of the business, but that never happened." A sad note carried on her voice, weighting it down. "Some say that's why he came back, to keep an eye on his beloved Adeline."

"I heard it was because of his ear. I understand he lost it in the explosion?"

"Yes, that's right," Minnie nodded. "Some of the men weren't so lucky, you know. Some were blown to bits. But when they dug Mac from the rubble, still wearing his favorite wool jacket and his placket-front shirt, the only thing missing was his ear. They said he almost looked peaceful."

Gera smiled at the old woman. Like Leo, she told a compelling story. She spoke with such sincerity, such emotion, that it was easy to imagine she had actually been there, all those years ago.

"You weren't by chance ever a tour guide, were you?" Gera grinned.

"No, no. Why do you ask?"

"Because you would've made an excellent one. Were you a history teacher, I hope? You could've really made history come alive for your students." Gera thought back to some of her own teachers, the ones whose lessons were drier than dust and as old and tired as the rote stories they retold, time and time again. There had been one teacher, however, who had made learning about the past fun and imaginative. Of all her teachers and professors, Mr. Camden would always be a favorite. Minnie's tales of the past reminded Gera of his.

"No," the old woman said regretfully, "I was never anything as noble as a teacher. I spent most of my career in housekeeping."

"Nothing wrong with that," Gera assured her.

Minnie folded her crippled hands in her lap and smiled up at her friend. "So, what do you've planned for today, my dear? Do you have a good angle for your story yet?"

"Not yet. I'm looking for… Uhm, wait. I never told you I was a reporter."

Minnie looked nonplussed. "You didn't have to, dear. I recognized your name."

"You did?" In spite of herself, Gera couldn't help but sound incredulous. Hardly anyone recognized her name, even within her profession. She was lucky if her own co-workers at the magazine recognized her.

"Yes. You wrote that riveting article on water bottle waste. I thought you made some excellent points."

"Oh, well, uhm, thank you." She was surprised anyone had noticed the article, given that it was tucked away at the back of the magazine. Filler, at best.

"Well, I don't want to keep you," Minnie said, quite out of the blue. "I know you have far better things to do than talk to an old woman. I'll meet you here again in the morning."

Gera was surprised by the abrupt brush-off, but perhaps Minnie was tired. She thought of her earlier spell, when the woman had zoned out for the better part of two minutes. "Are you sure you're feeling okay?" she questioned.

"My feet feel a bit tingly, but that's nothing new. Don't worry about me. I'm fine."

"I'll try to get here earlier in the morning. Maybe we can have breakfast together," Gera suggested.

"Fine, fine. You run along now, and I'll see you in the morning."

Gera got the distinct impression Minnie rushed her from the garden. "If you're sure you're all right…"

"I'm sure." Minnie's smile looked convincing enough, but her blue eyes weren't as vivid as usual.

Still, Gera did as her friend asked and gathered her dishes. As she had done the day before, she paused at the doorway to look back and wave.

Minnie was no longer on the bench. Tingly feet, chunky shoes, and all, her friend had already disappeared.

Securing an appointment with Grant Young was easier than Gera had imagined. All it took was one call, a few minutes on hold—during which time she listened to a canned message about interest rates and the friendly tellers at First Yavapai Savings—and she was in.

She took the last appointment of the day, which left her plenty of time to do her homework.

Grant Young, she discovered, was a third-generation resident. His grandfather and uncles ran a store here back in the day, and at least one Young had remained on the mountain, even during the lean years. When the town saw a spurt of regrowth in the eighties, Thomas Young seized the day and opened a savings and loan. Gera couldn't find much more about the bank around the new millennium, but plenty on golden boy Grant. After an impressive basketball career at Mingus High School and Princeton University, Grant studied finance and started his assent up the corporate ladder. His resume touted positions at institutions all across the United States, from Chicago to Los Angeles, each one higher than the last.

Ten years ago, Thomas Young had the first of several strokes. Grant, ever the good son, returned home and took the reins of the family business. After a prosperous career in some of the largest cities in America, Gera wondered how he had adjusted to life back here on the sleepy mountain. Any job here, even as president and CEO, must've felt like small potatoes to the man. A quick glance at the bank's financial statement told Gera he had made the best of the situation, turning it to his advantage. Under Grant's stewardship, First Yavapai Savings had enjoyed steady growth and a significant presence in local real estate. Grant Young maintained good relationships with banks and savings institutions all across the country, and served on numerous boards and advisory panels.

Definitely overqualified for a bank this size, Gera thought, but she had to admire the man's dedication to family and community.

She lucked out and found a parking spot along the street, right in front of the bank. First Yavapai took up a small sliver of space on Main, wedged between the *Cactus Bar* and *Spirit Books.* Even though the building was historic, the security and equipment inside were state of the art. Gera passed through a metal detector before she was ushered into the president's office.

"You must be Gera Stapleton," he greeted her with a smile. His large hand swallowed hers as they got the standard pleasantries out of the way. "Please, come in. Have a seat."

The photo on the internet didn't do Grant Young justice. It showed a tall, athletic man with dark hair and sharp, intelligent eyes, dressed impeccably in a pinstriped suit and diamond tie stud. Gera recognized the similarities, even though his current suit jacket hung from a hook on the wall and his simple navy tie swung free when he moved. Even without the hair—his head was now shaved completely bald—he was still the same attractive man. Yet the lens hadn't captured his charisma. It hadn't recorded his energy. Gera vaguely wondered how high an EMF meter would bing when directed his way.

Nor had the camera chronicled the way he tilted his head to one side, signaling his complete focus in the moment. She noticed the way he softly clicked his tongue, tucking it behind the pearl of his gleaming teeth as he studied her. Part of his charm was that he made the conversation about *you*, not him. Traits like those couldn't be frozen in time.

"So, I understand you're doing a magazine article on Jerome. As a life-long resident, business owner, and member of the Chamber of Commerce, I want you to know you're more than welcome here. Any exposure is greatly appreciated."

His response was quite different from that of Miles Anderson. Which left Gera to ponder... which man had Loretta described as sour and which as salty? No doubt, Jake Cody took the title of sweet.

"That should certainly make my job easier," Gera smiled. She pulled out a small pocket recorder. "Do you mind? I'll take notes, but I find a recorder helps fill in the blanks."

"By all means," he said, waving a dismissive hand through the air. His hand was large and his fingers long, perfect for handling a basketball. He leaned back in his chair and laid one long leg across his other knee, getting comfortable. His relaxed posture put Gera at ease.

She asked a series of routine questions, mostly about his background and his long connection to the town. A man in his position could've boasted, turning a few simple questions into a long, self-serving expose. Gera appreciated the way he kept his answers short and precise, if not modest. She noted he had described himself as a 'member' of the Chamber, when in fact he held the title of president. After inquiring about the organization and some of its activities in town, and after commending him on his leadership skills within the bank, she moved on to the questions she really wanted answered.

"I understand you were the one to discover Abe Cunningham's body."

A series of wrinkles worked across the top of his scalp, the progression more noticeable without hair. His eyes turned troubled. "Yes. Unfortunately, that is correct."

"I suppose you knew Mr. Cunningham personally?"

"Of course. The Cunningham family has been here as long as the Young family, if not longer. I've known Abe and Ruth my entire life."

"I understand there is a fund set up here at the bank, to help with funeral expenses?"

"Yes, when something like this happens in the community, we try to help in whatever way possible. The bank will match funds, dollar for dollar."

"That is very commendable of you, particularly given the recent troubles you had with Abe."

His relaxed posture never changed, but the audio recorder picked up the slight edge that cut into his reply. "Troubles?"

"I understand Mr. Cunningham had some unpaid taxes and got in somewhat of a bind. He borrowed money from First Yavapai against his property, only to have a lien placed on it by the state. Something about the money order he obtained from this bank wasn't valid?"

Grant Young waved those long fingers in the air again. "I appreciate your attention to detail, Miss Stapleton, and your fine investigative efforts. I know how it must look to a curious mind, but let me assure you, Abe was never in danger of losing his home. It was all a misunderstanding. I will admit, there was an embarrassing clerical error on our end, but we had it sorted out in a matter of days. And, as I'm sure you discovered, the entire ordeal was all for naught. As it turned out, the county treasurer's office was at fault, mistakenly tagging his account as delinquent. Taxes on the entire Cunningham estate had been paid like clockwork for the better part of a century."

"So, you released the lien on his property, as well?"

He did that thing with his tongue again, tapping against the row of pearly white. "I really should be insulted, you know," he said, but his voice held a teasing note.

Surprise hiccupped in her voice. "Insulted?"

"You know I cannot disclose a client's confidential information to you, Miss Cunningham. I should find it insulting that you would think otherwise."

"Naturally, I meant no disrespect."

"Naturally." He looked almost amused.

Gera tried to look contrite. If she was practiced at flirtation skills, she might try to be coy. Judging from the smile on Grant Young's face and his teasing tone, he was open to the possibility. But Gera never had been one for exploiting her feminine wiles. Perhaps, she was loath to admit, because she wasn't entirely certain she possessed any.

She went with a compassionate angle. "I suppose I'm just concerned for Mrs. Cunningham, now that her husband is deceased. I'd like to think that entire nasty business is all behind her."

"I think you can rest easy at night, knowing Ruth is taken care of."

"Oh, well then, good. That's good to know." She knew she nodded a bit too enthusiastically. *Get back on track, Gera,* she scolded herself.

"Can you please tell me about the moments leading up to finding Mr. Cunningham, and how it is that you noticed him?"

"I had picked up dinner at the café across the street and was walking back to my car. I was parked in the lot down on Hull."

"Excuse me," Gera broke in, "but isn't that a rather strange place to park, especially for take-out? That's like two streets over."

"One, actually, but you're right; it is a bit far. But it was Tuesday night poker, so there weren't many places left along Main. Besides, I enjoy the exercise. I spend far too much time behind a desk these days."

"So, you were headed to your car…"

"When I stopped to toss a coin into the pit." At her look of surprise, he grinned a bit sheepishly. "Old habit. As a kid, I never passed by there without tossing in a penny or two and making a wish. If I had saved that money, say put it into a high-yield money-making account, I could be a millionaire today."

"I saw your bio, Mr. Young," Gera said quietly. "And your bank's financial statement. I think you've already got that covered."

"Okay, I could've been a millionaire before I turned for-ty." Again, she arched her brows. He quickly amended, "Okay, thirty. The point is, over the years, I've spent a small fortune, tossing in one coin at a time."

She wasn't flirting, but Gera couldn't help but smile and ask, "And just what have you wished for over the years?"

He offered an easy shrug. "Oh, the usual. When I was a little kid, it was for BB guns and bikes. It slowly turned to things like making the team, winning the next ball game, making a home run, perfecting my mid-court aim." His smile turned lascivious. "Sometimes it was about girls. A wish that I could take Lisa Jensen to Homecoming, or Tiffany Braxton to prom." He winked, as if letting her in on a secret. "Big things like that were worthy of a silver-dollar coin toss."

"And did your bigger investment pay off?"

"Yes and no. Both girls said yes, but Tiffany dumped me at prom and left with Miles Anderson. I had rented a limo for the night, so I'd say I didn't get a very good return for my money."

So, he and the chief of police had a history. Gera filed away that tiny bit of information. "And what about that night, Mr. Young?" she asked. "On Tuesday night, what were you wishing for?"

He didn't respond immediately. She wasn't sure if it was because her question took him by surprise, or because he didn't want to answer truthfully. The slight delay gave him time to think of a lie, but he responded with, "You know, I don't recall. I guess with all that happened next, a silly wish didn't seem so important any longer."

"And what did happen next?"

"I saw Abe lying there. I knew by the unnatural pose that it wasn't good. His eyes were open, staring up at the sky..." Grant passed a hand over his face, as if he could wipe away the ghastly image in his mind as easily as one wiped away scribbles from a chalkboard. He shifted in his chair, uncrossing his legs and scooting up to the desk. Gera recognized the move as an unconscious gesture of having something to hide.

Perhaps he hid the fact that he had been afraid, Gera considered. He had discovered a dead man, after all. A *murdered* dead man. It was enough to frighten anyone.

"Did you notice anyone else around? Maybe while you were still across the street?"

"No, I'm afraid not. But as I told the police, I wasn't looking for anyone."

"And the gates were locked when you arrived?"

"Yes. I tried them, of course, trying to get to Abe." His voice dropped with regret. "I knew it was too late to help him, but I tried anyway."

"Do you have any idea why Abe was there?"

"No."

"Any idea how he could've gotten inside?"

"No."

"Some say," Gera said, careful to keep her voice devoid of judgment, "Mac is responsible for Abe's death."

"I know what you're doing, Miss Stapleton. You want to know if I believe in Mac's guilt or innocence. More importantly, you want to know whether or not I believe in Mac."

"And do you?"

Again, the banker was slow to reply. "You may find this hard to believe, but that's not as easy a question to answer as you might think."

"Oh? And why is that?"

"I grew up here, Miss Stapleton. I've heard the legend my entire life. Not just of Mac, but of ghosts in general. More importantly, I've *seen* things. Heard things, felt things. Sensed things. Things that cannot be readily explained. Call them what you may, but we have tangible spirits among us. I know it is difficult for an outsider to understand, but it is something that you have to experience firsthand to comprehend."

"I have a ghost tour planned for this evening," Gera offered. "Will that help?"

His smile was charming. "It's a start."

A gentle buzz illuminated the intercom on his desk. "I'm sorry to interrupt, Mr. Young, but you have an unscheduled guest."

"I'm in the middle of an interview, Sharon."

"Yes, and I'm so sorry, sir. But your guest is Ruth Cunningham." The worry in the woman's voice carried over the line.

"Please give me a moment." He sent Gera an apologetic look. "I'm sorry, Miss Stapleton, but I'm afraid I will have to cut our interview short."

Gera began gathering her interview tools. "Absolutely. I completely understand. And as I said, I appreciate you taking the time to talk with me today."

"If you need anything further, we could reschedule. Over dinner, perhaps?"

It was impossible to read his smile. Was he asking her out on a date, or simply being polite?

Her own smile was noncommittal. "Perhaps," she agreed. "Thank you again, Mr. Young."

Gera was slow to leave, stalling so that she might get a glimpse of Abe Cunningham's widow.

She knew her upon sight. The stout seventy-something woman looked pale and drawn, her eyes puffy from crying and her nose a bulging red bulb. Gera murmured a greeting as they passed, but Ruth Cunningham was preoccupied, and understandably so.

Before she wandered too far out of hearing range, Gera staged a mishap. She clumsily dropped her notebook. Another slip of her foot sent a handful of loose leaf papers sliding across the slick wooden floor, closer to Grant Young's office. She bent hastily to retrieve them, trying her best to look embarrassed, even though no one was in the hallway to witness her act. There were cameras, she knew.

She kept her face bent on task, but her ears strained to hear the conversation on the other side of the door. She was unable to hear anything after the initial greeting.

Just as she gave up and straightened to leave, she heard Ruth Cunningham wail, "But you promised! You promised you would drop this ridiculous farce!"

She heard the low murmur of Grant Young's voice, but his words were muffled.

"This isn't right, Grant Young, and you know it!"

"I'm afraid my hands are tied, Ruth."

This time, Gera heard his reply, meaning he was closer to the door. She hastily retreated, so that by the time Ruth Cunningham came storming out of his office, she was already well on her way across the lobby.

Gera waited outside, pretending to make a call on her cell phone. She watched as Mrs. Cunningham barreled through the bank doors, where a stocky middle-aged man joined her on the sidewalk. Her son, no doubt, judging from the family resemblance.

"What is it, Mother? I knew I should've gone in with you!"

"That lying little weasel," his mother all but growled. "He didn't tear up the papers. He claims he still has a mortgage on the property."

"But Dad said he handled that!" the son roared in disbelief.

"He did. Grant Young said he would tear up the papers, make the whole thing null and void."

"So what happened? What went wrong?"

He herded his mother to the car, but Gera heard her reply, loud and clear.

"He lied."

10

It troubled Gera, knowing that Abe Cunningham's widow
wasn't 'taken care of,' as Grant Young described it, after
all.

She didn't have long to dwell on the matter. She wanted
to make the last tour of the day at Douglas Mansion, now the
Jerome State Park. After that, she had the ghost tour with
Anise.

The mansion was interesting, and the short film playing
on a loop filled in a few historical blanks. However, she rushed
through the self-guided tour, knowing she had only a half
hour to be back in town. It gave her just long enough to grab
a soda, review her notes, and make her way to the next tour
with a few moments to spare.

Only four other people took the ghost tour, and she knew
two of them. Mr. Grump and Mrs. Gullible were already in the
small waiting room of the office, perched upon a ragtag sofa
across from two men. Mr. Grump looked more approachable
than he had before the first tour. The bulldog expression had
softened to that of a Saint Bernard.

Their real names, Gera learned, were Pete and Sandy Gibson. After a recent near-death experience, Sandy opened herself to 'new possibilities,' as she described it. Pete was still skeptical, but a restless night at *The Dove* had worn him down.

"Did you change rooms?" Gera wanted to know. She couldn't imagine Sandy staying in their original room, not after last night's hysterics.

"Yes, but I'm not sure our new room is much better," she fretted.

"Oh?"

"They moved us to the other end of the hall, but I swear I heard a woman scream last night. I kept hearing running in the hallway, but when Pete opened the door, no one was there."

"She got me up three times to check," he confirmed, none too happily.

"You heard it, too," his wife insisted. "And even you saw the shadow."

In spite of herself, Gera inquired, "Shadow?"

"There was no one in the hallway, but we both saw a huge, looming shadow. It hovered on the wall for a good five seconds before it faded away." Sandy nudged her husband in the ribs. "You saw it, Pete. Tell her."

"It's true," he said, his voice a sulk. "I saw the shadow. I have no idea where it came from, but I saw the shadow."

"And this morning when we woke up, our electronics were all unplugged and our soap was missing. Has anything like that happened to you?"

Gera didn't want to encourage the woman. There had to be a logical explanation for it all. "I had a little trouble with my remote," she acknowledged. "And the maids left all the lights on in the room while I was out, but that's all."

"I doubt it was the maids. It was more likely the spirits," Sandy predicted.

Before Gera could put up an argument, their tour guide arrived.

She introduced herself as Anise, their spiritual pilot for the evening. Dressed for the part, she wore long flowing robes of gauzy white, bound at the waist with a wide, printed sash. Even Gera recognized the pagan symbols scattered across the swatch of cloth. Many of the same emblems dangled as amulets from around Anise's graceful neck. Wisps of palest blonde escaped from the turban she wore, the pale green wrap positioned upon her head like a crown. Long feathers dangled from her earlobes to complete her outfit.

The clothes, Gera knew, were a persona. All part of the job she did. Even her soft, whispery voice could be practiced and perfected. But Gera had no explanation for their guide's ethereal complexion. With skin so pale it was practically translucent, and eyes a faint, watery blue, the woman could almost pass for a ghost.

If I believed in such a thing, Gera reminded herself.

Anise asked the group to introduce themselves. Sandy spoke for her and Pete, eager to share their spooky experiences at *The Dove*. Josh and Eli were from San Francisco, here to celebrate Eli's birthday—ghost chasing was a favorite weekend hobby for the couple. Sensing that she was the only non-believer in the group, Gera admitted only to being a journalist, writing a story on supernatural powers.

Anise welcomed them with an airy smile and arms spread wide. She gave a nice spiel about the journey they were about to embark upon. She encouraged the group to keep an open mind. If the spirits sensed they were among friends, they might be willing to speak with them, interact with them. She had tools to help detect when a ghost was present—EMF meters, infrared thermometers, ultra-sonic listening devices, flash photography—but the best tool was an open mind and a positive attitude.

Gera did her best to get into the spirit of the hunt. *No pun intended,* she snickered to herself. These people were believers. And even she wasn't so rude as to insult them to their face.

She couldn't help but think of Grant Young as they began their rounds through town. He was an intelligent man. Well educated and revered among his peers. Yet he, too, was a believer.

She suspected Jake believed, as well. He hadn't come out and said as much, but it took a person secure in one's position—someone such as Anise, for instance—to openly admit to believing in ghosts.

Anise not only admitted to her belief in other worlds, she embraced it. She spoke freely about séances and spiritual rituals. She talked about spirits she had called forth, conversations she had led. She talked about guiding lost souls back to the inner realm so that they could peacefully cross over into the next life. That was her sole purpose of ghost hunting, she insisted. She wanted to help those trapped within the in-between realms of now and the hereafter.

To that end, she claimed she had a good rapport with most spirits. They sensed that she was here to help them. A few, however, had turned out to be bitter and uncooperative, but she tried to help those, as well. Sometimes all they wanted, Anise explained, was to have someone listen to them, someone to care. Ghosts weren't so different from mortals, having been one themselves at some point in time.

They began the tour at twilight, that mystical, mysterious time of day when things weren't always as they seemed. A play of light could fool the mind. Shadows could play tricks upon the eye. Anise used the fading light to her advantage, her whisper-soft voice enhancing the mood of secrecy and mystification.

Aside from the running commentary about ghosts, Gera learned a great deal of valuable information about the town. Jerome, once hailed as the wickedest town in the west, had a vivid and interesting past. Minnie and Leo had shared some of that history, but most of their stories had revolved around *The Dove*. Anise offered a more well-rounded version that included the entire community. It turned out the town was full of colorful characters. And, if Anise was correct, many of their ghosts still lingered today.

By the time they reached the *Sliding Jail*, darkness had set in. Their leader offered a riveting tale about the historic structure and some of the spirits she had encountered there throughout the years. As they left the jail and headed toward the shadowy corner of town that housed the *Cuban Queen Bordello*, Anise launched into a lively tale of its owner Anna, and her jazz musician husband. Both were known to practice voodoo, she told her followers.

"Ouch! What was that?" Eli cried, stumbling a bit as they crossed the uneven terrain of the city park. "Someone pulled my hair!"

Anise stopped suddenly, creating somewhat of a pile up amid the group following closely upon her heels. "Please, everyone. Shh. A spirit is among us." She nodded to the hand-held meters gone silent. While in search mode, the meters gave off a steady hum of static. Silence signaled an energy source was near.

Sandy fumbled in her pockets and pulled out her thermometer, waving it around to see if the numbers plummeted. Josh moved closer to his boyfriend.

"Eli, ask your friend if he or she can present themselves," Anise suggested.

"Is—Is anyone there?" the man asked, his voice timid.

"If you're there," Anise said, "please know you're among friends. We would like to help you. Please give us a sign."

"I felt it!" Josh insisted. "Something—someone—brushed against my arm."

"Good, good. They're making contact. Eli, is there anything you would like to ask our friend?"

"Uhm, sure. So, are you a dude? Or a female?"

"A different format, please," Anise murmured. "Remember, our meters can only detect yes and no answers. One spike is yes, two is no."

Eli gave a nervous nod. He held his meter out like a flashlight, waving it through the air. "Are you male?"

There was a brief burst of static as the needle spiked across the grid one time. "Okay, good. Were you ever a guest at the jail?"

The response was delayed, but finally there were two bursts of static. "So no jailbird. Cool. Hey, are you Mac?" he asked hopefully.

Gera had been studying the town from this vantage point, trying to judge the most probable path used by Abe's killer. Hearing mention of Mac, even she turned inward and awaited the 'answer.'

The meter rattled out a single gust of static.

She was standing next to Eli, if not a few feet behind. She could play this game, too. She quickly stepped up and asked the next question. "Did you kill Abe Cunningham?"

The group held a collective breath as they waited for the answer. When the meter began to crackle and hum, they sighed in disappointment. "We lost contact," Anise said. "Perhaps he was insulted." She didn't verbally chastise Gera for her question, but her pale eyes were full of censure. "Those of us who know Mac know he could never commit such a heinous crime. Mac has a good, gentle soul."

"Have you ever seen him?" Gera asked, refusing to apologize for scaring away a ghost. And wasn't that an oxymoron, at any rate?

"Why, yes, many times."

"Why do you believe he hasn't crossed over? What keeps holding Mac here?"

"I believe that Mac feels responsible for the blast of '38. Do all of you know the story?" When all heads nodded, she continued, "I think he made a commitment to the town, to stay behind and watch over us, to keep us safe in the afterlife, even though he was unable to do so during his mortal life."

"So, you don't believe he is responsible for all the mischief that has taken place recently?" Gera pressed.

"Of course not. Mac is too honorable to do any of those things. Please, if you take nothing else away from our search tonight, please know that Mac McGruder is a good, kind, gentle soul. He will be your friend, if only you allow him to be." She stressed her sincerity to the group, her pale face practically aglow in the dim moonlight.

"Let's continue," Anise said, starting to walk again. "Eli, I believe that Mac may have been trying to guide you through the park. The ground is uneven here. He may have sensed you were about to stumble, and pulling your hair was his way of warning you. Now, up ahead, as I mentioned, is what remains of the bordello. This was a very fancy establishment in its day, with gambling facilities, a full-service saloon, musical entertainment, and, yes, girls of the night. You'll notice…"

Gera fell slightly behind, only half-listening to what Anise had to say. She was tempted to drop out now, before she wasted an entire evening listening to this charade. A ghost, trying to warn a man about stumbling? She snorted in disbelief. She didn't care if her meter had gone silent again. It didn't mean that a ghost walked beside her.

She looked back over her shoulder, still trying to imagine the path Abe's killer had taken. How long would it take to get from the crime scene to this darkest corner of town? Bare minutes, particularly at a run. That could explain how someone could kill Abe and escape without being seen. By the time Grant Young wandered along, the killer could've been hiding here in the shadows, watching from a safe distance.

Gera realized that by lagging behind, she had allowed the group to wander further ahead than she intended. She would need to hurry to catch up. The night was dark and her flashlight was prone to moments of flickering light. Anise suggested it was indicative of a ghost nearby, taking its energy from her battery, but Gera knew it merely meant the batteries were weak.

She saw the others up ahead, rounding the corner to head up the rugged path of First Avenue. Another skeletal building loomed in front of them, an eerie but beautiful structure in the moonlight. No street lights illuminated this sad stretch of pavement.

Her flashlight dimmed on her again, going almost completely out. Just her luck, it happened at the precise moment the moon tucked beneath a cloud. Gera almost stumbled in the darkness, but she managed to keep upright and moving. Her gracefulness surprised even her.

But as the moon came back out and the others noticed for the first time that she wasn't among them, the hairs on Gera's arms ruffled to attention. She had the oddest sensation of being watched. It wasn't someone in the group, but someone who studied her intently, their gaze pointed. Someone watched her, she was certain of it.

After that, she made a point to stay with the group. They made their way back up the steep assent of First Avenue, pausing at various points as Anise shared one story or another. Gera snapped pictures with her cell phone as the guide relayed her tale. Let the others think she was trying to catch an orb; Gera was trying to catch a killer.

She blamed what happened next on the fact that she knew someone watched her. She had to admit, she was a bit spooked by the fact. Her defenses were down, she decided. That was why she reacted the way she did when Anise told a poignant tale about a group of children, the tale about Mac saving a group of school children, rushing them out of harm's way.

Gera felt a shiver of cold pass through her.

It was an emotional story, she reasoned. It was only natural to get chills. Didn't mean a ghost was present, even when her meter fell silent. Even when she snapped a photo of the dark street beyond and noticed a tiny speck of light on the preview screen.

Gera glanced up and checked the same spot with her naked eye. Nothing.

She snapped another photo. The light had moved, closer to her this time.

Again, she looked up. Nothing was in the street. Nothing she could see, but her mind insisted that it was a piece of trash, catching the light of her flash.

No one else seemed to notice. They were caught up in Anise's dramatic rendition of Mac's heroic deed. The chill crawled up Gera's spine, manifesting itself in gooseflesh that covered her arms. She could've sworn she felt a cool breeze swirl around her, but no wind stirred Anise's dangling feather earrings, nor the filmy edges of her flowing skirt. The night was still.

As the group trudged up the street, Gera was angry with herself. This wasn't proof of a ghostly spirit. This was proof of the power of suggestion. She, of all people, knew there was no such thing as ghosts, yet here she was, almost willing to entertain the notion of an unseen entity.

She was almost too aggravated to appreciate the fact that they passed right by the old *Bartlett Hotel*. It was hauntingly beautiful in the moonlight, its stark structure and elaborate ironwork a beacon in the dark night, even when swathed in crime tape. Out of respect to Abe Cunningham, Anise kept her commentary on the old building brief, but she hinted that spirits dwelled within.

Lastly, they crossed the street and visited the Upper Park, where of all things a miniature golf course was once the rage at the turn of the twentieth century. Dynky Lynx was gone, but swing sets and picnic tables now nestled amid the town's busiest streets, a tiny hidden oasis amid the trees. When the group aimed their temperature probes at the playground equipment and found the meters dipped as much as ten degrees or more, excitement stirred among them. They interpreted it as a sign that playful spirits lingered, particularly those of children. Gera attributed the sudden plunge to the cold, hard substance of steel, but she kept her opinion to herself.

Their final stop was the old Catholic church. As they climbed the steep incline, Cathy commented it wasn't far from their hotel, which sat higher up the hill. The roadway was dark, as were the steps up to the church. Gera found it a bit disconcerting to visit a church on a monetized tour, and, yes, just a little creepy. In spite of the dark, she still felt as if someone watched her.

The chapel was dim, the only light coming from the flicker of a hundred prayer candles. Behind the altar, dozens of decorative crosses and stained glass caught bits of light and seemed to dance across the back wall with a life of their own.

Anise spoke in hushed tones and guided the group about with reverence, careful not to disrespect the house of worship. They stopped briefly in the cemetery out back. Despite the beautiful landscaping and its aura of peace and tranquility, Gera still found the visit in poor taste. It left a negative vibe that nibbled at her conscience.

And even as they traveled back down the hill and dispersed as a group, Gera still couldn't shake the sensation of being watched.

Most disturbing, however, was the sinking feeling that she, of all people, had succumbed to the greatest evil of all.

She had fallen victim to the power of suggestion.

⚘

Gera woke in the night, hearing voices.

She had drunk too much wine last night. She hadn't been drunk, merely aggravated. The ghost tour left her restless and in a bad mood, and dinner at the *Spirit Burger* hadn't sat well on her stomach. Sulking, she had come back to her room and consumed the better part of a bottle of wine.

Now, drawn out of a deep sleep, she was slow to clear the cobwebs from her mind.

She heard a child crying. A baby, from the sounds of it. Perhaps more than one.

Gera sat up in bed, still trying to get her bearings. Was that a car she heard? And where were those voices coming from? Last night her room had been so quiet and peaceful, but tonight a low din of noise came from outside.

A draft wafted through the room and pushed against the drapes, playing among the long wispy panels.

"I bet the doors came open," she said aloud.

Using the light on her cell phone, Gera padded into the sitting room, where she found the French doors flung wide open, just as Jake had warned they might.

She started to shut the doors, but decided to step out on the balcony and see what the commotion was.

The night was quiet. Warm. Somewhere in the distance, she heard the purr of an engine, but it couldn't have been what she heard earlier. There were no voices now, just the hushed sounds of a town, fast asleep.

She looked up the hill to her right, to the house she knew belonged to Ruth Cunningham. The house was dark, save for a single light in an upstairs window. She wondered if that was the master bedroom, and if Abe's widow was having trouble sleeping. From this distance, it was hard to be certain, but Gera thought she saw a person's silhouette against the light.

Even more impossible, she could've sworn she heard crying. Not a baby this time, but the sounds of a woman sobbing. A woman with a broken heart.

The sound echoed in her head, even as she moved inside. Gera closed and latched the doors, making certain the lock was secure.

The baby next door had stopped crying. Gera thought she heard someone singing a soft lullaby.

As she went back to bed, she failed to notice the paper airplane crashed at the edge of the sofa, nor the half-eaten lollipop stuck to the cushion.

11

Gera had trouble falling back to sleep, so she overslept again the next morning. This time, she completely missed breakfast. And Minnie was nowhere to be found.

Grumpy and out of sorts, finding the half-eaten sucker was the final straw.

Gera stopped by the front desk, determined to give the staff a piece of her mind. While she was at it, she would complain about the thin walls. Perhaps even ask for a different room, on a floor devoid of infants.

Someone different was at the desk this morning, a middle-aged woman with coiffed hair and a matronly smile. Her nametag identified her as Terri. She smiled at Gera as she approached.

"Good morning, Miss Stapleton. How are you today?"

Gera answered with a terse, "I'm fine, thank you," even though her inner voice said, *A little weirded out that you know who I am, but whatever.*

"How may we help you this morning?" Terri smiled.

Gera set a napkin upon the counter and opened it to reveal the half-eaten sucker. "I found this in my room." Irritation sharpened her words. "Apparently, the maid left it on my couch when she cleaned yesterday."

Terri scooped up the napkin and whisked it out of sight. "Those naughty children," she clucked.

"There were *children* in my room?" Gera asked incredulously. "Are those the ones I heard crying in the night? Please tell me why—and how—they had access to my room?"

"Oh, dear," Terri murmured worriedly. Her eyes darted about, searching for reinforcements, but there was no one else in the lobby to help field the complaint. "I—I'm afraid it's the children again, playing tricks." Her hands became animated. Her fingers twitched as she fingered the edge of the counter. Straightened the collar of her blouse. Tucked a wisp of hair behind her ear. "I'm so sorry they bothered you, Miss Stapleton. This—This really doesn't happen very often, you know." She soothed her hands over her hips, pressing out imaginary wrinkles. Fingered the clasp on her watch. "Not all the time, at least."

The woman was a nervous wreck. Something in her face gave Gera pause. "You bring your children to work with you?" she asked in surprise.

This could be a story. Her mind raced ahead with possibilities. A single mother, perhaps, trying to make ends meet. An innovative childcare option put in place by management or, better yet, the hotel's owner. She liked that in a man, too, by the way.

Busy thinking of angles for such a story, Gera almost missed Terri's reply.

"Oh, no, not *my* children! Miss Cordelia's."

Flabbergasted, Gera stared at the woman. She actually blamed a ghost for the maid's incompetence! The only thought Gera could muster was, *And she looks so normal.*

"This isn't the first issue I've had, you know," Gera continued. "The first day, the remote was hidden under the couch cushions and the batteries were missing. The next day the maid left on all the lights in the room and toys on the bed. Don't try to turn this into a marketing ploy, the way Leah did. I see it for what it is, a pattern of incompetence."

Terri began to wring her hands. Her next words came out in a breathless rush. "Let me call for Lucy." She reached for an outdated rotary phone and dialed a two-digit extension. Turning slightly away from her guest, she spoke into the receiver with urgency. "We have a bit of a situation. Please come to the front desk."

Terri turned back to face Gera, attempting a smile that was meant to be bright and reassuring. The nervous warble of her lips ruined the effect. Her fingers worried the edge of her collar again as she said, "Lucy will be with you shortly."

"You know what? It's just a sucker. Forget it," Gera decided, trying to calm down. She knew she came across too strong at times. She certainly hadn't meant to cause this woman a nervous breakdown.

"No, no. Lucy will know what to do. She's on her way."

With a sigh, Gera stepped back from the counter and waited on Lucy, head of Housekeeping.

A few minutes later, a heavy woman came puffing into the lobby, clearly winded. Gera didn't know if her breathlessness was due to excitement, age, or weight. Perhaps it was a combination of the three. The old woman waddled when she walked, wiggling in distinct layers—first her broad hips rolled, which caused a wave to move across her belly, which in turn sent an upward swell jiggling across her enormous bosom. Unbothered by it all, the woman's black face split with a wide smile. Freckles scattered over the bridge of her nose, her skin pulled too taut for wrinkles. It was impossible to guess her age, but her thinning hair was a wiry cap of solid gray.

"Well, well, who do we have here?" she asked in a deep, booming voice, beaming at Gera as if she were a shiny new bauble. "Ain't you a pretty little thing? Nerva told me you were a looker, but I didn't know she meant *this* pretty!"

The woman's warm greeting—and her reference to the deceased Minerva Cody—caught Gera off guard.

"I'm Lucy. You met my Leo the other night." Her voice dropped with feigned accusation. "*He* didn't tell me you were this pretty, either." She nudged Gera with a beefy elbow and belted out a hardy laugh, setting off another jiggle of her bosom. "Ain't that just like a husband? After all these years, afraid I might be jealous!"

At a loss for what to say, Gera went with a meek, "I'm Gera."

"Oh, I know who you are, honey. What I don't know is what's troubling you today." It took effort, but she whirled around to face Terri. "What's this situation you called about?"

"It's the children," Terri reported nervously. "They're up to their tricks again. They left this lollipop in Miss Stapleton's room." She presented the half-eaten sucker for inspection.

Lucy looked relieved. "I thought you were going to say it was the babies. The speaker system broke again and the babies cried all night, least ways 'til Nerva started singing to them. I was afraid the babies kept her awake, like they did the guest in 407."

"Wasn't it their baby?" Gera broke in with a speculative frown. "It sounded like it was right next door to my room."

"Oh, there aren't any babies in the hotel, Missy. No mortal babies, that is. But don't you worry, we'll get the system up and working in no time. Nerva sang so much last night, she's got herself a sore throat, so we'll have to get it fixed for sure. We can't have those babies crying again all night."

With a defeated sigh, Gera said aloud, "Look, I'm sorry to have bothered you. I should've never mentioned the sucker to begin with. I just thought perhaps you would like to know your cleaning staff needs to do a better job while in the rooms, but—"

"This wasn't from *my* cleaning staff!" Lucy huffed. "None of my girls would've left that there." She jabbed a fleshy finger toward the offensive sucker.

"You really can't be sure of that," Gera protested. "But forget it; it's not a big deal. I—"

"I most certainly can be sure of it!" Lucy insisted. She propped her hands upon her ample hips. "See those teeth marks? Sonia is in the process of getting dentures. There's not a single tooth in that woman's mouth! And what color is that sucker?"

"Red," Terri supplied.

"Shawna is allergic to red dye. That little white girl's skin is so fair, she breaks out if she even gets close to anything with red food coloring." Lucy shoved a finger in her mouth to expose her gums, trying to talk with her lip hiked at an angle. "Gets these tiny wittwe bwistas, aw awound her gums." Dropping her hand, she finished her argument. "And Justine is down in Tucson, taking care of her sick momma. So, it couldn't have been any of my girls." She gave a smart nod of her head and concluded, "Had to have been the children."

Of course, she blamed the children. She thought she conversed with Minerva Cody. Gera knew she was fighting a losing battle. She muttered beneath her breath, "I'm stuck in the *Twilight Zone.*"

But she presented a bright smile to the other women and pretended all was normal and right. "Again, I'm sorry to have bothered you. Thank you for coming down and clearing everything up."

"Anytime, sweet thing. Anytime," Lucy chuckled, setting off another wave of jiggles. "You should join me and Nerva for tea. She likes you, you know. Thinks you make a nice match for her grandson."

"Oh. How… flattering."

Gera backed her way out of the lobby, strangely reluctant to turn her back on the old woman. You never knew what an unstable mind was capable of, she reasoned, even if the person seemed all sweet and grandmotherly.

She called Jillian the moment she cleared the doors. Getting through to her editor proved more difficult than getting through to the local bank president. By the time she heard the familiar voice on the line, Gera was already in her car and had the air at full blast, chasing away the heat.

"What's up, love?" Jillian asked.

"Jillian, I want you to know I tried. I tried to make this story work, but I just don't think I can do it anymore. This town is nuts. Literally, I mean nuts. Bonkers. Every single one of them believes in ghosts." She adjusted the air vent to keep it from blowing directly in her face. "Okay, all except the guy with the overpriced collectibles. And maybe the sheriff. But everyone else is a believer, including the bank president. And *he* went to Princeton!" she threw out, as if that made a difference.

Jillian had the audacity to laugh at her. "What, do they have an anti-ghost clause for those attending Princeton?"

"I'm just trying to point out that, to the naked eye, these are seemingly normal, sane, educated people. But beneath the surface, they're nuts. Absolute nuts. You cannot even imagine the conversation I just had."

Had to have been the children, the woman had said, as if that were the logical conclusion.

"Gera, as a reporter, you know the importance of keeping an open mind. Just because some people see things differently than you do doesn't necessarily—"

"You don't understand, Jillian," she interrupted her boss. "I don't really care if they think a ghost helped them find a lost ring or kept them from stumbling in the dark or even if they think a ghost sang herself hoarse last night. Whatever. Whatever floats their boat. But I'm talking about murder. These people are content to blame the death of a man on a *ghost*. Someone killed Abe Cunningham. The police are being very tight lipped on how he died—"

"He was stabbed," Jillian supplied. "We have a confidential source that just confirmed details this morning."

"Okay, so someone stabbed Abe Cunningham and left him there to die. Did you see the pictures I sent you? There is no way a man as old as Abe could've scaled that fence and gotten inside, unless he entered through the gate. But people here are literally claiming that Mac, the once-friendly ghost, somehow picked him up, magically transported him over the fence, stabbed him, and left him to die. Never mind that a real murderer is still roaming the streets. They blame it on a ghost."

Jillian was quiet on her end of the line, presumably pondering the issue. "Everyone?" she questioned.

"No, not everyone, actually. There are many in town who insist that Mac is a good, decent soul and would never do such a thing. But don't you get it, Jillian? The point is, they believe it is possible that a ghost *could* kill a man. Maybe not this ghost, but a ghost in general. A tangible spirit. They. Literally. Believe. In. Ghosts."

"But you believe someone else killed this man."

"Of course! Of course, I believe someone else did it. Someone mortal!"

"Then prove it."

Gera dropped her head back against the headrest and groaned. She had fallen into that trap quite nicely. "How, Jillian?" she asked wearily. "The chief of police has made it abundantly clear that he doesn't want me interfering in his case. No one else in town seems worried about finding the true killer. They're far more concerned with defending or attacking Mac's character, whichever the case may be. Honestly, I feel like I'm caught somewhere in the *Twilight Zone.*"

"Ask yourself this. Why would someone want to kill Abe Cunningham?"

"I have no idea."

"Then you need to find out."

Gera was quiet for so long that Jillian had to ask, "Hello? Are we still connected?"

"Yes. Sorry, I was trying to think of reasons someone might want Abe dead."

"Motive, Gera. Find your motive, and you find your killer."

"I'm not a detective, you know." Her tone was testy. Jillian asked the impossible.

"Of course you are! You're a reporter, and that is essentially the same thing. Look, when I sent you on this assignment, I thought it would make a great side piece for our October issue," Jillian confessed. "A bit of a twist to the old ghost and goblin story, if you will. But you've stumbled upon something, Gera. A murder. You say the town is unconcerned with finding the true villain. Why is that? Do they have something to hide? Why else would they be content to blame such a heinous deed on a ghost? These are the questions, Gera. Find the answers."

"I'll try," she promised on a sigh.

"What was that?"

Gera straightened her shoulders and spoke with something that sounded enough like conviction to please her boss. "I said I will."

Jillian chuckled. "That's the spirit."

"Thanks, Jillian. I needed a little pep talk right about now."

"Oh! I think I saw a note here on my desk for you. Let me just find it…" There was the sound of shuffled papers and a brief pause, filled with bumping and one muttered curse. At last, Jillian came back on the line. "Yes, here it is. Ramon had a tip for you. He said to be sure to ask about something. Frankie D. and the hidden gold."

"Who? What is he talking about? And what hidden gold?"

"Beats me, but unfortunately, you can't ask him right now. He's having all four wisdom teeth extracted and will be out until next week. And you know how loopy medication makes our friend."

She did. With a sigh, Gera said, "Okay, thanks anyway."

With new determination, Gera pulled out of the parking lot. She made a mental list of things she needed to do today, angles she needed to explore. Jillian was right. Every crime had two elements: motive and opportunity. If she found these, she could find the killer, and just maybe the cover on the October issue of *When It Happens.*

Stopped at the foot of the hill by the church, Gera remembered the creepy feeling she had while there the night before. She considered the possibility that she simply had an aversion to religious institutes. Perhaps, she decided, she associated churches with death. Her last several visits to a church had been for funerals.

Her attention snagged on the police cruiser making its way up the hairpin curve from Main, climbing onto Clark Street. As the car passed directly in front of her, she saw the unmistakable profile of Miles Anderson behind the wheel.

Gera didn't have to think it through. She eyed the cruiser until it disappeared, inching her way out enough to watch it round the mountain and head out of town. Then she whipped her own car in the opposite direction and drove directly to the police station. She took a parking spot at the far end of the street and hiked back up the sidewalk. The exercise was good for her adrenaline.

She was in luck. Officer Mike Cooper was at the desk when she walked in.

She popped in with a bright smile. "Hi, remember me?" She didn't wait for his answer. "Mike, isn't it? I just dropped by for that list Chief Anderson left for me."

He gave her a blank stare. "Uh, list?"

"Yes. I'm working on that magazine article, you know, and I'm here to pick up the list he made. Is he in?" She continued to smile expectantly, pretending to search the station for sight of him.

"No, he had to go into Prescott. You just missed him."

She looked crushed. "Oh, great," she muttered. "Just great." She consulted her watch. "I need to be somewhere in a half hour. I don't suppose you could be a lifesaver and just give me the information yourself?"

Officer Clark glanced around the empty office. "Uh, what information did you need?"

"The list of witnesses to the current crime spree. Oh, and the names of people who have access to the Bartlett building." She tried to come across as casual. She hoped her blatant audacity didn't bleed through in her voice.

The surprise on his face was comical. Gera bit her upper lip, trying not to smile. She hoped her one and only acting class was preparation enough to pull this off.

During a low point in her life, amid four jobs and the most recent rejection from the newspaper office, she wavered in the focus of her studies. Maybe journalism wasn't the right thing for her, after all. When one of her online classes fell victim to technical difficulties, she snapped up the last spot in a theatrical night course. One drama class was all it took to reaffirm Gera's commitment to becoming a reporter, but she had to admit, that one class had proved invaluable. Good acting skills were a must for any reporter.

The key to acting, the coach had told her, was believability. It helped if you were an accomplished liar—which, she noted, Gera was *not*—but there were ways to imply a lie, without actually telling one. Similarly, there were ways to imply believability, even when acting. It was all in the details.

"And he said he would *give* you a copy?" The officer's voice was incredulous.

Gera nodded with enthusiasm. "He had a list." It was true, she was sure. He just never said he would share it with her.

"Uh... well, okay then. Let me see if I can find it." Clearly confused, the officer lumbered to his feet. He ran a hand up the back of his head, unsure of where to start and what to do.

For good measure, Gera glanced back at her watch. A small enough detail, but the officer noticed.

"Yes, appointment. Right." He shoved aside a few papers, looking for a note in the chief's handwriting, or an envelope with her name on it.

She spotted the thick folder that topped the stack. "Isn't that the case file? Maybe it's inside."

He flipped the file open, making a show of thumbing through the pages. "Nothing," he reported. Seeing her deep frown, he lifted the folder by its covers and flipped it over, to prove there was no envelope tucked inside. He yelped when several papers floated free.

Gera bit back another smile as he scrambled to gather the loose papers and stuff them inside the bindings. Some were photos, some were jotted notes. Others were newspaper clippings. Her eyes tracked the progress of one small slip of paper. It floated independently of the others, sliding neatly beneath another folder. She didn't bother pointing it out to the officer. He looked frazzled enough.

"I'm sorry, I don't see anything with your name on it," Cooper said.

Gera's sigh was clearly discouraged. "Does he do this often? Get so busy he forgets to do as he promises?"

The officer gave her a sympathetic smile. "All the time," he admitted. "He's a busy man."

She drummed her fingers on the counter. Glanced worriedly at her watch. "How long does it take to get to Cottonwood?" Not that she was headed there, but Cooper didn't know that.

"Depends on what side of town you're going to," he said. "If you're headed to Police Headquarters, it will take a good twenty minutes."

Gera squeezed out a groan. Shifted on her feet. Shifted again. Her mannerisms *implied* that she was torn, trying to decide between keeping an appointment and waiting for the promised information. She even tipped her head, suggesting she favored one silent option over the other.

It took him longer to respond than she anticipated. Gera stalled, blowing out a discouraged breath. Cheeks puffed, she let her shoulders sag. *Come on, have a heart,* she silently pleaded. *How much more pathetic can I look?*

He finally took the bait. "I don't see anything he left for you, but I guess I could give you the notes myself." He still sounded unsure about the whole thing. He pierced her with a direct look. "And he said you could see the files?" he clarified.

"Not the entire thing, obviously. I mean, I'm sure that's classified." She flashed her palms with an implied hands-off gesture. "But he was making a list." She bobbed her head in a show of certainty, without actually telling a lie. What investigation didn't require a list? "The string of recent misdemeanors and the witnesses who reported seeing Mac at the scene. Oh, and I wanted a copy of the coroner's report," she added. She threw in a little tidbit for added credibility. "Any word on the type of knife used?"

"Oh, so you talked to him this morning," Cooper surmised. Last he heard, they were keeping the cause of death under wraps. But if the chief shared that much with her, he apparently didn't mind sharing the rest.

With a shrug, the officer picked up the file folder and carried it to the ancient copier at the back of the room. "We just got that report back."

The moment his back was turned, Gera slipped her hand over the counter and snagged the previously floating slip of paper. Tucking it into her pocket, she offered a suggestion. "You know, instead of making a copy, I could just snap a few pictures with my phone. It would be quicker." She darted a glance at the clock on the wall.

Accustomed to doing things old school, it was obvious the thought had never occurred to the officer. He blinked into action. "Right. You have that appointment in Cottonwood." He brought the folder back and flipped it open, pushing it toward her. "It will be quicker if you just do it yourself," he said. "You know what you need."

Gera knew a golden opportunity when she saw it. She wasted no time in snapping off photos of as many pages as possible. She ignored the nibble of guilt tugging at her conscience. Officer Cooper committed a huge breach of confidentiality. It could cost him his job, should her source of information be discovered. She would just have to make certain it never was.

"If you like, I can call Detective Chao and tell him you're running late."

She had no idea what he was talking about, but she played a hunch. "How did you know my appointment was with Detective Chao?"

"Easy," Cooper shrugged. "He's Macandie's alibi. Naturally, Billy Boy was our first suspect. It's kind of ironic how he's turned out to be our ace witness, but you can't get a more solid alibi than Chao."

One thing acting class didn't teach her was how to successfully hide her own feelings of surprise. She was afraid it showed now on her face. She had no idea who Billy Boy Macandie was, but he obviously had something to do with the case.

"You know what? Don't call Chao just yet. I'm done here, and with any luck, I can make our appointment by the skin of my teeth." Gera flashed a smile bright enough to give the sun outside a complex. "You, my friend, have been a lifesaver."

Her flattery wasn't lost upon him. "Now don't you go off, speeding down the mountainside," he warned gruffly, shaking a finger for emphasis. "The roads are dangerous enough without adding speed as a factor."

"Hey, I'm no daredevil," Gera promised. "Thanks, Coop."

Gera waltzed out of the station, feeling quite proud of herself. She had the information she wanted—and more—and she hadn't told a single lie to get it.

Yep, once again, that acting class had more than paid for itself.

12

Still playing a hunch, Gera decided a visit to Detective Chao wasn't a bad idea. She ducked into the café next door and did a quick search for the Cottonwood police department on her phone. As it turned out, even getting through to a high-level detective on a busy police force was easier than getting through to her editor. Within minutes, Gera had an appointment scheduled for early afternoon.

Having missed breakfast, Gera decided to multitask. She would grab a bite to eat while searching for information on this Billy Boy Macandie. The last thing she wanted to do was go unprepared into her meeting with the Detective.

Since she carried her iPad and notebook in her purse, Gera whipped them out and set up shop. She typed in Macandie's name and waited for the page to load.

"My, my, what a busy boy you've been," she murmured.

Robert 'Billy Boy' Macandie was a low-level thug with a string of questionable acquaintances and minor skirmishes with the law. In his late twenties, he had stopped short of committing any serious crimes, but he was a person of interest in numerous cases involving organized crime. He managed to graduate high school but had an employment record with huge, gaping holes. Having lived his entire life in a twenty-five-mile radius, Billy Boy showed no visible prospects of expanding his borders, unless it happened to be the state penitentiary over in Phoenix.

"Here's your pancakes," Loretta said, sliding a fluffy stack between Gera and her iPad. She looked at the social media page splayed across the screen. "What you doing looking up that boy? He's nothing but trouble. You need to concentrate on Jake Cody. Now there's a fine catch."

Surprised by the woman's candid invasion of privacy—not to mention her attempt at matchmaking—Gera quickly choked back any indignation she might have felt. Loretta could be a valuable source of information.

"I don't know," Gera said, trying to sound thoughtful. "You don't think he's sort of cute?"

"I don't go for all the rings and baubles stuck here and yonder," Loretta snorted, running a finger beneath her nose. "You know some of those have got to hurt."

"Do you happen to know where I could find him?"

"Sure. Walk across the street and ask for the bartender at *The Cactus*. But mark my words, girl. He's nothing but trouble."

"I'll keep that in mind."

"Say, did you get in touch with Anise?"

"Yes. As a matter of fact, I went on a tour with her last night."

"Oh, yeah?" Loretta grinned. She was already moving away as she asked, "What did you think about it?"

"It was very interesting," Gera answered in all honesty.

A deep, pleasant voice spoke from behind her. "I hope you're referring to your conversation with me." She turned to see Grant Young smiling down at her. "Hello, Miss Stapleton. How are you today?"

"I'm fine, thank you."

He nodded to the empty chair across from her. "Is this seat taken? Would you mind some company?"

"By all means…" she invited, scrambling to scoop up some of her scattered papers.

"Don't mind me. I just came in for coffee."

"They don't make coffee at the bank?"

His eyes twinkled as he admitted with a charismatic smile, "All right, I admit it. I saw you in the window and came to say hello."

Not sure how to respond, the best Gera came up with was a lame, "Oh. Well, then… hello."

He found her discomfort amusing. And yes, Gera decided, the man was flirting with her.

"I see you're having a late breakfast. By the way, the pancakes here are fabulous. Please, don't let me keep you."

"Brunch," she corrected. "Saves time, not necessarily calories." This, as she drowned the stack in maple syrup.

"No need for you to worry about that," he murmured in appreciation.

Gera cut into her pancakes with precise detail. Anything to keep from acknowledging his flirtatious remark. She still wasn't certain how she felt about that.

"I see you've been busy making friends here in town." There was a slight tone of disapproval in his voice. His eyes indicated her iPad.

It seemed to be a common practice here in Jerome, nosing into someone else's business. Closing the page and pushing the device aside, Gera shrugged. "Not really. Just surfing the net."

"My advice? Keep surfing. Macandie is bad news."

"Loretta said the same thing."

"Listen to her. The only positive thing Macandie ever did was finger Mac for the crimes that have taken place recently. Thanks to him, the police have positive identification. From what I understand, Macandie is a key witness in at least two of the crimes."

Not knowing how to respond, Gera stuffed a pancake into her mouth.

People are allowed their own opinions, Gera. Keep an open mind.

Another voice spoke in her head, taunting her. *Yeah, and look where an open mind got you last night!*

The pancakes really were delicious. Gera made a show of chewing well and swallowing. What could she say, without insulting the man's intelligence? She may have seriously questioned that intelligence at the moment, but she couldn't be so rude. Chewing gave her time to formulate a plan.

She could try her hand at acting again. Maybe she could *act* as if she didn't think he was nuts.

Details, she reminded herself. Gera tilted her head just so, to indicate her thoughtful interest. "From what I understand, Mac has gone from being friendly to antagonistic. Why do you think that is?"

Nice save, Gera girl, she congratulated herself. Now to remember to nod a lot and act convinced, no matter how ridiculous his answer.

"Good question. My opinion?"

"Yes, definitely. Absolutely." She bobbed her head with enthusiasm.

Grant Young leaned in across the table, dropping his voice to a confidential tone. "I think he's trying to drive people off the mountain."

"But, why? Whatever for?"

"There has been... talk." He chose his words carefully, as if deciding how much information to confide in her. "Rumors that there is another slide coming, a substantial one. Geological studies have confirmed that eventually, the entire town will slip off the side of the hill."

"You mean, like they predict California will eventually break away from the continent?"

"Exactly." His eyes sparkled, appreciating her sharp interpretation. "I have friends within the field, highly renowned scientists, who confirm that early test results show the slide will occur within the next few years."

Gera frowned. "This is public information?"

"Not exactly," he admitted.

"But—shouldn't you tell them? Isn't this information the public deserves to know? Aren't you putting their lives at risk by not telling them?"

He looked around in concern, afraid someone had overheard her hissed remarks.

"Shh, please," he urged, leaning even closer. "This is highly confidential. And believe me, it is for the safety of the community that we don't release this information to the public."

Gera had heard enough. The man truly was nuts. "Oh *really*?" she asked sardonically, leaning back in her chair.

"Please, hear me out." He motioned her forward. "The scientists tell me that if there were to be a mass exodus off the mountain, it could actually cause immediate danger. Something to do with pressure points, calibrations of the earth's vibrations, undue stress on specific fault lines, and whatnot." He talked with his hands, indicating movement. He flashed a disarming smile. "To be honest, it's above my head. I deal with numeric equations, not scientific ones. But I understand the basic principle."

She nodded. "Like displacement of weight, triggering detonation of a bomb."

"Exactly! In fact, my friends used that very analogy. They stressed the importance of not causing a panic within the community and having everyone leave at once."

"So, what? You just leave them here like sitting ducks?" Gera scoffed.

Loretta came by with the coffee pot, filling the cup already on the table. The normally vocal waitress looked at them with curiosity, noting their proximity and the urgency within their hushed voices, but she made no comment. The look in her eyes spoke for her. She didn't trust the banker. Gera didn't have time to wonder if her distrust was directed to all people in that profession, or him specifically. Grant Young spoke again as Loretta moved away.

"Think of it this way. People in California know an earthquake will happen, and that sooner and later, it will be devastating. The same can be said for the people in Oklahoma and Kansas, with their tornadoes. And for people along the coasts, with the very real threat of hurricanes and floods. None of us are completely safe from the elements, no matter where we live."

"Okay," she said with grudging reluctance, "I guess I see your point."

"So, I don't have to worry about seeing any of this conversation in print?" He tipped in closer, just enough to make the conversation feel intimate.

"It's a little late to worry about that now, isn't it? How do you know you can trust me?"

His eyes were warm. "I just do."

They had gotten far off topic. The last place Gera wanted to go was to where the look in his eyes led. He was an attractive man and apparently quite the eligible bachelor, but he was at least fifteen years older than she was. And he believed in ghosts.

So does Jake, a voice whispered in her head.

Oddly enough, that last realization hurt, far more than it should have.

She shook her head free of the distractions. "What does any of this have to do with Mac?"

"I think he knows the slide is coming, and in his own unique way, he is trying to save the town. Scare people away slowly, one household at a time, so that everyone is safe."

"That is a nice theory, I suppose, except for one thing."

"And what would that be?" He studied her intently, waiting for her valued opinion.

"Abe Cunningham. What was that, a sacrifice killing?"

A frown tugged the corners of his mouth. "That's a rather crude way of putting it, of course. However, it is possible, now that you mention it. Perhaps Abe knew about the impending slide and wanted to release the study. Abe may have been trying to stop him."

"Wait. I never said—"

"No, no, you make a valid point," he murmured. "It would make sense, now wouldn't it?"

They were discussing a supposed argument between a man and a ghost. No, none of it made sense! Very little in this entire town did.

Instead of answering, Gera went back to her pancakes. Grant drained his coffee cup, his eyes thoughtful.

"Would you care to have dinner with me this evening?" he asked, quite unexpectedly.

"Uhm, I'm afraid I already have plans." Again, not a direct lie. At some point this evening, she would have a meal and go to sleep. However loose and undefined, those qualified as plans, didn't they?

"I understand. Perhaps before you leave town?"

"At this point, I can't make any promises. I have a very busy schedule."

"I understand busy schedules," he smiled. "In fact, I have one of my own that I'm sorely neglecting." He stood from the table and pulled several bills from his wallet. "That should cover things."

"Oh, you don't have to—"

Her protest was cut short when Mike Cooper came into the café. Not only was it the happening place in town, apparently, she was in the happening seat. The officer stopped behind her and looked down at her in surprise. "I thought you had an appointment with Chao?"

Gera was proud of her quick reply. "You were right. I would've had to drive too fast. I have a one o'clock appointment now."

"Ah, I'm glad you rescheduled. Drive safe." He shook hands with the banker as he passed on to an open booth in the back.

Grant Young smiled at her. "Well, Gera, I hope you have a lovely day." The use of her first name and the warmth of his large hand cupping her shoulder had an intimate feel. "I hope to see you again soon."

She wiggled her fingers in farewell. "You too, Grant."

⚘

"You really go for the bad boys, don't you?" Loretta said, shaking her head with disappointment. "Poor Jake doesn't stand a chance, does he?"

The waitress' tendency to butt in grated on Gera's nerves. "Two things," she said, indicating them with her fingers. "First, I don't *go* for Grant Young, nor this Billy Bad Boy. Two, what is it with you and Jake? Are you secretly in love with him or something?"

Loretta flashed a toothy smile, propping a hand onto her hip. "Ask my husband, it ain't no secret," she drawled. With a flip of her hand, she admitted more seriously, "I just think he's a sweetheart, is all. He hasn't had a girlfriend since he came back here to run the hotel. I worry about him being lonesome."

"I can assure you, if Jake Cody is lonesome, it's of his own choosing."

Loretta grinned even wider. "You like him, don't cha?"

Gera gave her an evil eye. "What, are we in junior high?"

The waitress completely ignored her and launched into a round of advice. "If you want to have a chance with Jake, don't let him see you getting friendly with the banker. Those two don't exactly get along."

"I'm not getting friendly with Grant Young," Gera denied. "I just met the man yesterday."

"You sure looked cozy to me."

Hearing the accusation in the waitress' voice, Gera surmised, "I'm sensing you don't like the man, either."

"You could say that."

"Anything you'd like to share?"

"I went to school with him. You know the type. Super jock, super cool, super rich, super smart. Super jerk."

"Really? I didn't get that impression at all." *In fact, I think he's really nice,* she thought to herself. *A complete nut, but nice.*

Loretta sniffed. "Maybe having to come home to his old stomping grounds took him down a peg or two. He was a real hotshot, you know, traveling all over the world, making a name for himself in the corporate banking world. Then his father had a stroke, and he had to come back here. To this." She spread her hands, indicating the tiny little town beyond the plate-glass windows. "You know it had to take some of the piss and vinegar out of the man."

"That's commendable though, don't you think, coming home to take over the family business?"

"Like he had a choice!" she harrumphed. "The way I hear it, that's one of the conditions of the trust. A Young has to remain on the mountain, no matter what."

Gera thought of Grant's tale about the impending slide. Would keeping his family fortune be so important to him that he stayed here, no matter the danger? Somehow, she doubted it. There had to be a legal loophole that accounted for such a thing.

"Anyway," Loretta continued, "I just don't like the way he lords over the town, doling out money at his discretion."

"Well, that's kind of what bankers do," Gera reminder her.

"I guess. Me, I avoid the whole lot of them, as much as possible." She scooped up the bills on the table and counted them out. "Your bill isn't half this much. I'll be right back with the change."

"Keep all of it," Gera insisted. "Compliments of Grant Young."

The *Cactus Bar* stood on the corner, next to First Yavapai Savings. According to Loretta, it was one of Mac's favorite haunts, and the place she saw him most often.

Gera eyed the elaborate fireplace in the back of the room, situated behind several card tables. Someone said this was where the Tuesday night poker game took place, but the space currently did double duty as a crowded lunchroom.

It seemed everyone favored the place, not just Mac, the one-eared ghost.

Billy Boy Macandie was working today, and as long as Gera was willing to order drinks, he was willing to talk to her.

No surprise after seeing his social media account, but tattoos covered most of his visible skin. They trailed up his long arms and wrapped around his neck, reminding Gera of a snake. Behind the piercings and the ink, she imagined he might be a rather nice-looking man, but it was difficult to know for sure. His hair was dark and cut in a strange wedge that was clipped close and short on one side, left long and full on the other. She wondered if he had trouble finding a hat to fit. Not that he looked the hat sort of guy. Beanies, most likely, and hoodies. Billy Boy was tall and lanky, and no longer a boy.

"Yeah, I saw him," he said in answer to her question.

"What was he doing?"

"Just walking. Headed away from her car. Then the chick came out, opened her door, and started yelling that her purse was missing."

"How did you know it was Mac?"

"Saw his coat and hat."

"Did you see his face?"

"Had his back to me."

"What about when Megan McCracken was assaulted? I understand you witnessed that, too."

His smile was almost attractive, but his tongue ring was designed like a snake's head. And like a snake, Billy Boy liked to flick his tongue out. Gera found the habit disgusting.

"I have a one-drink-one-question minimum."

Gera pulled another bill from her purse. "I'll take another."

Billy Boy grinned, flicking the snake her way. "You haven't finished that one yet."

She tried to suppress a shudder. "Don't worry about me. I'll catch up."

When he came back with a second glass, he noticed her first was now half-empty. "You're getting there," he said with approval. "So, what else did you want to know?"

"Megan McCracken. I understand you saw Mac assault her on the sidewalk, right outside the window."

"Yep."

"And?" she prompted.

"And you ain't finished your drink yet."

Tired of the game he played, Gera downed it in a single gulp. She refused to cough, no matter how badly her throat burned.

He laughed and pushed the second glass her way. "It was closing time, 'bout one or so. Megan had just left and was going out to her car. Mac came up and pushed her. She staggered around and fell, right out there." He pointed toward the windows.

"Are you sure she wasn't just drunk?"

"Don't matter. A gentleman should never push a lady." His grin was lascivious as he leaned inward, a little too close for Gera's comfort. "Wanna hook up later? I get off at eight."

She ignored the offer. "It was dark at one o'clock in the morning. How do you know it was Mac?"

He leaned closer. "Take a sip," he urged provocatively, "and I'll tell you."

This drink burned worse than the first. She couldn't help but clear her throat this time.

He laughed softly. "How did I know it was old Mac?" His eyes danced with mischief and he spoke so quietly, she had to lean in to hear his whispered words. He paused for effect, before stretching out the words, "I saw his coat and hat."

"Newsflash," Gera said, matching his delivery. "A lot of people wear coats and hats."

He had grown weary of his game. Pushing his lanky form away from the bar, he said abruptly, "You want anything else from me, you gotta pay again."

"Sorry. For no more information than that, your prices are way too steep."

She stumbled ever so slightly, killing the effect of storming away. Whatever he put in those drinks had been some powerful stuff.

And she still had to drive down the mountain.

13

Gera stopped by the local coffee shop and ordered their strongest cup. She needed something to clear her head. As she made her way back down the sidewalk, she imagined she felt Billy Boy's eyes following her, searing into her back.

She started the descent down the mountain, already nervous about driving at such heights. Being a fan of roller coasters, it was odd that she should be so apprehensive. She chalked it up to the fact that she didn't drive the coasters, just rode them.

"Don't look down," she said aloud to herself. "Keep your eyes focused on the road. None of this blurry stuff. Focus, Gera." The white line swam before her, multiplying by two.

She took her hand off the wheel just long enough to chug her coffee. "Damn, that burns!" she cursed, even though it wasn't a habit of hers. "Wait, wait, wait! Why are there three lines now?" she wailed. "They're multiplying like rabbits! This is so not good."

She slowed down, even when the car behind her honked. Repeatedly.

"Go chase your own rabbits," she snarled. "There, that's the spirit. Shoot me the bird as you go flying past. Fly away, little birdie."

She drained the last of her coffee. "Last chance to sober up, Gera girl. I don't know what he put in that drink, but it was some strong sh—"

She never finished her sentence. Something shiny caught her eye. It stretched along the side of the highway, fender high. She knew, because she nudged it with her bumper. Bounced right off it, too, right into the other lane of traffic. Where a pickup truck was traveling.

Someone in the car screamed. By the time Gera jerked the wheel and came back into her own lane, she realized the scream had been hers. Knowing she was in real trouble now—most likely drugged, more than drunk—Gera looked for a place to pull over, but she was headed down a long, thin ribbon of road that barely left room enough for two vehicles to pass. The ribbon zigzagged down the mountain, switching back and forth with dizzying frequency. With a car on her bumper, she couldn't give into the urge to just stop, right there in the middle of the road. She had to keep going.

"Talk it out of your system, Gera girl," she said aloud. "Don't let that little punk get the better of you. Snake Boy was playing games with you, but you won't let him win, will you? No. You will win, because you're smarter than he is. And you're smart enough to get yourself out of this mess. So let's think. Think, think, think, think, think."

Her bumper brushed along the guardrail again, ever so slightly. The car behind her honked.

"Yeah, yeah, I'm not asleep. But thanks. Thanks for looking out for me, whoever you are. Who knows? Maybe you're Mac. Maybe good ole Mac will follow me down the mountain and make sure I make it in one piece. Wouldn't want me to *sliiide* over the edge." She drew out the word as if she were actually sliding. Judging from the rough tug on her front fender and the horn behind her, she might have been.

"Oops, back toward the middle, Gera. Keep your eyes on the triple lines there in the middle. Can't go sliding down the mountain like Bozo the Banker says the town will do. No need to race it to the bottom." She giggled at her own brilliance.

Giggled again, at the lack of his. "Can you believe that dude? He's a millionaire. Handsome as sin. A little bit sexy, too, though not as sexy as Jake. But he's nuts. Bonkers. He thinks Mac murdered Abe to keep some big secret that the town will slide down the hill like a giant melting snow cone. Why is it all the good ones have some fatal flaw, like believing in ghosts?"

She started to mewl just a little. She knew she was doing it, but she couldn't seem to help herself. She was trying to talk it out, trying to keep herself awake and conscious and between the white lines, no matter how many of them there were. Most of all, she was trying to keep herself alive.

"He could be the perfect man," she whined aloud. "Smart. Handsome. Successful. And sweet, so sweet. But Jake believes in ghosts. And did I say how sexy he is? Clark Kent and Superman, all rolled up into one gorgeous body and the bluest eyes I've ever seen. Face it, Lois Lane, you'd like to jump his bones."

She attempted a song, but it sounded more like the range from a deep-toned gong, reverberating in her chest. "Bones,

bones, bones." She hummed another bar, off-tune, before stopping abruptly. "Wonder if Mac has bones? If he doesn't, how does his coat stay on his shoulders? Do ghosts have shoulders? I'll have to ask Minnie, if she comes to the garden tomorrow. I like Minnie. Minnie knows everything. Minnie is like a freaking walking ogle." She giggled. "Now she has me doing it, calling it ogle. I wonder if I googled 'ghost bones' what it would say."

She straightened in her seat and spoke in a sharp, authoritative voice, as if she were speaking to an employee. "Gera, take a note. If you make it out of this mess alive, find out if ghosts have bones. If not, find out how they can wear coats and hats and go around scaring people. Most importantly, find out how they can stab another man to death. How the heck would they even hold a knife?"

She looked down to examine her own hand and drifted a bit into the other lane. Horns from either direction alerted her to her mistake. However, she saw only five fingers on her hand, which was a good thing. She quickly kept up her banter, knowing it was the key to staying alert.

"Okay, so whatever he gave me is fast acting. No trace left to linger in my blood. Blood, blood, blood. I hate blood. No, oops, get back on track. Think about bones. Ask yourself if ghosts have bones. Jake has bones. I bet he has really nice, long bones… No, no, nice image, but no, back on track here. To stab a man, you have to be able to hold a knife. To hold a knife, you must have a hand. To have a hand, you must have bones. So either a) ghosts do, indeed, have bones, or b) a ghost didn't kill Abe Cunningham. What's that you say, Lois Lane? You say b? Why, yes, I do believe you are correct. Let's go for the bonus round. True or false? If Abe Cunningham wasn't killed by a ghost, he must've been killed by a mortal. True?

You are absolutely correct! We will let Clark Kent deliver your prize later this evening."

Gera smiled at the thought of that. The way her girl parts zinged, she suspected she wasn't quite as drugged as she had been ten minutes ago.

In fact, she saw only one white line in the center of the road now. And look. Up ahead was a small patch of dirt, wide enough to accommodate a car. Judging by the tracks, cars pulled over here all the time. She put on her blinker and slowed down enough to safely exit the road. The car behind her beeped its horn as it whizzed by.

Gera jammed the brakes harder than she intended, but at least she was no longer moving. With great concentration, she put the car into *Park* and got out for a breath of fresh air. Mere inches away, cars whizzed past on the roadway, oblivious to her troubles. She should've pulled over a bit further. Her legs were unsteady as she made her way around the car and checked the front bumper.

Ouch. She hoped her insurance covered all those scratches.

Gera stood on the side of the road for at least ten minutes, trying to clear her head, her lungs, and her smarting pride. Billy Boy Macandie had outsmarted her. If anything could sober her up, it would be plotting her revenge.

Picking her way back to the driver's side—timing it between oncoming cars so she could safely open her door—Gera happened to glance into her backseat.

A man's hat rested on the seat. Tall and black, it was the same kind of stovepipe-style hat they claimed ole Mac wore.

Just another reminder that someone still stalked her.

As she suspected, Detective Chao could divulge only limited information. Even if she had been mentally up for the challenge, she doubted the hardened detective would fall for any of her tricks, not the way Mike Cooper had.

Now that her mind was clear, Gera remembered the trick she had played on Cooper and felt more than a little guilty. Maybe she deserved whatever it was Billy Boy gave her.

She told Detective Chao about the visit to the *Cactus Bar*, but she declined his offer to press charges. She had no evidence. The drugs were long gone by now, out of her system with no lingering effects. He suggested she go to the emergency room as a precautionary measure, but she knew there was no point. Just as there was no point in testing the stovepipe hat for prints. Both efforts would be a waste of time.

All the detective could tell her was that the Jerome police had questioned Robert Macandie in connection to a robbery that took place there six weeks ago. At the time of the robbery, Billy Boy sat in the same chair Gera now occupied, answering some questions Chao had concerning a separate matter.

Like Cooper said, he couldn't have a better alibi than that.

Before tackling the mountain again, Gera drank plenty of water and another cup of coffee. She took a third cup with her, just in case.

The drive up was dull in comparison to her earlier adventure. Slow and steady, despite the trail of cars stuck behind her.

Dull, Gera decided, was nice for a change.

Jake was working the desk when she returned to the hotel. It was the first time she had seen him since their late-night dinner two nights ago, and she realized she was hungry for the sight of him.

Bones, bones, bones.

She shook the echo away and wiggled her fingers as she headed for the elevator.

"Hey, Gera, do you have a minute?"

"Uh, yeah, sure." After the day she had experienced, she was hot, sweaty, and tired. The Arizona heat and random drugs weren't her best source for beauty, she knew.

Jake stepped out from behind the desk and motioned her toward a nearby settee.

"I understand you had a problem this morning."

A gross understatement, at best. "You'll have to be more specific than that."

"I understand you had concerns with housekeeping?"

"Was that just this morning?" she murmured, raking her fingers through her hair. She really couldn't do it any more damage than was already done.

When he gave her a strange look, she simply said, "Busy day."

"It must've been," he agreed, the expression in his vivid blue eyes somewhere between sympathetic and amused. *Incredulous* was a good word for it, Gera mused, staring into his eyes. They were such a gorgeous shade, even behind the lens of his glasses.

"Gera?"

She blinked slowly, realizing he had caught her staring. It had taken drugs to make her admit, even to herself, that she was attracted to him. Now that the secret was out, there seemed to be no controlling her raging hormones. Her girl parts were on full alert.

"Sorry. I guess I'm more exhausted than I thought. But yes, back to your question. I did have a bit of a problem, but it's okay. I'm good now."

Jake wasn't easily convinced. "Seriously, if there's an issue with housekeeping, I want to know so that I can address it properly."

"It was me," she admitted. "I didn't sleep well and I was in a really grouchy mood this morning, and I let it get off with me. I made a big deal out of nothing, and I think I almost caused your receptionist to have a nervous breakdown. But honestly, it was nothing."

"It didn't sound like nothing, not if she called Lucy." Tiny laugh lines creased the corners of his eyes. A sea of deep blue twinkled from behind his lens. "Calling in Lucy is like calling in the big guns."

Gera laid her hand onto Jake's arm. "Believe me when I say, I'd already forgotten about it. It's not a big deal."

"If you're sure…"

"I am."

Her hand lingered on his arm, where she detected a very long, strong bone. His hand came up to cover hers. "Are you too tired to join me for dinner tonight?" he said, his voice warming with hope.

Gera felt a surge of energy flash through her. "Not anymore."

"We'll try to beat the clock tonight. Eight o'clock?" he suggested. "Or we could go out, if you'd rather."

"No, here is fine." It was probably the safest place on the mountain.

The bell at the front door jingled. Jake released her hand and stood. "Duty calls. Guests for the weekend."

She no longer worried about being the only guest at the hotel. She had bigger things to worry about. Things like crazy bartenders, crazy bankers, and crazy citizens. Things like getting Mike Cooper fired and bringing Miles Anderson's wrath down upon her. Things like people who stalked her and drugged her and left warnings in her car.

Things like staying alive.

14

Gera had packed two decent outfits for her stay in Jerome. She chose the paisley print sundress, the one in shades of blue that left her shoulders bare and swirled around her knees with a decided nod to femininity. It wasn't her usual attire, but it was perfect for tonight.

After examining the information she gleaned from the police files—'gleaned' was a much nicer word than 'stole'—Gera indulged in a long, soaking bubble bath. Today of all days, she deserved such a treat. She shaved her legs, applied makeup and a generous dousing of perfume, and found a suitable way to style her hair. She was ready long before eight, but hated to look too eager. At five until the hour, she called for the elevator.

She was actually nervous as she crossed the lobby. Had it really been so long since she last had a date? She did a quick calculation in her head. Sadly enough, it had been over five months.

Jake was there at the desk, talking with another guest. Gera stood back and watched him, admiring the easy way he had with people. He had such a friendly, open smile. Such expressive eyes. And don't get her started on the sensual curve of his mouth.

He looked up and saw her, and she swore she saw his eyes smile, even from here, even from behind his glasses. He excused himself from the guest and came to greet her.

He, too, had showered and shaved. He had the tiniest nick at the edge of his squared jaw, and Gera had to resist the urge to reach up and kiss it all better. Perhaps later. Later, when Lois collected her reward from Clark.

What is wrong with me? she wondered. *Are the drugs not out of my system?*

But as he took her elbow and led her back across the lobby, she knew the answer. This drug was Jake Cody.

"Let's take the elevator," he suggested, when she would've started for the stairs. She gave him a quizzical look, but allowed him to lead her to the antique car.

Once the doors shut and the button pressed, Jake turned to her and gently tugged her into his arms. "Just so you know," he murmured against her lips, "this is a date."

She wound her arms around his neck. "Duly noted."

His lips were soft, but firm. Warm. Heat surged through Gera's body. They reached the lower level all too soon, but Jake continued to kiss her. The doors on vintage hand-operated elevators, Gera remembered, didn't open automatically.

She was suddenly very fond of vintage elevators.

A buzzer sounded, and the elevator slowly lurched into action. "Someone is calling the car," he murmured.

Gera pressed herself against him. "I hope it's the third floor," she whispered.

The car stopped in the lobby. With a reluctant groan, Jake set her away and reached for the door. His arm stayed around her waist, however, not wanting to break their connection.

Again wondering what had gotten into her—she normally wasn't so greedy, not on a first date—Gera paid no attention to the two men who stepped into the car. She spotted a smudge of her pale lipstick at the edge of Jake's mouth and wondered if her own lips were a fright. Turning so she could catch her reflection in the brass tiles that lined the car, she ran her thumb around her mouth and called it good. As she lifted her eyes, her gaze tangled in the shared reflection of Grant Young's eyes.

She whirled around in surprise.

"Why, Gera," he said in a pleased voice. "Fancy meeting you here."

"I—I'm staying here at *The Dove*."

"Really?" He seemed delighted, until he noticed the arm hooked around her waist. His gaze followed the arm upward, to the terse expression on Jake's face.

"Grant," Jake acknowledged. Gera had never heard him sound so formal.

"Cody." Grant didn't even bother with first name pleasantries.

Jake was polite enough to greet the second man, a hint of a smile in his voice as he extended his hand. "Clyde, good to see you."

"Good to see you, too, Jake," the other man said, clueless to the tension that hung in the air as heavily as smoke. "We thought we'd come out tonight and have one of your fine steaks."

"We're glad that you did. I'll send the chef out to take your order personally."

The other man chuckled in pleasure. When the elevator stopped and Clyde slid the door open, Gera accepted his invitation of ladies first.

Grant raised a questioning brow, knowing the elevator had just come from the lower level. "Missed my floor earlier," she murmured, without quite looking anyone in the eye.

Clyde was eager to step out and claim his steak, but Grant lingered in the car with Jake. "Making out in the elevator with a guest, Cody?" he murmured. "Hardly professional. I must take that issue up with the Hospitality Board. I do believe that falls under Sexual Harassment."

Jake made no comment. He stepped out of the car, slid his arm around Gera's waist, and guided her quickly away.

"What was that all about?" she asked, glancing over her shoulder to find Grant's searing gaze upon them.

"Old history," was all he offered. He led her to the back of the dining room, to an area she had never noticed before. Not completely private, but a heavy brocade curtain draped low, offering a measure of seclusion. A round table waited for them, set with white linen cloth and candlelight.

"Ooh, this *is* a date," she grinned in approval.

Jake pulled her chair out for her and excused himself, leaving her for a moment as she got settled. Through the veil of the curtain, she saw him disappear into the kitchen. At the front of the restaurant—which happened to be crowded tonight—she caught a glimpse of Grant and his friend.

"I'm sorry about that," Jake said as he returned. He ran a hand along her bared shoulder, sending a shiver of delight to dance across her nerves. Grant's touch had felt nothing like this.

"No worries."

"So what would you like? The chef has given you permission to order anything you wish."

"In that case, I'll have the same thing I had the other night."

They made small talk until the waiter came. He brought chilled water, a bottle of fine wine, and a basket of Jake's favorite breads.

"Okay, we might as well address the elephant in the room," Jake said on a sigh. "How do you know Grant Young?"

"I asked for an interview with him yesterday. He was the one who found Abe's body, you know."

"So I heard."

In the spirit of full disclosure, she added, "And I saw him this morning at brunch. When he asked me out, I sort of fibbed and told him I already had plans. So thank you for keeping me from being a flat-out liar."

She could no longer resist the urge to swipe away the smudge of lipstick from his mouth. Her fingers lingered.

"My pleasure," Jake assured her in a deep voice, catching her hand and holding it to his lips. He pressed a kiss against her fingers. She pulled slowly away, letting her knuckles skim his lips, tugging them slightly apart. She had the craziest urge to skip dinner and go straight for dessert.

After that, Gera sat on her hands. Literally.

"So why did you turn him down?" Jake wanted to know, offering her the breadbasket. He raised a brow when she shook her head and kept her hands to herself, but he said nothing.

Her voice was quiet, her eyes wide and honest. "I'd already met you," she whispered.

A pleased smile hovered around his mouth. He noticed how her eyes hungrily traced the gesture. A faint blush stained his cheeks.

Mortified, Gera reached for her water glass and almost tipped it over. "I don't know what is wrong with me tonight!" she insisted.

"Relax, Gera," he urged. "Let's just enjoy our dinner and forget about everyone on the other side of that curtain."

"Not yet. Not until you tell me how *you* know Grant Young."

"I've always known him, of course, but I didn't really get to *know* him until recently, when I came back here to run *The Dove*."

"And now that you know him, you don't like him."

"That's one way of putting it." He paused to grin, the boyish gesture endearing. "Actually, that's the only way to put it. I don't like Grant Young. And as you can see, the feeling is mutual."

"I can't imagine anyone not liking you," she said. Then she went out on a limb and confessed, "And to be honest, I can't imagine not liking Grant, either. I found him to be very sociable."

"Hmm. I'm sure he came across as all charming and humble, particularly with you being a gorgeous female and all, but believe me, he is a shrewd and formidable businessman."

Gera interrupted him when she laughed aloud, amused by something he said. "Gorgeous female?" she hooted. "I've honestly never been called that in my entire life!"

Jake blinked in surprise. "I can't imagine why not. I don't need these glasses to see how beautiful you are."

Gera made light of his praise. Keeping her tone playful, she looked at him keenly and proclaimed, "I *like* you."

"And I'm so glad, being this is a date and all," Jake shot back dryly.

"Okay, sorry, back on track. You were saying?"

"There is a fine line between being a shrewd business man and being a cruel one. Grant has been known to cross that line."

Gera thought of the conversation she had overheard, when Ruth Cunningham visited the banker. "I know what you mean. And I think he could cause a problem for Abe's widow."

"How so?"

She told him what little she knew. Jake shook his head in disgust and said, "That sounds about like Young. For whatever reason, he wants that piece of property, and it seems he will go to any lengths to get it. He's tried a similar tactic with me, but it won't work. We don't owe a dime on *The Dove*, and I plan to keep it that way. The last person I want to be indebted to is Grant Young."

"Isn't there anything Ruth Cunningham can do?"

"I don't know, because I don't know exactly what's happened now. My guess is there's probably some tiny little technicality, like an unpaid filing fee of fifty dollars, or some such nonsense. I'll go over and talk to Ruth next week and see if I can help."

"You're a good man, Jake Cody," Gera smiled. "One last question and we will drop the subject of Grant Young forever, or at least until the next time his name comes up. What did he say to you in the elevator?"

"We both serve on the Hospitality Board, an organization my grandmother started to increase tourism here in

Jerome. He made some noise about reporting me for Sexual Harassment."

"Because we were kissing in the elevator?" she asked incredulously.

"Something like that. He's just jealous, and I can understand why." Jake smiled at her, his eyes warm. "I'll say it again, because it is true. You're a gorgeous woman, Gera."

"Is it harassment," she asked breathlessly, leaning in close, "if both parties are willing participants?"

The waiter came with their meal. Talk turned to lighter subjects. The sounds of their laughter floated out into the main dining room and drew the attention of others, but they were cocooned in their own little world.

Gera went easy on the wine. She didn't need anything that would lower her inhibitions any more than Jake Cody had somehow managed to do, simply by being himself. She couldn't remember ever feeling so alive.

"Dessert?" the waiter offered.

Gera put her hand to her stomach. She was deliciously full. "Maybe after a while."

"We can always deliver to your room," the waiter offered.

When they exited the dining room, Gera was surprised to see that it was empty. They had unknowingly stayed well beyond closing time.

"I feel bad," Gera said as they stepped into the elevator. "I had no idea it was so late."

"I'll put a little something in their paychecks," Jake offered, inserting his key and pressing the button for the third floor. The old car chugged into motion. "It was worth it."

They didn't talk as they rode the elevator up. They stopped on the first floor to take on riders, stopped again on the second floor to deposit them. Reached the third floor with a new awkwardness between them.

"Would you like to see my personal residence?" Jake asked as they stepped out into the hallway.

"You live here?" she asked in surprise.

"I have an apartment at the end of this hall." He pointed in the direction opposite her room. "Come on, I'll show it to you."

"I never thought about it, but I guess it makes sense," Gera said, "to live here at the hotel. Except that you can't ever quite get away from work, can you?"

"Oh, you'd be surprised," Jake said, unlocking the door.

She stepped inside and looked around. The space was spacious and airy, and much more modern than the rest of the hotel.

"And I am," she said. "Surprised, that is." She pointed to the spiral staircase. "There's a fourth floor?"

"Fifth, if you count the basement. But yes, there is a partial upper floor."

"May I?" she asked, foot poised on the bottom step.

"Be my guest."

The upper level was one large room. A wall of floor-to-ceiling windows offered a bird's eye view of the valley below. Or it would, in the daylight. Tonight, it offered her own reflection staring back at her.

She saw something else in the reflection. She saw Jake's massive bed behind them. And Jake's eyes, so vivid and blue, even when mirrored in glass.

"That's not why I brought you up here, Gera," he said quietly.

"It's not?" Even to her own ears, her voice sounded disappointed.

Throaty.

Needy.

"Not that I would object," he clarified. "But I don't expect it."

She searched the reflection of his eyes. "But do you want it?" she asked softly.

He stepped up behind her, placing his hands on her shoulders. His lips trailed over her bared flesh. Gera sucked in her breath. Dropped her head back to give him access to her neck.

"I most definitely want it," Jake murmured, running his tongue along the tiny pebbles of gooseflesh he discovered there.

"So do I," she admitted raggedly.

Gera had never had a one-night stand before. The idea was strangely exhilarating. Oddly depressing. Would one night with Jake be enough? She turned impatiently in his arms, pulling at his shirt. For once in her life, she didn't mind that the lights were on or that she stood in front of a bare window, allowing a man to peel her dress away.

"Something happened to me today," she said breathlessly, even as he pushed away her bodice, pooling it down around her waist.

"What was that?" he murmured, but his attention was on her two very fine breasts.

"I think someone drugged me."

She regretted her words instantly. Jake stopped what he was doing, and he had been doing it so well. Gera moaned, trying to pull him back to her.

"What? God, Gera, what are you talking about?"

She pulled his hand back in place, but his talented fingers were now idle. She dropped her head forward, resting it against his. "I went to the *Cactus Bar* today, to question Billy Boy Macandie. I think he put something in my drink. I felt very strange after I left. My vision was blurred, my feet sluggish. It was all I could do to drive down the mountain."

"You *drove* in that condition?" Jake exploded. "You could've been killed!"

"I did scrape the fender of the car," she admitted. "More than once. I knew I kept bumping into it, but I couldn't seem to do anything about it."

Jake ripped the shirt from his chest—reminding her, for a moment, of Superman—and put the garment around her, stuffing her arms into cloth still warm from his own flesh. It gave her a delicious thrill, stacking goosebumps upon her goosebumps.

"Let's sit over here," he said, leading her to a small seating area with a leather couch.

"I think it was some sort of date rape drug," she said. "I never blacked out, but I got all weird feeling. I had cognate thought, but it was uninhibited, you know? Silly, at times, like I was drunk. But I don't think I was. And then it cleared, and suddenly I was back to normal."

"Tell me you went to the police!"

"Not exactly." She explained her trip into Cottonwood, and why. The only detail she omitted was her acting gig with Mike Cooper, and that was for his own protection. She didn't want to cost the officer his job.

After a brief argument, in which Jake insisted she contact Miles Anderson and Gera steadfastly refused, they came to an impasse.

Jake ran his hand through his dark hair, ruffling it in disarray. He looked over at Gera and asked quietly, "And this?"

He passed his hand between them, and the dress still pooled around her waist. His shirt hung free, offering a tantalizing view of her exposed breasts. "Are you still under the influence?"

"I want to say no, but I'm not so sure," she admitted honestly. "I'm normally not so... eager."

His smile was bittersweet. "I thought it was a little too good to be true."

She grabbed for his arm. "No, Jake, you don't understand. I want this. I do."

"And so do I. But not this way."

"Okay, so maybe there's still a little bit of the drugs in my system, because I will be very honest with you right now. Tomorrow I might deny I ever said this, but you deserve to know." She took a gulp of courage and continued. "I was attracted to you from the beginning. But it took being drugged for me to admit it. I gotta tell you, Jake, thinking about you today got me all hot and bothered." She put her hand to his face and made sure he was looking at her so, so that he could see the truth in her words. "I don't know if this was the drugs," she whispered, "or just you."

Jake kissed her very gently, cradling her face in both his hands. The kiss was long and thorough and, oh, so sweet.

"Thank you for telling me that," he said in a soft voice. He set her away from him, pulling the shirt together to hide her from him. "Give me your key, and I'll go get your pajamas. I don't want you to be alone tonight. You take the bed, and I'll sleep here on the couch."

"No, Jake, I couldn't," she protested.

"I insist. Tomorrow we'll argue some more and I'll convince you to go to the police." His tone was confident. "But tonight, you're staying here, where I can keep an eye on you."

"And tomorrow night?" she asked.

"Tomorrow night, I may not be such a gentleman." He tapped the end of her nose and waited for her to hand over her key.

Gera stared after him when he was gone, breathing in his scent from the shirt that enveloped her.

"I may just hold you to that," she whispered to the empty room.

15

Gera slept soundly that night. No crying babies, no voices, no loud cars. No bad dreams, held over from the waking hours.

She awoke alone in the apartment, with a breathtaking view and the sunny promise of a new day. A note lay on her pillow, anchored by a Hershey's kiss.

Call me when you're awake. I'll send up breakfast, no matter the time.

His cell number was scrawled beneath the message in a broad, masculine hand.

By the time she went back to her own room to shower, the sun had crawled high in the sky. She had missed her garden meeting with Minnie again, if the old woman even came on weekends. Not for the first time, Gera wondered where her little friend lived. She had said nearby.

Pulling out of the driveway, Gera looked past *The Dove*, to the rather rickety old house next door. Was that where Minnie lived? It almost looked abandoned, if the darkened windows and sagging porch were any indication. The yard was nothing like she thought Minnie's might be. Instead of clusters of blossoms, mounds of old dirt lay, hardened and spiked with weeds, as if someone had dug holes all through the yard and not bothered to fill them back in. Gera imagined Minnie's yard would look much like the tiered garden at *The Dove*.

But perhaps, she considered, that was the reason the old woman came each day. Tending a garden demanded a certain level of physical fitness. Gera knew this from personal experience, citing memories of her summers with Grams, helping with the orchards. Grams had grown flowers and vegetables, too. Rose bushes with big, robust petals, and a vegetable garden with neat rows of peas, potatoes, and radishes. Gera never cared for radishes—she hadn't thought to list them, had she, when Jake asked her preferences—but she recalled the new potatoes as particularly delicious. She remembered sitting on her knees and digging in the earth, searching for the edible gems as if they were hidden bits of gold. Digging for potatoes had always been exciting, because she never knew how many she might find beneath the soil. And growing roses was quite the adventure, too. She remembered counting the blooms each day, delighted when a new bud appeared overnight.

Minnie, she knew, would never be able to bend and stoop as much as a garden would require. Her curled fingers were much too stiff to dig into the fertile soil and tug a root free. Gera couldn't imagine the old woman sinking to her knees and pressing her bare toes into that second layer of soil, the one that was always slightly damp and cool, untouched by the heat of the sun and the dryness of the wind. Plus, if by some chance she did manage to get down onto her knees, poor

Minnie would have a terrible time getting up. Even without the orthopedic shoes and heavy support hose, Minnie's legs didn't look very nimble.

Perhaps she came to *The Dove*, Gera decided, where she could enjoy the beauty of the garden without the fuss and bother of growing one herself. And a house that size—and that old—had to be difficult to maintain, particularly when she was alone and had lived the better part of a century.

As she took the road down into town, Gera's thoughts turned to Ruth Cunningham. Would she have the same troubles? Would the old house prove too much for her? She had children, but they might not live nearby. The sons might know more about building a portfolio than building a porch. The daughters might be afraid of ruining their manicures, or they might be too busy running their own households to worry with hers.

Or maybe none of them would ever have the chance to help, because maybe the bank would take the house away. Heavy creases lined Gera's forehead. Surely, Grant wouldn't let that happen. No matter the problem, he would help the widow find a way to keep her home.

Gera made the curve onto Main Street and found, to her surprise, that the sleepy little town had come awake. Cars lined the street, every parking spot occupied. There was even a traffic jam ahead, as a confused motorist couldn't quite comprehend that half of Main was one-way traffic only. People strolled up and down the slanted sidewalks, ducking into this store or that, and coming out again with colorful bags and lighter wallets. Gera had to make the loop, driving all the way down Main, jack-knifing back onto Hull, and parking in the lot across from the *Sliding Jail*.

Indeed on Saturdays, it seemed that more than just ghosts roamed the streets of Jerome.

Gera grabbed her camera and started up the steep embankment that was First Avenue. It was the same path she had taken upon her arrival in town, and the one Grant took that very same night, before he came upon Abe's body. The steep path led her handily up to *The Bartlett*, now free of its yellow crime tape bindings. That sort of thing would be bad for tourism, she supposed.

She took more photos of the scene, these without the little tented markers that had chronicled the recent crime. According to the leaked COD, Abe had been stabbed to death. Gera hadn't seen much blood, even that night. She thought maybe she had missed something before, but there were no traces of a deadly spill, no telltale stains on the sun-bleached tiles below. Nor had Grant mentioned the blood. He spoke of the unnatural pose, the blank, open stare, but not a word about the blood.

Was it possible, she wondered, that Abe had been killed elsewhere and his body dumped here for discovery? But how—and when—would someone manage to get his limp, lifeless body inside the empty structure without being seen?

First and foremost, that person would've needed a key, and only five people possessed one to the gates surrounding the old hotel. She knew this because she had snapped a photo of the chief's notes. Lucky for her, the man did, indeed, make lists. And filled them in quite nicely, too, with neat, handwritten notations beside each name.

The first name on the list had surprised her, but then made sense when she realized Grant Young was the president of the Chamber of Commerce. Since there were no notations beside his name, she assumed Miles Anderson had come to the same conclusion she did. Grant was a leader in the community and a stellar citizen, unlikely of committing murder. That was probably why there was also a blank beside his own name, second on the list.

Third was Harriett Nettles. The notes reported she was a retired librarian and currently out of the state. Fourth on the list was the highly esteemed treasurer of the Museum Society. The chief noted that Cora Hill came each month to collect the coins and deposit them into the Restoration Fund at the bank, but that she was currently ill with pneumonia and had a solid alibi for the night of Abe's death, having been in the hospital that entire week.

The last name on the list, and the only other person with a set of keys to the old structure, was Mayor Howard Strait, often referred to as Pastor Strait. That evening, he had been fulfilling his pastoral duties and visiting Cora in the hospital.

Besides a key, the killer would've needed opportunity. That meant a way to access the busy intersection with a dead body in tow, plus the time needed to get it inside.

Maybe she should scrub the idea of him being killed elsewhere. If merely imagining all the details involved were this difficult, pulling it off would've been next to impossible.

"Do you want to tell me exactly what is going on here?"

She hadn't seen Miles Anderson approach, but she definitely heard his snarled words. Gera turned around and saw the chief of police striding angrily across the street. He ignored the people milling around on the sidewalk and marched straight over to Gera, his face as dark as a stormy sky.

Gera played dumb. She looked over his shoulder, to the crowded streets and sidewalks. "I have no idea. The town is certainly busy today, though, isn't it?"

"I'm not talking about the tourists and you know it!" he barked.

She wasn't about to volunteer anything. And she had vowed to protect Mike Cooper, at all costs. Gera simply stared at the chief officer, waiting for him to yell at her again.

It took only seconds. "Do you want to explain the meaning of this to me?"

Poor Coop. She hoped he still had a job.

Before she could answer, the chief roared on, "Why the hell is Detective Chao of the Cottonwood Police Department calling to inform *me* of something that happened in *my* town? Do you have anything you want to tell me, Miss Stapleton?"

"No."

"No? That's all you have to say? I don't know who you think you are, coming into my town and stirring up a bunch of trouble, but you'd better have something better to say to me than that, little lady!"

She hefted out a sigh. People were looking at them strangely, wondering what she had done to deserve the lawman's wrath.

"Look, I didn't mean to be disrespectful, any more than I'm sure you meant to be when you called me *little lady*." Even though it was useless, she hit him with her mother's best smile.

The officer continued to glare.

Gera shrugged, continuing, "I don't have anything more to say because there is nothing more to tell."

"Detective Chao told me you went into the *Cactus Bar*, where Macandie slipped something extra into your drink. You dammed near killed yourself, driving down the mountain, but you refused to press charges because it was already out of your system."

"See? You already know the whole story. There's honestly nothing else to tell."

"Except *why* he might want to drug you." His tone held accusation. "What are you doing hanging around a lowlife like Macandie, anyway?"

"I'm not. I went into the bar and ordered a drink. That was the first time I had ever seen the man, and if I'm lucky, it will also be the last."

"I have to agree with you there," Miles Anderson said. "Billy Boy Macandie is nothing but trouble. But don't think I buy your little innocent act. You went into that bar for a reason. The same reason you went to see Chao. Spill it, Miss Stapleton."

"Okay, so it was the first time I had ever seen Billy Boy, but it wasn't the first time I heard his name. I know he is a key witness in the recent crime spree plaguing your city."

"And you know this how?"

"A good reporter never reveals her source."

He wasn't impressed with her mother's smile this time, either. "Stay out of my case," he growled. "You may not think so, but we're working each case with thorough precision. No need for you to butt in and try to solve them for us."

"That's not what I'm trying to do. In fact, I'm working an entirely different angle. Want to hear about it?"

He looked mildly bored. "Sure, why not?"

Gera glanced around, at people walking around them to access the sidewalk. "It's a little hot out here, standing in the sun. Can we find somewhere to sit?" she suggested.

She thought he would refuse, but curiosity won out. "We can go across the street," he said.

He led her across the traffic, again treating her like a child. There was a horrible moment when Gera feared they were headed to the police station, where Cooper might unwittingly mention yesterday's visit. She was so relieved to see they headed right, toward the park, that she forgot to be angry at his high-handed manner.

The chief found a shady section of the wide cement steps and motioned for her to have a seat.

"What are these, anyway?" she asked. "Steps? Bleachers?" Whatever they were, they stretched an entire city block, right in the center of town.

He shrugged his wide shoulders. "Both, I suppose. Steps to reach Upper Park, bleachers to watch parades. Whatever you need." He adjusted his cowboy hat as he sat down beside her. "So, Miss Stapleton, tell me the angle for your story."

"I've been thinking about it, and I have a new theory. You see, I think this entire thing has been a setup. I don't think it was ever about stealing that bike or breaking into that house. I don't think anyone had a grudge against Megan McCracken or ever intended to steal Ruben Gonzales's wallet here in the Upper Park. I think it was a setup, right from the beginning."

"Who, exactly, was being setup?" Despite a tinge of skepticism in his voice, she had snagged his attention. His eyes were thoughtful as he waited to hear the rest of her theory.

"In a way, it was the town." Her quiet words surprised him, made him draw in a sharp breath as he sat up, his posture now fully erect. She finally had his full attention. "Whoever did this," she continued, "whoever killed Abe Cunningham, knows the townspeople believe in ghosts. I think the killer used that to his advantage and created this series of minor incidents so that he could throw suspicion on Mac. All it took was a few witnesses to say they saw someone who looked like Mac, someone in a long coat and tall hat. It wouldn't take much for the rumors to get started. Rumors that Mac had turned on them."

"You make the townspeople sound a bit gullible, Miss Stapleton."

She was polite enough not to point out that these were people who believed in ghosts. In her mind, that spoke for itself.

"Is it such a stretch?" she said instead. "When bad things started happening, and when witnesses claimed they saw Mac at the scene, why not suspect him of turning on them? I think the killer counted on that, and it gave him the perfect setup for murder. Kill Abe Cunningham, have everyone blame it on a ghost, and get away scot-free."

Chief Anderson mulled over her theory. "No way to question a ghost," he murmured. "No defense argument. But I do see one problem with your theory."

"What's that?"

"Me." He stared at her with the same stony countenance of all sheriffs past and present from her father's favorite shoot-em-up westerns.

"*You* may not be so gullible, Chief Anderson," she acknowledged, "but you answer to the community. If the town's leaders, even men as influential and powerful as Grant Young, are content to blame a ghost rather than cast accusation upon one of their own, is there really anything you can do about it?"

His snarled reply surprised her. Not because of its venom, but because of its focus. He ignored all but one point she had made. "Grant Young isn't as powerful as he thinks!"

Gera vaguely remembered the banker's comment, something about a prom date, back in the day. Had the two men fought over a girl? Did an old rivalry still simmer between them, festering and feeding on bruised egos and scraped hearts?

"Still, I think it's a pretty good theory," she insisted. "So now the question becomes *why*. Why would someone want to kill Abe Cunningham? What would anyone have to gain? This took planning. This took weeks of preparation and manipulation. Why would someone go to such lengths to kill a seventy-five-year-old man?"

"This is your theory. You tell me."

"I suppose the first and most obvious motive would be a life insurance policy."

"Would be, but according to Ruth, it's hardly enough to get him in the ground."

"Inheritance?"

"Far as I know, all he really owns is that house and the little bit of soil it sits on. If you're staying at *The Dove*, you know there's not a lot of room for soil up there."

Gera chewed on the inside of her lip, pondering the possibilities. "There's got to be something else. Something important enough for someone to kill him over."

"Doubt it was a love affair gone bad," Miles Anderson offered. "He and Ruth have been happily married for close to fifty years."

"What about the trouble he had with his taxes?"

"I told you before, I have nothing to say on that matter."

"Yes, yes, I understand that. I'm not asking for information. I'm just wondering who could benefit from something like that."

"Theoretically, it would be the State of Arizona. Property can be seized and put up for auction. Any monies collected go toward satisfying unpaid taxes."

Gera stared down the street at the bank, thinking aloud. "Unless you take out a loan on your property, so that you can pay those taxes. Which is what I understand Abe Cunningham did at the bank. Then it all turned out to be a big mistake, so Abe returned the money. And now for whatever reason, the bank still holds a mortgage on the house."

"Who told you that?" the lawman asked sharply. "Where did you hear such a crazy thing?"

"From Ruth Cunningham, herself." Which was true. She just wasn't speaking to Gera when she said it. Not that the chief needed to know that.

"Damn that Grant Young, this time he's gone too far!" Anger flooded into the officer's face, twitching at his handlebar mustache. A curse hissed through his clenched teeth. "That house belongs to Beverly Ruth. Or it will, one day." When he banged a clenched fist against the concrete steps and never once flinched, Gera realized he could be a strong and dangerous man. He leapt to his feet, his voice like the roll of summer thunder. "He can't do this!"

He was already two steps down, almost at the bottom, when he remembered Gera. He turned back with a cryptic message. "Your theory has holes, Miss Stapleton. Take care not to fall through them. You might get hurt."

He whirled around and marched off, striding angrily across the street. Gera stared after him in shock, cringing when a car had to lock up its brakes to avoid hitting him. Miles Anderson yelled at the driver to slow down, but kept to his own hurried pace.

"I have no idea what just happened," Gera muttered aloud. "But I swear, that last part sounded like a threat."

16

Grams had once told Gera that one of her biggest liabilities—which, in an odd twist of nature that only God above could understand, also turned out to be her greatest asset—was the fact that she was fearless. She faced her problems head on, never shirking from the possibility of a fight.

It was that head-on approach that landed Gera in the principal's office, the second day of third grade. A boy tried to bully her, having had limited success with the same technique the year before. However, Gera would have none of it. She marched up to him on the playground on that second day of school, popped him in the nose, and watched the blood trickle out in a slow, red pool. The boy didn't flinch when she hit him. But at the first sight of blood, he dropped to the ground in a dead faint.

She had no more problems from that boy, ever again. In fact, they became good friends, partially because Gera brought him brownies the next day, with enough extra for the whole class to enjoy.

That same fearless nature was the reason Gera adored roller coasters and scary movies. She wasn't sure why the notion of driving down the winding mountain had frightened her, but now that she had managed it half-drugged, she knew she had conquered her fear. Head on, minus one or two sideswipes to her bumper.

And it was that fearlessness that kept her going when her mother died at an early age, and when Grams got the dreaded diagnosis of cancer. Gera fought the doctors, argued with the technicians, yelled at the nurses who poked her grandmother with needles and tubes and that horrible stuff they called chemo. What the disease didn't kill, the medicine did. Grams succumbed to both, but Gera was a fearless warrior, coming to see her every day, right up until the end. She was a cheerleader when Grams got discouraged, a nursemaid when Grams got sick, a rock when Gram grew weak.

And so today, unsure whether she acted upon the liability or the asset, Gera tackled another of her troubles. Head on.

She marched into the *Cactus Bar* and took a seat at a table, making sure she had a clear view of the bar and the man behind it.

When Billy Boy Macandie saw her, he took a double take. Then a slow smile touched his face, and he flicked his tongue, just like the snake that he was. Gera stared back at him, unamused.

Customers came up to the bar and drew his attention. Gera used the opportunity to study the back wall with its mantled fireplace, where Mac's image was often seen. Now that she had latched onto the theory of someone framing Mac, she liked it more and more.

Her first inclination was to think that someone could have slipped inside the bar via a secret back entrance, donned a hat and coat, and posed as Mac there by the fireplace. Yet that idea didn't make sense. First, why would someone stand there all night long, on the off chance someone might come along, see them, and mistake them for the legendary ghost? Second, the bank wrapped around the bar, effectively cutting off any notion of a hidden back door. No need to worry about security when your walls bordered a bank; few other buildings were sealed and secured as surely as a bank building. So no secret entrance.

But there could be a projected image, Gera thought. She strained her neck to see around the room, but there were too many people. She did spy one cable that looked a bit out of place. It ran across the ceiling and came down the wall adjacent to the fireplace, about a dozen feet or so out. The angle and placement would be right, she decided, for some sort of laser device, but a table of rowdy drinkers obstructed her view.

She felt Billy Boy watching her. He made no secret of it. He even followed the path of her eyes, staring at the cable. Was it her imagination, or did he look amused, as if imagining ways in which he could strangle her with that very cord?

She was being ridiculous, of course. She could see no such thought in his face.

A few moments later, a waitress came to her table. "Compliments of the bartender," she chirped, sliding a drink in front of Gera.

Gera glanced up, catching his satisfied smirk. She refused to blink, refused to look away. She met his glare, head on. Her eyes never wavered from his, but she knew when the smirk slid from his lips. Knew when he cleared his throat and swallowed. Hard. Smiled, ever so slightly, when his eyes took on a nervous tick.

Eyes still on his, Gera stood from her table, took her untouched drink, and walked to the bar, putting a bit of swagger into her hips.

Billy Boy misread the signs. His nervous tick relaxed. His tongue ring flicked out. Writhed in slow and explicit implication, as his eyes darkened with excitement. Gera kept coming, even when her stomach threatened to turn. Billy Boy grinned. He let down his guard.

Gera leaned over the bar, motioning him forward with her finger. He laughed as he leaned in, tongue writhing. Most tongue rings made a clicking sound against teeth. His, she discovered at close range, made a hiss. Disgusting, she thought, even as she crooked her finger into the neck of his t-shirt and pulled him forward.

"Thanks for the drink," she purred. She tugged again, stretching the shirt. "But you keep it."

Her words were so quiet, so sultry, that he never saw it coming. Like a snake, her strike was swift and silent.

Before Billy Boy Macandie ever knew what was happening—in the middle of the packed bar, with patrons and co-workers there to witness it all—Gera dumped her drink down the front of his shirt.

Sensing she was no longer welcome in the bar, Gera left. She heard laughter behind her, as well as the string of obscenities that spewed from Billy Boy's mouth.

There would be no conciliatory brownies after this showdown.

She took the side street, opting off the busy hustle of Main. Before she reached the end of the block, another pedestrian practically plowed her over.

Her first thought was that Billy Boy had come after her. Gera reached for her mace. But the face she saw was a pleasant one, devoid of inks and piercings.

"Oh, good Lord, Gera, forgive me!" Grant said, clearly as flustered as she was. "I didn't even see you there! I am as clumsy as an ox." He made certain she was steady, then brushed at his own clothes, soothing away unseen wrinkles from his impeccable attire.

"Is the bank open on Saturdays?"

"Half a day," he confirmed.

She thought of how Miles Anderson had stormed over there, less than a half hour ago. What a letdown it would've been for him, had he risked his life crossing the street and arrived, only to find the doors locked.

"You must've been in quite a hurry to leave," she smiled.

"I was. I was on the phone, and I just plowed right into you. I'm so, so sorry." He looked genuinely contrite.

Why did some people find him so unpleasant? Gera liked the man. Not *that* way, not the way he had hoped she would, but he was always pleasant and polite to her. Okay, a tad bit nuts, perhaps, believing in ghosts and towns that slid off mountains, but nice, nonetheless.

"Well, I know you must have somewhere pressing to be, so I'll let you get there. Have a nice day, Grant." She wiggled her fingers and started back on her way.

When she realized he was following her, she looked back with a question in her eyes.

"Headed to my car," he explained, "down here on Hull."

"That's where I'm parked."

His lips lifted in a smile and he picked up his pace, catching up to her in two long strides. "Then allow me to walk you there."

They made small talk as they walked along the side of the road. When the sidewalk played out, Grant took her elbow and helped her along the sloping path.

"Which one is yours?" he asked as they approached the crowded lot.

"Red Mazda, second row."

"The one that looks like it has a flat tire? It's sitting a bit oddly."

"What? You've got to be kidding me!" She pulled free of his hand and ran toward her tilted car. She groaned in defeat, even before she reached it.

"And what about these dents and scrapes on your fender?" he asked in concern. "Isn't this a rental?"

"Yes, but those are mine." She waved away his confused look. "Long story. But look at this tire! Completely flat."

Grant squatted down to examine it more closely. "Not just flat, I'm afraid," he reported. "There's a huge hole it in."

"A hole?" Unease skittered along her spine.

"Yeah, like a chunk, just taken out of the rubber."

A hole.

Like the ones Miles Anderson warned her about, perchance?

Grant insisted on calling a garage he used down in Clarksdale. They would replace the tire and deliver the car to her hotel by afternoon.

He also insisted upon driving her back to *The Dove.* Gera resisted, thinking she should call Jake, but Grant was adamant. His conscience would never rest, he claimed, knowing he left her there to fend for herself until her ride arrived. He could drop her there himself. Five minutes out of his way.

She could think of no polite way out. It wasn't as if she was accepting a date, she was merely accepting a ride. And even though Jake didn't like nor trust the man, he had been nothing but polite to Gera. She had really no good reason not to slide into his Saab and wrap herself in the luxurious comfort of cooled, buttery-soft leather.

"Nice ride," she grinned.

"My other car is a Prius."

She might as well use the short drive to her advantage. "So you said you grew up here, huh? Went to school in Cottonwood?"

"That's right."

"So you and Miles Anderson have been friends all this time?"

His expression changed, but marginally. *Remind me to never play poker with the guy,* Gera thought to herself.

He avoided a direct lie. "We've known each other for a long time," he agreed.

"But aren't necessarily friends," she read between the lines. Gera tilted her head and studied him. "So who got the girl in the long run?"

"Girl?"

"Prom girl. Tiffany, I think?"

"Ah, yes, the lovely Tiffany Braxton. Well, neither of us, I suppose, not in the long run. She was actually Anderson's first wife, but they were divorced within a year, from what I understand."

"First wife? How many has he had?"

"Two? Possibly three. That's not counting Beverly Ruth. They never actually divorced, even though they've been separated for years."

"Beverly?"

Grant nodded, carefully maneuvering the chuckholes and dips marking the roadway like a moldy slice of Swiss cheese. *Holes*, Gera thought, as he elaborated. "Yes. Beverly Ruth Cunningham."

She stared at him in surprise. "What? Abe Cunningham was the chief's ex-father-in-law?"

"Technically, I believe he's best described as his late father-in-law. No divorce, remember?"

"I can't believe this! I've spoken with him several times, and he never once mentioned that the murder victim was his relative!"

"I don't think they thought of themselves as family."

The car glided to a smooth stop, but the lack of motion was slow to register on Gera's stunned mind.

"Gera?" he asked gently. "We can go for a ride, if you'd like."

"What? Oh, no, I'm sorry. I didn't realize… I'm just so stunned about what you just told me!"

"Obviously." His gaze traveled to the hotel behind her. Just for a moment, a look of pure envy stole across his face. His eyes seemed to caress the old girl, traveling over her railed porches and towering heights. His eyes shuttered when he sensed Gera watching him. "Shall I see you in?"

"No, no, I'm good."

"At least let me get your door." He exited the car gracefully, his long legs making short work of the distance between his door and hers. He helped her from the soft leather, his hand lingering on her arm.

"Thanks again, Grant. I appreciate the ride, and especially you calling the garage and arranging for a new tire."

"It was my pleasure. If Mondo doesn't arrive as promised, you let me know. In fact, here's my card." He pressed a finely textured card into her hand. "That's my personal number. Feel free to call. Anytime." Still his hand lingered. "About anything."

She stepped away as quickly as politeness would allow. "Okay, thanks," she said, trying to disengage her arm from his.

She hurried up the steps of the hotel. Just a few days ago, she had found the noisy protests of the creaking boards and the wail of the old front door a bit foreboding. Now she welcomed the sounds.

Jake was behind the desk again, helping guests. Two women, as it turned out, and both were flirting shamelessly with their handsome host. But when Jake looked up to greet whomever had come through the door, and when his eyes met hers, his smile deepened. Totally free of yesterday's drugs, Gera tingled from the look he sent her. This was definitely all Jake.

"Hey," he said softly as she came up to the desk. "Be right with you."

One of the women actually sighed. "Come on, Shelli," she told her friend. "We can probably find the vending machine on our own."

He hid a smile and Gera scrunched her nose as the women passed behind her.

"So how is your day going?" Jake asked.

"Not so great. Town is crazy busy, and I had a flat."

"Do I need to fix it?" he offered.

"Thanks, but it's all taken care of. Actually, Grant came to my rescue. And don't make that face. He was perfectly nice. He even gave me a ride home. And I think he may have gone on up the road to drop in on Ruth. Oh, and guess what I found out? You probably already know this, but I just found out that Miles Anderson is Abe and Ruth's son-in-law!"

"Ex son-in-law," Jake corrected.

"Grant says they never divorced. Which, come to think of it, may be why the chief was so upset about the lien still on the house. He insisted Beverly was set to inherit it. Which," she reasoned, "means he might have some sort of claim to it. Eventually."

Jake looked a bit confused. "Not sure what all you're talking about," he admitted. "And I wish I could say you could tell me over dinner, but Terri called in. I have to pull a double. I'll be stuck here until eleven."

She looked as mournful as he did.

"Make that ten thirty," he amended. "I'll grab a shower and give you a call, if that's not too late."

"It's not too late."

He glanced around, saw no one in the lobby, and jumped forward, just enough to hang on the edge of the counter and brush a kiss onto her lips. "See you later then."

"Shall I grab something from the restaurant and bring it to you? We could still eat dinner together."

"Thanks, but Saturday nights are usually pretty busy. I probably won't get much of a chance to eat."

"Okay. Text me if you find a few spare minutes."

"Will do." The switchboard behind him rang. "See what I mean? The later it gets, the worse it gets."

As she threw him a kiss and went toward the elevator, Gera heard Jake apologizing to a guest. "No soap? Or batteries in your remote? I'm so sorry about that, Mrs. Abas. I will send some up immediately."

And here we go again, Gera sighed to herself. *The children.*

17

With no available car and no plans for dinner, Gera spent the afternoon doing research. A slow internet connection made gathering what she needed that much slower. When she needed a break, she went down to the restaurant, ordered a snack, and went out to the terrace. A little fresh air and warm sunshine would do her good.

She tried to sort it all out in her head.

A town that believed in ghosts.

A town that blamed a ghost for a death.

A chief of police whose father-in-law was the victim.

A widow who might lose her house, because of a bank president many disliked.

A bank president whom she liked, and one who *really* liked her.

A sexy hotel owner she couldn't resist.

An unknown enemy who stalked her, leaving her subtle threats.

A bartender who drugged her.

A town that believed in ghosts.

A town that blamed a ghost for a death.

As the loop played again in her head, Gera put her hands over her face and groaned.

"Is everything all right, dear?"

She jerked her head up in surprise. Minnie sat on the bench beneath the arbor, a smile upon her frail, wrinkled face.

"Minnie! When did you get here?"

"I've been here a few minutes, dear. You looked deep in thought, so I didn't want to disturb you."

"I've missed seeing you the last two days."

"Yes, well, one morning I just couldn't quite pull myself together," the older woman admitted, with somewhat of a sheepish smile.

"I understand. That was my excuse this morning."

"No worries, dear. We can visit now. So tell me, why do you look so deep in thought? Are you having trouble with your article?"

Gera's laugh held no humor. "You could say that. I thought of a new angle, but it's proving a bit more difficult than I imagined."

"Anything I can help you with? You remember, I know a lot of the town's history."

"You certainly do. So, what can you tell me about Miles Anderson?"

"The chief of police? He's a nice enough fellow, I think. Dedicated to his job. Has his hands full at the moment, trying to find the person responsible for the recent crime spree in town. And now poor Abe's murder!"

"I didn't realize until today that Abe was his father-in-law. I understand he's still married to one of Abe's daughters?"

"His only daughter, actually. Beverly Ruth. But they broke up years ago."

"But I hear they didn't divorce, so they're technically still married."

"I wonder if Peggy Running Branch knows that," she mused aloud. "I understand she and Miles have been keeping time lately."

The late afternoon sun beamed down on Minnie, illuminating her silvery cap of curls, making her pale skin almost glow, much as the moonlight had done to Anise.

"Would you like to sit over here, out of the sun?" Gera offered, motioning to the chair beside her. "That metal bench must be warm."

"Oh, it is. Feels divine," Minnie said dreamily. "Great source of energy, too."

It was an odd response, particularly on a hot day like today, but maybe Minnie was particularly cold natured. She wore that shawl again, the one that wrapped around her shoulders like a giant bandage. Gera remembered Grams had gotten cold a lot, especially near the end.

"Do you know anything about Miles Anderson's first wife?"

"Hmm, let me think. I believe... yes, he married a girl he went to school with. They weren't married very long. She ended up pregnant."

Gera looked at her friend in surprise. "He didn't want children? So he divorced her?" Her opinion of the policeman rapidly deteriorated.

"I don't know about *wanting* them, but I do know he couldn't *have* them. He shot blanks, as they say. So when his young bride came up with child..."

"Oh. Oh, I see." Now she felt sorry for the man.

"He married another girl a few years later, but she had her sights set on Hollywood. Their marriage lasted until a movie producer came to town. They were filming a show about the lost gold of Sycamore Canyon, and when he pulled out and went back to LA, she went with him. And then he married Beverly Ruth, and they had an on-again, off-again sort of marriage."

"I suppose it's currently in *OFF* mode again."

"I suppose."

"What's that about gold?"

"You're not familiar with the legend?" Minnie asked, her eyes twinkling at the prospect of telling a new story. When Gera shook her head in the negative, Minnie clapped her withering hands together and launched into her tale.

"It is said that in the 1500s, a Spanish Expedition came into Sycamore Canyon and mined for gold. They dug excavation tunnels and found a rich vein, carrying samples back with them to Mexico City. But they were denied access back into the region, and the mine fell idle. It was years before another expedition found the mine and tried again. Through the ages, many different explorers came, and mined, and were eventually chased away by hostile Indians. The Indians would hide the entrance to the mine, wanting to keep it for themselves. Early Indians mined the deposits here in Jerome, too, you know, but the vein in Geronimo's Cave was said to be far better, and worth a great deal of money. In the 1870s, the Indians hid the mine entrance once and for all. People still come here today, trying to find the lost gold mine. Many get lost out in the wilderness. Some have even died."

"And where is this canyon?"

Minnie raised her hand and pointed in the distance. "It's in some of those magnificent red rocks yonder. Not far from here, only twenty miles, at most. It is a beautiful canyon, as much as seven miles wide at some points, and empties into the Verde River. A lovely spot, but it can be deadly, if you go deep into the wilderness."

Gera smiled at the older woman. "I like your stories."

"And I enjoy telling them, my dear. An eager audience is always appreciated."

"Do you have any more?"

Her vivid blue eyes sparkled. "I have plenty of stories, my dear."

A belated thought occurred to Gera. "I guess your gold story is what my friend Ramon was talking about. He said something about Frankie D and the hidden gold. Do you know who Frankie D was?"

"Of course. Franklin D. Roosevelt."

"FDR, the *president*? He looked for the lost gold?"

"No, dear, this is another story altogether."

"Can you tell it to me?"

Minnie hesitated for a moment. She glanced up at the sun, which already didn't seem to burn as hotly as it had a few moments ago. She touched the bench with her curled fingers, testing it for warmth, and shifted her slight body, just enough to feel the full heat of the sun's rays.

"All set," she murmured, before adjusting her hands and beginning a new tale. "I don't know if you keep up with government issues past and present, but one of the darkest eras for the American people came during the Great Depression. The stock market crashed, the dollar lost its value, and our president, FDR, issued an executive order in which he confiscated all gold and silver holdings in the United States."

Gera frowned. "That can't be right," she started to object.

"It is, dear. You can find it in any library, any ogle search. Our president demanded that all citizens tender their holdings within fourteen days. Safe deposits at all banks across the country were immediately sealed, so that people couldn't access their vaults without a federal agent present. People weren't allowed to buy, sell, trade, move, or hoard their private holdings of gold and silver. The government confiscated it all."

This didn't sound like her government. "But, *why?*" Gera asked.

"To manipulate the economy. They paid people for their gold, of course, but in paper dollars. The dollar was immediately devalued, and the price of gold, which now belonged solely to the government, soared."

"That's an incredible story. I've never heard it before. Are you—Are you certain it is correct?" Gera asked carefully, afraid she might insult her friend. Minnie was getting older. Perhaps her memory failed her.

"Absolutely. Executive Order No. 6102, to be exact," the older woman said with great clarity. She leaned slightly forward, her voice taking on a confidential hush. "But there's more to the story."

"Oh?"

"The mines here in Jerome didn't produce just copper. There were substantial deposits of gold, silver, and zinc. A by-product, as it were, of excavating the copper. With the mining company's focus on copper, they stockpiled the other metals aside, as incredulous as that may seem. And so, when the order came to relinquish all gold… well, some of those stock-piles disappeared."

"Can I find this on Ogle—I mean, Google—as well?"

"Oh, no." Minnie looked around, making certain no would could overhear their conversation. A lone couple sat on the tiered garden above, lost in one another's arms. Minnie frowned and veered slightly off track. "There are perfectly divine hotel rooms just feet away," the older woman murmured in disapproval. "Why must they behave so wantonly in public?"

"I think they assume they're hidden," Gera said, noting a flash of bare skin. Unconcerned with the couple's exploits, she turned back to her friend. "What happened to the gold?"

Minnie looked uncertain again. Her eyes searched Gera's face. It was clear she was deciding whether to trust the younger woman.

"I know you're a reporter, Gera," she said softly. "I know you're looking for a story to tell. Nevertheless, what I'm about to tell you… There is more at stake here than merely selling an article, dear. Please, remember that. Please weigh the value of a salable story against the value of a family legacy. Perhaps against the value of life, itself."

Her words seemed almost ominous. Gera leaned forward, her breath but a whisper in her lungs.

Minnie was still hesitant. "Can I trust you, Gera?" The older woman pinned her with her intense blue eyes.

It was the look in Minnie's eyes, as much as the question itself, which gave Gera pause. *Could* she be trusted? She was a reporter. She researched stories. Dissected them, ferreting out what was truth, what wasn't. That was what she did. Her curious mind demanded answers. Moreover, she made her living by sharing the best of those stories with the public.

So, *could* she be trusted?

Gera sucked in her breath. "I think so." Her answer was stark and honest.

"I appreciate your honesty. And I'm counting on your integrity. Because I will tell you something, my dear. Many will say it isn't so, but I know it for a fact, Gera. Much of that gold was hidden, right here on the mountain. And it remains hidden today."

"But..."

"Very few people are privy to this information. As you might imagine, if this knowledge fell into the hands of the wrong people..." She stared into the distance, toward the fabled canyon, where adventurous men and women were willing to die in order to find the entrance to an ancient gold mine. Minnie need not say more. What might a greedy soul do to discover a hidden hoard of mined gold, more easily accessible?

"Why did you tell me this?" Gera cried in quiet dismay. "A story like this..."

"Knowledge is power, Gera. Knowledge often means the difference between life and death."

What did that even mean? Gera's forehead pulled together in a wrinkled seam.

Minnie recognized her distress. "I've overwhelmed you. I'm so sorry. Let me tell you another story, while I'm still able."

Gera wasn't sure her mind could absorb any more, but Minnie had already begun.

"I know you aren't a believer, dear. You can't understand an entire town openly embracing the idea of ghosts among us, of welcoming a connection to the spiritual world."

"No, I can't," she agreed honestly.

"Some say it started with the Indians. If ever there were a people who were mistreated and misunderstood, it is the Native Americans. Have you been two hours north of here, to the Navajo Nation? No? Be prepared for heartbreak. Much of the land they were given is worthless, full of huge ravines and rock. Some believe the rocks are red because they're soaked in the blood of our native ancestors. It is no wonder that their spirits still roam these hills, searching for peace."

Gera struggled to keep an open mind. She wanted to understand. She would never believe, but perhaps, at the very least, she could understand. "What do the others say?"

"Do you know much about mining, Gera?"

Her shoulder lifted in a shrug. "I've seen movies. Been through a few museums."

"It was hard, back-breaking work. And very dangerous. There could be a cave-in at any moment, burying men alive. A dynamite blast could go wrong, leaving men disfigured for life. These men knew the risks when they took the jobs. Still, when the job claimed a life, it was customary for the mining company to offer a bereavement package of three hundred dollars to his family, to pay for funeral expenses and the like. But times were hard, and people did what they had to do in order to survive. Most people took the money and invested it in a sure thing. Most opened their own brothel, the surest way to make a living in a mining town."

Gera suspected there was more to the story. She took the bait. "Then how did they pay for the funeral?"

"I'm not saying it is fact, but rumor has it that they by-passed the funerals altogether. The smelters and kilns blazed day and night. Who's to say that a body wasn't tossed into the fire? It was a fast, convenient, no-cost method of disposal."

Gera recoiled in disgust. "That's horrible!"

Minnie shrugged, causing the lacy shawl upon her shoulders to bunch as surely as Gera's face. "I'm not saying it's true. But local lore has it that in time, the ashes of those men worked their way into the product. By century end, there was an ordinance that all buildings had to be made of brick or stone to combat fire. Many were reinforced with metals made here in the smelters. Some folks believe that, in a very real sense, the spirits of early miners are ingrained in our town's very infrastructure."

Gera stared at the woman in a mixture of fascination and horror. She finally found her voice. "That—That's incredible."

"With a history as rich and rowdy as Jerome's, is it any wonder the spirits have trouble finding peace?"

"You said before that most spirits had missions to complete. Is that their mission, to find peace?"

"Perhaps. Perhaps some stay behind to protect their loved ones. Maybe they're watching over them, or trying to relay a vital message to them. Perhaps they know a secret, or something that could make a profound difference in their lives."

"Something like the hidden hoards of gold?" Gera murmured.

Minnie's gaze was intense again. "Perhaps."

They fell silent for a few moments. When Gera glanced at her friend again, she seemed paler than ever, and not as alert. The sun was sinking lower in the sky, beginning its evening decent. As the day lost its energy, so, it seemed, did Minnie. She seemed to be wilting, as surely as one of Gram's prized roses. Gera remembered how the petals would curl into themselves at night, tucking aside the heat of the day for the coolness yet to come. Minnie seemed to do the same thing.

"Minnie? Are you feeling all right?"

"Mm, perhaps you could bring me a glass of water?"

"Certainly!" Gera jumped to her feet, eager to help. "I'll be right back."

Yet when she returned just moments later, the old woman was gone. The couple on the upper terrace hadn't seen her. They hadn't even noticed her talking with Gera.

Gera returned to the restaurant, searching for her friend. When she didn't find her in the dining room or the restrooms, she dared stick her head into the kitchen. Someone suggested she check the back hall. Sometimes guests wandered the wrong way, they said, or tried to take the back stairway up.

She doubted Minnie was capable of taking the stairs, but it was worth checking. Gera found the hall beyond the kitchen easily enough, the one where the prostitute Penelope was murdered. The lighting was still dim here, as it had been the other night. But without Leo's dramatic prologue, the space wasn't nearly as eerie.

Until the lights went completely dark.

As blackness swooped in and filled the narrow space, causing the air to go stale and Gera's feet to stumble, she thought she heard someone behind her. It sounded like a woman's voice.

"Minnie? Minnie, is that you? Are you all right? Have you fallen?"

"Help me," the voice whispered.

"Yes, yes, certainly. Where are you?"

"Family."

"Do I need to call your family? How do I contact them?" Gera felt around in the darkness, trying to locate the other woman. She brushed along the floors, afraid her friend lay hurt or bleeding.

"I must protect them." Her voice was fading, perhaps retreating further down the hall. Gera started after the voice, intending to follow. Somehow she stumbled, as if someone had shoved her, knocking her to the ground. By the time Gera struggled to her feet, the lights were again burning low and she was alone in the hallway.

She ran down the hall to the stairwell entrance. No one was there.

There were other doors along the hallway, ones she hadn't noticed on the tour. Gera pushed on one and found it locked. The next one opened into the laundry room. A quick search revealed piles of dirty linens, but no people.

When she opened the third door, she was surprised to find herself in Lucy's office.

"Why, it's pretty little Gera. Come right in. Nerva and I were about to have tea. You can join us."

"Uh, thanks, but I can't stay. I was looking for a friend of mine. Seventy-ish, curly white hair, white shawl."

Lucy looked at the empty chair across from her desk. "Nerva?"

Great. Lucy would recruit her imaginary friend to help Gera look. "That's okay, I can see you're busy," she said hastily. "Thanks." She hurried out and shut the door behind her.

Clearly, Minnie wasn't in the hallway, nor in the restaurant. Most likely, the older woman had decided to walk home.

Gera should return to her room. Her mind was awhirl after Minnie's stories.

And it was still several hours before ten thirty.

18

For the past hour, she had watched the clock in sixty-second intervals. She changed her mind at least a dozen times.

When Jake called, she would make an excuse. She wouldn't go.

But what excuse was good enough to miss a night in his arms? She would go.

She couldn't go. Why start something that had no chance for a happy ending?

Why not have one perfect night, if nothing else? Go.

Don't go. *You don't know him well enough.* What if he's the killer?

He has killer blue eyes. You know you'll thank yourself in the morning. You gotta go, Gera girl.

She had finally decided that no, she couldn't go. The reasons were long and many, all well thought out and perfectly rational. But they all came down to one fundamental flaw in the otherwise nearly perfect man. He believed in ghosts.

Her phone rang at 10:38 p.m.

"Hey." His voice was low and sexy, and almost her undoing. *Stay strong, Gera girl. You're saying no.*

"Hey."

"Sorry, I just got away."

"No problem. I was working and didn't even notice the time." *Liar,* her mind screamed.

"I'm starved. I called for a bite to eat. You want something?" *We practiced this. Say no. You're tired and going to bed.*

"Sure."

Gera smacked herself in the forehead. Where had that come from?

"Great. I'm going to jump in the shower. I'm leaving the door cracked for room service, so come whenever you want. I'll be out in five."

"Let me put things away and I'll be over in a little while. Call me if I'm not there when the food arrives."

"Will do."

Gera berated herself as she jumped from the couch and checked the mirror, for what had to be the millionth time. She had worn her dress last night. Tonight, she had decided on jeans and a tee. Changed into a pair of lounge pants. Changed back to jeans. She was currently dressed in striped lounge pants, a white cotton cami, and house shoes, because her last decision—before she heard his voice again—was that she was going to bed. She wasn't about to change again. Because no matter what nonsense she spouted to him about putting away her work and coming in a little while, she knew it would be all she could do not to take off running, all the way to the far end of the hall. She could be there in less than sixty seconds.

She took time to swig a sip of mouthwash, squirt one last spray of perfume, and run her fingers through her hair. Then she was off down the hall, her nerves tapping out a pace even faster than her feet.

Room service arrived at the same time she did. Blushing, she took the tray from the man without quite meeting his eyes and shut the door behind him. She could hear the shower still running upstairs. On shaky legs, Gera carried the tray up the spiral steps.

She stood in the middle of his bedroom, trying to formulate a plan, when the bathroom door opened. Steam escaped around him, so that at first she didn't notice he wore only a towel at his waist. When she did notice, her mouth went dry. She almost dropped the tray.

"Hey!" he said in surprise, a smile spreading across his face. "I didn't know you were already here."

"I—I should go," she said suddenly.

"Go?" he asked in confusion. "But the food is here." He took the tray from her and turned to put it on a table in the sitting area. Muscles rippled along his back with the movement. "Aren't you hungry?"

It was an innocent enough question, but Gera, fully under the influence of the heady and gorgeous drug called Jake, answered with a breathless, "Yes." Her eyes devoured him, taking in the sculpted pecs and bulky shoulders. Slid low, to where the towel hung on the barest thread of decency, barely covering him.

If she had had the nerve, she would've been waiting for him on the bed, naked, alongside the tray. When he came into the room, she would've asked in a sultry voice, "See anything you like?"

But she didn't have the nerve. The girl who punched bullies in the nose and defied the ravages of cancer and poured her drink down bartenders' shirts lost her nerve when it came to this. She had no skills at seduction. No flirting finesse.

But she did know what she wanted.

And she wanted Jake.

"Gera?"

She met him halfway across the room. He held his arms wide and let her fall into him. Kissed her until she almost forgot her newest and most brilliant plan. *Head on, Gera.*

"You're way over-dressed for this dinner party," he murmured, just as she reached for the tail of her camisole. She whipped it off and flung it over her head.

His eyes darkened. Without his glasses, the color was even bluer than before. Gera could drown in the blue of those eyes.

Jake kissed her again. His deft hands pushed at the waistband of her pants, pushing them down to pool around her feet. When she stepped out of them, he kicked them aside and pulled her backwards, a few steps closer to the bed.

"Are you sure?" he murmured. "No lingering drugs?"

"I'm high on the best drug of all," she said, pushing her tongue into his mouth. He tasted like toothpaste and cinnamon. "Jake Cody. This is all you." Before she lost her nerve, she tugged his towel free.

"Then forgive me, my beautiful Gera," he murmured against her throat, trailing his mouth lower, hot and hungry, as he disposed of first her bra, and then her underwear. "But I have no intentions of being a gentleman tonight."

It was midnight when they finally ate. The rolls were cold and the strawberries were warm, but they were both starving. Gera was amazed at the ease she felt, crawling naked onto his bed with a plate filled with food and eating it, right there among the tangled sheets.

They talked about everything and nothing, much as they had done before. But this time, they did it with no clothes on, and stopped intermittently to nip the other on the shoulder, or to kiss the tip of a nose, or the back of a knee, or in that sweet spot between the neck and the collar bone. And when Jake proclaimed they had talked enough and it was time for dessert, she didn't think she could reach such heights again, but he proved her wrong. Her pleasure came in waves, washing over them both and whisking them away to a place only they could know.

He held her afterward, guiding her safely back to Earth. She came down slowly, not wanting the magic to end.

"Jake?" she murmured groggily.

"Yeah?"

"Something you said," she said, running her hand across the muscled planes of his chest. "You said you indulge Leo and Lucy, because they're like grandparents to you, and you can't bear to send them away. What did you mean by that?"

His attention was on the creamy lobe of her breast, and how it fell perfectly into the palm of his hand. "Just that I let Leo do his puppet show, as you call it, because it seems to make him happy, and I go along with Lucy when she thinks she talks to my grandmother, because I don't want her to know that I know."

"Know what?"

"That she's losing her mind," he whispered, the words too painful to admit in a normal voice.

"But, if you believe in ghosts"—and this was the most difficult part, because if not for the ghost angle, she could easily fall in love with this man—"why do you think she's losing her mind? Why don't you think she's really talking to your grandmother?"

"I never said I believed in ghosts, Gera," he answered quietly.

"Yes, you did," she argued.

"No, you said it for me. I just didn't disagree."

"Then you aren't a believer?"

He stroked her ivory skin, testing the weight of first one breast, then the other. He was fascinated by their symmetry, their smooth flawlessness. "I think there is *something*," he answered thoughtfully, "some... spirit. Some connection. Something that doesn't always end with death. There are days that I think I can almost hear my grandmother's voice. Other days I get this odd chill, and then a warm sensation comes over me, and for no reason at all, I think of my grandmother. I feel really close to her again in that moment. But that's not a ghost. It's the spirit of love. So no, Gera, I don't believe in ghosts."

A huge smile spread across her face. Her mother's smile, the one that had beguiled her father and kept him deeply in love with his wife, even all these years after her death. Jake blinked beneath the brilliance of that smile. Swallowed hard. Forgot even to breathe, or to fondle her breasts. His heart hammered in his chest, his mind struck senseless by her smile.

"You, Jake Cody, may truly be the perfect man," she whispered through her smile. "Definitely my very own Superman."

She came awake to the sound of his voice.

"Good morning, Lois Lane."

"Morning, SuperClark." She had given him the adapted moniker sometime deep in the night, when their bodies melted together for yet another time.

"I have the next two days off," he announced with a smile. "What would you like to do? Anything you want, you name it."

"Anything?"

Jake laughed, seeing the hungry look in her eyes. He stopped her hand before it could wander too far. "Even Superman has to have a break now and then, and Clark definitely does. And both need food. Lots and lots of food."

"Which of us gets the shower first?" she asked.

"Ladies, of course."

As she turned on the multi-jets in the over-sized stall and the room filled with steam, she heard Jake call out, "Want me to order breakfast in the room?"

"Sure. One of everything." She stepped beneath the hot water and let it sluice over her body, reviving her sore body and abused muscles. Both had quite the workout last night.

She had suds in her hair when she heard the bathroom door open and shut. Jake silently joined her in the shower and adjusted one set of jets to suit him. Peeking an eye open, Gera yelped as suds trickled down her forehead and stung her eyes.

"Who else did you think it would be?" he laughed. "I thought we cleared up the ghost issue last night."

"Can't ever be too sure," she said. She thought again about her initial fear of coming to the hotel, based on a slasher movie. There had been a shower scene in that movie, too.

Not that she had to worry about that now. She trusted Jake. "Did you order breakfast?"

"Sure did. One of everything, just like you said, but double pancakes and double bacon."

"Speaking of ghosts…" She put her head under the spray and washed the suds away. "Minnie told me an incredible story about ghosts yesterday. Have you heard the legend of miner's ashes in the steel?"

"Yeah, that's an old local legend. My grandmother told me about it when I was a kid."

"I hate to say it, but I do believe the part about some of the families skipping the funeral and going straight for the money."

"Times were hard. People did what they had to do."

"What about some sort of Executive Order, when Franklin Roosevelt confiscated all the gold and silver in the US and paid people back with devalued cash? Have you ever heard that one?"

Jake scrubbed shampoo into his scalp and rinsed it free before answering. "That's not legend. That one is fact."

"Really?"

"Really. Look it up."

"I will." She sighed as she picked up a bar of soap and absently began to lather Jake's back. "I intended to look up all sorts of things on the internet yesterday, but at one point, everything was down, even my hot-spot. What's up with the service around here?"

He looked over his shoulder and grinned. "You know what they're saying. Mac."

"So I'll just have to pick *your* brain. What can you tell me about Minnie?"

"Switch," Jake said, turning around and motioning for her to do the same. As he took his turn lathering her back, he asked, "Who?"

"You know, the old woman who lives next door."

"No one lives next door."

"Really? I just assumed she lived in that old run-down house. I think she might be poor. Not like starving-and-can't-afford-to-eat poor, but like take-advantage-of-the-free-coffee-and-flower-gardens poor."

"Who is this again?"

"The old lady I told you about, the one I see out in the garden most mornings. She was out there yesterday afternoon, and told me all sorts of great stories."

"Well, she doesn't live next door. It's been empty for about ten years. I remember MiniMa told me the owner died and didn't have a family, so the bank owns it now. Not that they've done anything with it." His soapy washcloth ran along her arm as he grumbled, "I wish they would at least clean it up. At the very least, fix the holes they left in the yard."

"You have a Mini Me?"

"Not Mini Me, MiniMa," he corrected. His cloth slid around to her belly, causing her to suck in her breath. He continued unabashedly, "Hey, don't judge. Some people have a Granny, some people have a Nana, some people have a Meme. I had a MiniMa."

"I—I had a Grams." It was almost sacrilegious, uttering her name with Jake doing the things he was beginning to do to her. She felt him press himself against her back. "I thought SuperClark wasn't up to the challenge."

"I was wrong," he murmured against her ear. "You, Gera Stapleton, are my new energy source."

19

"Can I ask you something?"

Jake paused, a cinnamon bran muffin halfway to his mouth. "Please don't ask for the muffin," he said, his face filling with mock horror. "It's my favorite."

"No, silly, I'm not asking for the muffin."

"I'll share," he offered.

"Eat your muffin. I want to ask you a serious question."

"It's a little early in the day for serious questions, but I'll make an exception. Go."

"Your apartment is on the third floor. Well, all except the planet of dreams." She pointed to the bedroom suite above them.

"Planet of dreams, huh?" he grinned. "I like that."

"Yeah, I thought you might. But seriously. You live on the same floor I've been staying on. Have you ever heard 'the babies' crying at night?"

"No, of course not. It's all in people's imaginations. Power of suggestion, and all that." He scooped the last of the scrambled eggs onto his plate. "Want any more?"

"I can't believe you're still eating. We had a ton of food, and it's almost all gone."

"Growing boy," he said with a wink. "Storing up energy, in case my Gera battery gets weak."

"I heard them, Jake."

"Heard who?"

"The babies."

He looked at her oddly for a long moment. Saw that she was serious. He pushed away his plate and reached out to take her hand. "It's getting to you, isn't it?" he said softly. "I can see how it would. Total immersion in a new place, where people are throwing ghosts at you at every turn. The mind is a powerful thing, but it can be tricked at times—"

"I'm not being brainwashed, Jake," she snapped. "I know what I heard."

"I didn't mean—"

She shook off his apology and started over. "I should start at the beginning. I have a theory about what's been happening in town. I think that someone has manipulated the townspeople into believing that Mac is responsible for the recent crime spree, so that they will also blame him for Abe's death. I've been studying reports of the Mac sightings. Most of them are in relatively the same location. Which led me to another theory, one concerning the hotel."

"Is that why you were looking through the ghost journals, the ones where guests record their own sightings and experiences here at the hotel?"

"Yes, and I discovered a pattern here, too." Gera took a deep breath and plunged in, head on. "What if it's rigged, Jake?"

"What do you mean?"

"Think about it. They have the perfect setup, the perfect opportunity. Leo and Lucy have the run of the hotel. Keys to every room. A reason to go inside when guests aren't present. What if they're the ones rigging the hotel, to have babies crying in the night and children's toys appearing out of nowhere? What if they're the ones taking the soap and the toilet paper and extra washcloths?"

"What—What are you accusing them of? You think they killed Abe?" His voice was sharp.

"No, no, no," she was quick to assure him. "This has nothing to do with Abe or Mac or any of the things happening in town. This is about *The Dove*. I know what I heard and what I saw, but since there are no such things as ghosts, then there has to be a logical explanation for all the odd things that happen here."

His Adam's apple bobbed. "But what you're suggesting is dishonest. Borderline fraud."

She grabbed his hand in both of hers, pressing warmth into fingers turned cold. "I don't think they see it that way, Jake. And I don't think they've done it to be dishonest. I think they were trying to save the hotel, and at the time, it seemed the logical solution to a very real problem."

"I—I don't know…"

"When did these supernatural sightings begin to take place?"

"After MiniMa died."

"When did Leo take charge of the hotel?"

"After MiniMa died. But that doesn't mean…" He pulled his hand free and got up to pace the room. He shoved his hands through his hair and left it spiky and unkempt, and oh, so sexy. "Oh, God, what if I've been defrauding the public all this time?"

"*You* haven't defrauded them, Jake."

"I'm the majority owner. I'm the one responsible for everything my staff does. Leo and Lucy have a share in the company, but I'm the president and CEO. I'm the one who is ultimately responsible."

"I could be wrong, Jake," she offered softly.

"It makes sense. Now that I think about it, it seems so obvious." He brushed a hand over his face. "How could I have been so blind?"

"You said it yourself. You love them. They've been like grandparents to you. And no matter what means they used, they kept this hotel afloat after your grandmother died." Gera got up to stand in front of him, effectively putting an end to his pacing. She wound her arms around his waist and lay her head against his bare chest, listening to the steady pump of his heart. *Such a good heart*, she thought with a smile. *Such a good man.*

"I looked into the financial records of the hotel." When he stiffened, she assured him, "Public records, nothing more. Before the internet went on the blink again, I checked out some of what I've learned the last few days. I remembered you told me about Grant Young, trying a similar tactic with you to get title to the hotel. I remembered it yesterday, when he dropped me off here. When he looked at the hotel, I swear he had a look of… almost lust… upon his face. Definitely greed. Envy."

"Maybe he was thinking about you, imagining you in my bed," Jake murmured, his voice a rumble in his chest. "Definitely envy worthy."

"Not to sound full of myself, but I thought of that," she admitted. "But no, this was something different. It wasn't about me, it was about the house."

"What does this have to do with Leo and Lucy?"

"When your grandmother died, she owed quite a bit of money."

"Yeah, she mortgaged the hotel to make improvements. You have no idea how much money it takes, keeping a hotel up to the expected standards of its guests. People want to stay in a historical property, but only if it comes with granite countertops and flat screen TVs and high-speed internet."

"Let me guess. She took out the loan, shortly after Grant Young took over the bank."

"I don't know, maybe." He ran the timeline through his head. "Probably."

Gera nodded. "When Grant took over at First Yavapai, he did wonders for their bottom line. Business tripled, mostly because he convinced half the town to refinance their loans or take out new ones. I'm guessing your grandmother was among that half."

"So when Leo took over, he took over a property deep in debt."

"I think he came up with a brilliant solution. That was about the time all those ghost shows popped up all over television. And let's face it, people here in Jerome were easily convinced. It probably didn't take much to get the legend started."

"Then why did he resort to trickery?" Jake's voice was clearly distraught.

"Granite countertops," Gera murmured. "The public always wants more."

They stood for a long time, arms locked, and Gera could've sworn she heard the sound of his heart breaking, there inside his chest. Her own heart ached for him.

"I can't let them continue," he whispered, his voice rough. "I've got to stop them."

"There is an upside to this," she told him.

"Yeah," he quipped. "A gorgeous reporter came to town, blew my mind, then blew my whole world apart. Left me broken hearted, in more ways than one." He sounded mournful. "At least we had last night."

She dropped her arms and stepped back. "So, what? You're going to blow me off, just like that?"

"You're leaving in a few days, Gera. We both know that." He sounded miserable.

"Can we please just tackle one problem at a time?" She sighed, taking her turn at torturing her own hair. "The whole time I've been here in this very strange town, I've been hit with sensory overload. Ghosts, murder, sexy hotel owner, an Old West sheriff and a charming banker, an old woman who keeps disappearing on me, a snake-loving bartender who drugs me, someone else who's trying to scare me, imaginary children who play in my room… I could go on, but you get the drift. I literally feel as if I'm caught in the *Twilight Zone*. The only way I can take all this in is to dissect it, one piece at a time. So, please, help me out here."

His tone was less than helpful, more like skeptical, when he asked, "I think you mentioned an upside?"

"Yes, there is. One, your loan is paid in full. No matter what happens in the future, you don't have to worry about losing the hotel your grandparents started so long ago. The legacy can remain in your family."

"So, the upside is that when we start losing all our guests, the only thing we have left to lose is electricity, and running water, and food to serve in the dining room. Which won't really matter anymore, because we won't have any customers. Sweet."

"Sarcasm doesn't become you, SuperClark. No, the upside is that your hotel will be solvent, and you can rely on things like your reputation, not your trickery, to keep guests coming."

For the first time, he looked hopeful.

"You can still do the ghosts tours. You can even play the lullaby in the hallway, with the whole spiel about comforting the babies. The legends can stay. But the trickery needs to stop."

"No more recordings of babies crying and pranks on the guests."

"Exactly. I wasn't at all fond of the sticky sucker or the blaring television set. Believe me, people can fill in the blanks with their own imaginations. Let them hear what they think they hear, see what they think they see."

He caught her by the waist, puffing her hair in disarray when he blew out a warm sigh. "Thank you," he said softly. "It wasn't something I wanted to hear, wanted to know, but it could save my family's legacy. All we need is a lawsuit and I could lose everything my grandparents worked so hard to build. And thank you for making me see that this isn't the end, but an opportunity to be new and improved. And that's always what guests want, isn't it?"

"Please don't look so sad. I feel like I just broke your heart."

"And now I have to go break the hearts of two people I adore. They'll think I'm disappointed in them."

"Then tell them how much you appreciate what they did. That they saved your hotel financially, and now you have to save it legally." She reached up to touch his face, caressing the strong curve of his jaw. "You're a very persuasive man, SuperClark. I should know. I was all set to say no last night, but I'm so glad that I didn't." She pressed a chaste kiss onto his lips. "And you're a good man. You can do this."

"Come here, Lois Lane. I need some of your amazing energy source right about now."

But instead of making love to her, he merely held her, gathering the strength he needed to face Leo and Lucy.

20

"One piece of the puzzle is in place," Gera said with satisfaction as she pulled out from the hotel. She had a brand-new tire and a shiny, buffed fender, free of any telltale scrapes. She would need to call Grant and thank him. "Now for the other nine hundred and ninety-nine pieces."

While Jake began the difficult task of talking to his surrogate grandparents, Gera decided to run into town. There were several things on her to-do list.

As she entered the hairpin curve where Clark Street segued into Main, she got a whiff of a strange and foul odor.

"What is that?" she said aloud, sniffing. "Did the mechanics leave something in my car? It smells sort of… musty. Cloying." She sniffed a few more times, curling her lip in distaste. "Whatever it is, it reeks."

She saw movement out of the corner of her eye, on the passenger side, just as something flashed in the rearview mirror. It hit her at once, where she knew that smell, and what moved in her backseat, and on her floorboard. Snakes. Plural.

"Don't panic," she told herself, but her voice was unnaturally high. Her eyes darted around, searching for a place to pull over, even as she frantically tried to keep track of the snakes. Off the top of her head, she counted six, all slithering and slimy and darting out their forked tongues. She couldn't help but squeal. She was in the middle of the curve, with no place to go. A car was behind her, already dangerously close.

Gera saw a seventh snake, this one dropping down from the visor and dangling between her and the windshield. When it twisted its scaled body and darted its tongue, appearing ready to strike, Gera knew what she would do.

She jerked her steering wheel hard to the right, directly in front of an oncoming car. She didn't care whether or not the car—a blur of blue shiny metallic and a god-awful horn—made the curve as it quizzed past her with only inches to spare. She didn't care about the car on her bumper, or whether the other cars ran into a ditch or into each other. All she cared about was vacating her own car.

She was more or less on the road in front of the fire station; the Mazda bounced along the edge of the pavement, passenger tires in dirt. Not much of the town lay beyond, primarily a utility works and access to the mine roads. Without preamble, Gera opened her door and bailed. Her saving grace was that the car rolled along at no more than fifteen miles an hour. Curling herself into as small a ball as possible, she tried to protect her head, knowing she was about to hit asphalt. *Tuck and roll, Gera. Tuck and roll.*

It was a huge ordeal. An even bigger spectator event.

By the time the medics ran from the firehouse, Gera was on her feet. Her arms were scraped and leaking blood, but the rest of her seemed to be in one piece.

One would think she was the first person to ever jump from a moving vehicle. The first person to create a roadway of her own, her car rolling along at a slow, unassuming speed as snakes slithered out from the opened door. The first person to have her car roll to a slow, peaceful stop, atop a three-story building. It was, after all, a town layered in tiers.

Tourists and townspeople alike came out to take pictures. The fire trucks cranked their engines and fired up their lights, with sirens screaming the entire four hundred feet it took to reach the car.

Chief Anderson and Royce Gibbons, the officer she met when she first came to town, were two of the first on the scene. Her little escapade interrupted their Sunday dinner at the café, which Gibbons assured her was of no concern. Miles Anderson made no such claim. He eyed Gera as if it were her fault her car had become a rolling snake den. The fact that two of the snakes were endangered species—and highly venomous, no less—only added to his aggravation. Arizona Fish and Game had to come out and remove the snakes and safely relocate them to their natural habitat. It seemed a waste of time and effort, considering their natural habitat was mere yards away, amid the rocky terrain of Mingus Mountain.

Gera was tempted to call Jake, but she didn't want to upset him further. She had caused him enough trouble for one day, and it was only an hour past noon. After the medics patched her scrapes—and after steadfastly refusing transport to the local hospital—she accepted the chief's offer of a ride.

He insisted on getting her official statement.

"*Now* do you want to press charges, Miss Stapleton?" Anderson asked as she sat at his desk.

"Is there any way to prove Billy Boy put the snakes in my car?"

"Probably not."

"Then what's the point?"

"Might make you feel better," he offered. "Like the wheels of justice are at least attempting to turn."

She lifted a shoulder and discovered that it hurt to do so. "Why bother with the red tape?"

Miles Anderson leaned back in his swiveling chair, rocking it so far back she feared he might tip it over. He studied her coolly. "I don't know what we'll do with you, Miss Stapleton."

"Well, let's see. So far, your fair city has drugged me, stalked me, ruined my tire, possibly ruined my rental car, left me presents of stovepipe hats and poisonous snakes, and attempted to trick me into believing in ghosts. What else is left?"

"Attempts have been made on your life, Miss Stapleton. I wouldn't sound so flippant, if I were you."

"Did you consider my theory, Chief?"

"I considered it."

"And?"

"Still has holes."

Gera rolled her eyes.

"I'll talk to him, Miss Stapleton. I'll let Macandie know that we're watching him and that if he tries anything else, or if he makes contact with you in any way, we'll haul his ass back to jail. Not that it will be too big of an inconvenience for him. It's his home away from home." He tossed his pen onto his desk and muttered, "Good thing I'm no longer married to his momma. Can you imagine if that punk was actually my stepson?"

Gera stared at him. The man was just full of surprises. "You were married to his mother?" she asked, mouth agape.

"For six glorious, ignorant, stupid-blind months. Right up until I realized the kid she carried wasn't mine."

"Prom girl," Gera whispered in complete surprise.

"What's that?"

"Uhm, Grant told me about prom. About how you stole his date."

"Only because he stole her from me first, luring her away with a big fancy limo and some sort of smelly flower he had flown in from Tokyo. Too bad that expensive corsage ended up crushed in the backseat of my Ford Mustang. Ground the stink right in," he complained, some thirty years later. "And it was a brand-new car," he lamented.

"But you won in the long run, right? I mean, you married the girl, even if it didn't last."

He narrowed his eyes. "I always suspected she was still fooling around with Young, even after the wedding, but she married Bart Macandie. Said it was his kid." He shrugged his shoulders, in a show of no longer caring about the past. He was more concerned about losing the new car smell than he was about losing his marriage, Gera realized.

"How much longer are you in town for, Miss Stapleton?"

Her answer was deliberately vague. "A few days."

"Can I trust you to stay out of trouble from here on out?"

Gera got to her feet. "The question to ask, Chief Anderson," she said in an even, head-on voice, "is whether or not I can depend on you to help me out, should that possibility arise."

Does not play well with others.

Wasn't that what her report card used to say, more often than not?

"You're still up to your old tricks, Gera girl," she said aloud as she escaped the chief's angry glare and hurried out onto the sidewalk. "What was it Grams always said? Don't burn your bridges? At this rate, you'll be swimming back to Indiana."

When Jake called, Gera answered with a direct and breathless, "How did it go?"

"Better than I expected," he admitted. "To be honest, I think they were relieved to have it all out in the open. They said they had felt awful, hiding it from me for all these years."

"See? I told you."

"You did. Thank you." His voice was soft.

"So now what?"

"Now I have to bail on you. I'm sorry, but there's some things I have to take care of here. Some of their tricks are on timers, and unfortunately, through the years they've forgotten some of the finer details."

"Such as?"

"Where all the lasers are hidden, what the passwords are, that sort of thing. They both swear they don't have a recording of babies crying, but I think they've simply forgotten. Now I have to tear this place apart, looking for it."

"Sounds like a mess."

"To say the least. I'm sorry, babe. I really wanted to spend the day with you."

"Tomorrow," she said. "Tomorrow, I want us to do something."

"What?"

"Anything. Do you realize I've never seen you out of your natural habitat? We need to at least leave the hotel."

"I promise. What time will you be in tonight?"

"Uhm, an hour or so after dark. I'll call you."

"Okay. Hey, and be careful. I hear there was a wreck today, right in front of the fire station."

"I'm pretty sure I'll do most of my research on foot," Gera said. "In fact, that new tire looked a little iffy. I may call you to pick me up, if that's okay."

"Absolutely."

"Thanks, Jake."

"No problem. Later, babe."

She hung up, knowing she had left huge gaps in their conversation. No need to tell him that the tire looked iffy because it sat upon the roof of the old Hermann Building, tangled up somehow with the air conditioning system.

"Hey, guess what, folks?" She mimicked the voice of a cheery radio announcer. "Come on down, we now have *rooftop parking*, right here in downtown Jerome."

Gera made a round through town, stopping by a few of the businesses on her list and talking with anyone who would spare her a moment or two. She was surprised at how quickly word of her mishap had spread through town, and how it actually helped to endear her to people. Often leery of speaking with a reporter, most people she came across couldn't wait to talk with her today. They were more than willing to answer her questions, as long as she gave them a firsthand account as to how her car came to rest atop the newspaper office. If she heard it once, she heard it a dozen times: Now *that* was a story!

She showed up for the ghost tour, ten minutes before their scheduled start time. There were more people on Anise's tour tonight, which was fine with Gera. It would make slipping in and out less noticeable.

"I'm so pleased you chose to join us again," Anise said in her serene voice, delighted to have a repeat customer twice in a matter of days.

"Your tour was so informative," Gera said. "I'm afraid I couldn't retain it all, hearing it just once."

"I think you will be especially pleased tonight." The guide raised her arms so that her flowing robes danced around her arms as she gathered her group all in. "Please, come closer. I have wonderful news to share with you. I don't know why," she said, keeping her voice hushed and confidential, as if she shared a shiny secret with them all, "but often Sunday nights prove our best night for tours. Perhaps it is the sheer spirituality of a Sunday itself, or perhaps it is simply because it is the start of a new week. Nevertheless, quite often, we make wonderful contact on Sunday evenings. So come, let's get started. We don't want to miss a moment of opportunity."

The tour followed in much the same pattern as before. They began at twilight, when the fading light of day gave way to the dark of evening, and played its tricks upon the human eye. Gera hung to the rear of the group, her eyes darting all about, watching the town around them as much as she watched the tour.

Her eyes skimmed rooftops along the far end of Hull. She just happened to be watching when it came on. Just a tiny spec of blue, indicating an electric timer. Gera checked the angle of the light and snapped a photo with her phone.

"Did you find an orb?" someone from the group asked her.

"No, just snapping randomly," she smiled.

"I sure wish we could see one of these orb things," the man grumbled. "This is the fifth or sixth ghost tour my wife has dragged me around to, in at least four different cities, in three different states, for crying out loud. For once, I'd just like to see a return on our money. Is a freaking orb too much to ask for?"

"Maybe tonight will be your lucky night," Gera said. She moved subtly away, downwind of his whiskey-tainted breath.

Sure enough, just one street over, they saw the first of the orbs. Unlike most orbs that were best detected on cameras with a flash, these were visible to the naked eye. A stir of excitement moved through the crowd. They picked up the pace, eager to see more.

"See? I told you I had a good feeling about tonight!" Anise beamed, her face aglow with excitement.

Poor thing, Gera thought. *She has no idea she's being set up, right along with the rest of the town. They think it's real.*

Because it was a Sunday, Anise didn't take the group to the church tonight. Instead, they visited the Upper Park and parts of Main Street early in the tour. Anise took them along the street, telling stories about historical businesses that once occupied this building or that.

They stopped in front of the *Cactus Bar* and heard the tale of a murder that had taken place there in 1899. Gera didn't remember hearing the story on the first tour, but she noticed that several of the tales were different. It was good to have a repertoire, she supposed, so that the guides didn't bore their own selves.

Gera pushed close to the plate-glass window, trying to get a better look inside the empty bar. It was actually closed for the evening, in deference, she supposed, to the Sabbath. She still didn't have a clear view of the wall just beneath the extended cable, but perhaps if she leaned down…

"Are you okay?" Whiskey-Breath asked, spooking her. She whirled around, embarrassed to be caught peering so intently into the storefront.

"Y—Yes. I hear that Mac has often been spotted at this particular bar, so I was just hoping…"

She let her words slide away with a shrug. The group moved on down the street, toward the next point of interest. She lingered behind for one more look.

Gera turned back around to face the bar and had a terrible fright. Billy Boy's face pressed directly against the other side of the glass, aligned almost perfectly with hers. Had the glass not been there, his vile mouth would have touched hers. Gera bit back a scream, but she stood her ground. The man rammed his face into the glass, knowing she couldn't deny an involuntarily flinch, no matter how many times he did it. Each time was as shocking and revolting as the first, especially when he would flick his tongue out and make the metal snake dance. She could hear his laughter on the other side of the glass.

She waited until she was turning away, and then she whirled so suddenly, it was Billy Boy flinching this time. Gera flicked out her fingers, like fangs of her own, and made a hiss so loud it carried through the thick glass. A satisfied smirk lingered on her face as she caught up with the tour. She hadn't anticipated seeing the snake man tonight, but in a way, it was an added bonus. If he thought a car full of snakes would stop her, he had another think coming.

Gera paid close attention as they approached the shadowed edge of town, particularly Queen Street. As she explained to Jake, she had studied the list of Mac sightings over the last few years and she had noticed a pattern. It was true, he did 'appear' most often on Sunday evenings, and usually within the same general vicinity. Not every Sunday, of course, and not always in the same location, because it would be too obvious. What Gera found most odd was that witness accounts of Mac's recent crime spree, including the details by Billy Boy Macandie, centered on much the same information and location as these random sightings. Hadn't Miles Anderson ever noticed the similarities?

Tonight, much like before, darkness cloaked the old *Sliding Jail* and the streets beyond. Gera felt it again, the sensation that someone watched her as she followed a few steps behind the group. It was difficult to keep up with them and keep her eye on a prime spot for a Mac sighting. She knew the general area she suspected, but the exact location was iffy. The same laser that created the orbs earlier could, conceivably, cast its beam just a bit further now, and show a nice shadow that could be mistaken for Mac McGruder's ghost.

"Look!" someone suddenly cried from the group, excitement coloring her voice. "Is that him? Is that the killer ghost?" A chorus of gasps rose up from their midst, as a woman pointed in the direction well ahead of Gera. It was roughly the very location she had been eying, for it was documented in two police reports and numerous random sightings.

Before Gera could throw her phone up for a picture, a hand snaked around her throat and jerked her so violently she stumbled. The group had their backs to her, their attention focused in the opposite direction. When the hand moved from her neck, Gera knew a moment of relief, but the abatement was short lived. A thick cord, the size and texture of a slithering snake, slipped over her head and tugged against her vocal chords. Her air was immediately denied.

Gera tried making a noise, but it came out a mere gurgle. She tried fighting, but when she swung her arms, they struck empty space. She settled for tugging on the chord and trying to get a finger wedged between it and her skin, but it was impossible. The binding was too tight.

Gera tried tangling her feet with that of her attacker, but it took effort to move, and to think. Her energy was flagging at an alarming rate. Blackness inched in around her peripheral vision, turning the night darker than it already was.

"H—H—Help!" she warbled again, but it made no more sound than a raindrop falling on the water. She swung her foot again, a last-ditch effort to fight for her life. The tip of her shoe made contact with a small pebble. It flew through the air and pinged one of the other tourists in the calf.

The teenage boy turned around, ready to snap at the person responsible for the painful sting. Then he saw the struggle taking place a few feet away, and the color fled from his face. He opened his mouth to scream, but just like Gera, no sound came out.

She thought that would be the last thing she ever saw, the boy staring at her with bulging eyes, his mouth opening and closing like a fish. But he finally made a noise, a small strangling sound that drew his mother's attention, and she turned to see what was the matter.

The mother had no trouble screaming. The sound arched to the sky and reverberated off the adjacent buildings, held there for a moment in time, suspended between the crumbling bricks and the hallowed-out spaces, before ending on a shrill, shrieked note that repeated itself, over and over again. Where the son couldn't begin to scream, the mother couldn't stop.

The cord dropped from around Gera's neck and she felt herself go limp. She sagged to the ground in an unceremonious heap, but as she fell against the pockmarked pavement, she thought to look back toward her assailant.

It was no surprise to see a long, dark coat and tall stovepipe hat disappear behind the *Cuban Queen*.

21

"Please, stop staring at me." Her voice was still raspy, even after a half night's sleep.

"I can't help it," Jake whispered, smoothing the hair back from her forehead. "I almost lost you yesterday. Twice."

"But you didn't. I'm fine, Jake."

"Do you know the worst part about it all? I might not have ever known it, not until I heard it in passing." He mimicked the sound of a random bystander's voice. "Say, did you hear about that reporter the other day, the one that jumped out of her moving car and cracked her head wide open? Or— Did you know Mac claimed another victim last night? That pretty little reporter staying up at *The Dove.* You know, Jake, the one you've been sleeping with. Didn't you know?" She heard the pain in his voice, bleeding through the heavy slant of sarcasm.

"I'm sorry, Jake. I'm truly, truly, sorry. I didn't want to cause you any more pain or trouble than I already had. I was trying to spare you," she said, stroking his dark head as he lay it against her chest.

"By scaring me half to death when Mike Cooper called, saying he was taking you to the hospital? Do you have any idea how I felt, especially to learn it was the *second* time someone had tried to kill you in one day?"

"I know. I'm sorry."

"God, Gera, don't ever do that to me again." He pulled her close, absorbing the shudder that moved through her body and echoed within his own.

They settled among the pillows and held each other for long, silent moments. Jake finally broke the silence.

"What is going on, Gera?"

"The less I tell you, the better off you'll be."

"Nice try, no sale. What's going on?"

"I told you. Someone tried to frame Mac's ghost for the recent crime spree, knowing he would also be blamed for Abe's death."

"So this was premeditated."

"Yes."

"What were you doing last night, going on that ghost tour again?"

"Looking for evidence."

"Why? Is that some sort of scam?"

"Not the way you're thinking. The tour guides are victims, too, in a way. They don't realize the visions they see are being projected around town, set on timers, and controlled by the killer. They think they're truly seeing ghosts."

"But they've been doing those ghost tours for years."

"I'm not saying that all the visions are fake, even though we both know my opinion on that. I'm saying I found a pattern, dating back about two years, that revolves around the image of Mac McGruder. What Anise and the other tour guides thought was their special 'spiritual connection' was an image on a timer."

"Who is it, Gera? And why haven't you gone to Anderson with this?"

She fingered the cloth of his t-shirt, dancing around a direct answer. "How well do you know Miles Anderson?"

"Well enough, I guess. I've always known *of* him, but he's several years older than I am. We never traveled in the same circles. I've gotten to know him better since I've moved back. We serve on several committees and boards together." He shrugged. "Seems to be an all right guy. Why?"

"I know this will sound crazy, but… I'm not so sure that Miles Anderson isn't the killer."

"What? You've got to be kidding!"

"I wish I were. There are just so many coincidences. I admit, most of what I have is circumstantial evidence, but it just seems to keep coming."

"You do realize the man is the chief of police, right? A highly respected member of the community."

"Yes, I do realize this. But it all comes down to motive, opportunity, and means. I hate to say it, but so far he appears to have all three."

"What would his motive be?"

She gingerly shifted positions, mindful of her battered body. The stiffness had set in now, seeping into her muscles and settling like cement. The entire right side of her body, the side that absorbed the brunt of her unceremonious slam onto the pavement, was bruised and beginning now to turn a kaleidoscope of colors. Her scrapes were still raw and oozing, and required bandages that itched. Careful to avoid as many of the sore spots as possible, Gera eventually settled into place.

"Sorry," she apologized.

"Do what you need to do to get comfortable. Can I get you anything?"

"I'm good." She propped her arm on a pillow and continued with her theory. "I think it's about the Cunningham house."

"I suppose it's in a prime location and has some historical value, but it's hardly a mansion. I can't see it being all that valuable," Jake reasoned.

"Did you know Miles Anderson was involved in a lawsuit two years ago? They settled out of court so that it wouldn't affect his career, but he's making some hefty restitution payments. Since his wife is in line to inherit the house, it means he might have some claim to it, too, once Ruth passes away. An inheritance might come in handy when paying off a lawsuit."

"But Ruth is still alive, so the house is still hers."

"But she's getting older, and it was a pretty big settlement."

"What about opportunity? Means?"

"I'm working on that, one piece at a time. The chief is one of five people to have keys to the property, so he had the means to lure Abe inside. And of course, he has access to a knife. I'm also working on the set-up. Two of the witnesses who named Mac's ghost as the perpetrator have recently had minor charges against them either dropped or reduced. A third witness—to two of the crimes, no less—was almost his stepson. Turns out, Billy Boy's mother was Anderson's first wife."

Jake blew out a low whistle. "You're right; it's all circumstantial, but it does look suspicious."

"Add in the fact that the chief was conspicuously absent after I was attacked last night. I know the man has to have a little time off, but even Cooper didn't know where he was."

When Jake's phone rang, he carefully extricated himself from the bed and padded across the room in his boxer shorts. *SuperClark, indeed.* She reined in her lustful musings when she realized he answered with short, terse responses.

His expression was grim when he came back into the room.

"What's wrong?" she asked.

"They just found Ruth Cunningham's body in her yard."

"Oh no! What happened?"

Jake touched her hair as he replied quietly, "Apparently, she died of multiple snake bites."

Gera's nostrils flared as memories of the previous day flooded into her mind. She thought she could smell it again, that unmistakable musty reek of a serpent. When she closed her eyes, she saw a replay of that moment when the snake fell from her visor. Her eyes popped back open.

"It's okay, sweetie." Jake said, stroking her hair.

Gera's gray eyes clouded. "Aside from the fact that the house will soon belong to Beverly Ruth—and, hence, her husband—I think the snake connection is a bit too coincidental." The image of Billy Boy and his disgusting tongue ring slithered into her mind, mingling with the leftover images of snakes from her car. "I hate to say it, but it's just that much more evidence against Miles Anderson."

"Here you go, madam. Your suitcase." Jake deposited the piece at the foot of the bed with a flourishing hand movement.

"Is that your fancy bellhop move that wows all the ladies?" Gera teased.

His eyes twinkled with mischief. "It's one of them."

"Thanks for bringing the rest of my stuff."

"I'll issue you a refund, by the way. No need paying for a room you aren't using." He dropped a kiss on the top of her head and asked, "Why are you getting dressed? You need to stay in bed."

"No way. This doesn't change anything. I still want to spend the day with you. Outside this hotel."

"You should rest. You had a rough day yesterday. Your body needs time to recuperate."

Gera pulled a brush through her hair. "I didn't say I wanted to hike Sycamore Canyon, but I do want to get out and do something. But the canyon may be something we can do later. Maybe on my next visit." She checked her appearance in the mirror. A red bruise circled her throat, a vivid reminder of last night's horror.

Jake came up from behind, studying her reflection in the mirror. "Will there be a next time?" he asked quietly.

Her heart thudded in her chest. "*I* want there to be a next time. Don't you?"

"Not only a next time, but a time after that, and a time after that."

It was just the right thing to say. Sweet. And so typically Jake.

Gera gave him a saucy look, but her eyes were unusually moist. "Good answer."

They headed toward Sedona and spent much of the day driving through the countryside, seeking views of the iconic rock formations. Gera was too sore for hiking, but they ordered sandwiches and ate at a picnic area in the Slide Rock State

Park. They splashed for a while in the creek, holding hands and laughing like youngsters, and Gera discovered that the water—and Jake's easy company—was therapeutic for her stiff muscles. They sat upon the rocks to dry, where the hot sun and wind made short work of the job. In Camp Verde, they found a barbecue shack and stopped for dinner, and listened to a live performance by a local band. What the group lacked in talent, they made up for in enthusiasm.

And that night, when an electrical storm moved across the plains and lightning danced in the clouds and lit the dark sky with fantastic streaks of color, they lay in Jake's bed high upon Mingus Mountain and made slow, sweet love.

Neither could imagine the brewing storm that was yet to come.

22

The pieces to her puzzle were slowly coming together, connecting one into another to form a better overall picture. Some pieces were still missing, some irregular-shaped edges that just didn't quite fit, but Jake was right. It was time to talk to Detective Chao.

Gera insisted on going alone, even though Jake wanted to be there with her for moral support. She knew he had a business to run, and even though he tried to hide it from her, she knew Jake was still worried about Leo and Lucy, and the untenable position they had inadvertently thrust him into. Though Gera found Grant Young to be a likable enough man, she had no doubt he could be a formidable opponent in business. What if he somehow discovered the old couple's well-intended shenanigans and used it against Jake? She could imagine a scenario in which Grant pressed charges against Jake for a host of unethical business practices, all in hopes of ruining him and swooping in to claim the spoils of war.

No, it was best that Jake stay at the hotel and protect his empire, particularly if it meant erasing any last vestiges of the old couple's deeds. It was bad enough that she had to borrow his pickup; when they pulled her car from the top of the Hermann Building, something underneath was damaged. With no rental facilities on the mountain, her only choice was to take advantage of Jake's generosity.

Such a good guy, this Jake Cody.

With time to spare before her appointment with the detective, Gera couldn't resist another visit to the scene of Abe's murder. She had been here a half dozen times, but something about the old building spoke to her, pulling her back time after time. If only there was a way to get inside! Gera believed the key to Abe's murder lay inside the railed arches of the skeletal structure.

Caught up in her musings, Gera didn't realize she had attracted company.

"It really is a beautiful old building, isn't it?" Grant spoke just behind her, frightening her enough that she gasped. When she jumped, her nose skidded against the cold metal rails.

"I'm sorry, Gera. I didn't mean to frighten you." His voice was rich with concern.

"I suppose I'm a bit skittish."

"And with good reason. I heard about what happened. Please, tell me that you're all right?" He touched her arm, the one not sporting a bandage. Dark bruises splotched her arms, but the worst bruise was the one around her neck, not so much in appearance, but in implication. The source of that bruise had very nearly been the death of her.

"Yes, I'm fine. Thank you for asking."

"*Now* do you understand?" Grant's fingers pressed into her arm with urgency. "Mac, for whatever his reasons, has become dangerous. I beg you, Gera, please back away from this. Your life is in danger."

"I appreciate your concern, Grant. I truly do. But I came here to write an article, and I can't leave until I have the answers I'm looking for."

"I've given you the answers, Gera. Mac is to blame. He attacked you, tried to strangle you. You have the proof on your neck!"

"No, I don't know that it was Mac." She spoke evenly, resisting the urge to point out that the man he spoke of had died some eighty years ago.

"There were a dozen witnesses!"

"What we saw was someone in a long coat and tall hat. It could've been anyone."

He was more agitated than she had ever seen him. Grant Young was normally suave and composed, but her stubborn response left the banker disquieted. "Why must you do this? Why must you persist, when it puts your own life in danger?" he cried. He scrubbed his hand over his bald head and made a final plea. "Let it be, Gera."

"I can't," she answered simply.

She turned back to face the gutted building. Its stark beauty called to her. *Maybe it's whispers from the ashes,* she mused. *Miners' ashes, stirred into steel.*

Seemingly resigned now to her tenacious dedication to her craft, Grant moved alongside her and joined in the quiet contemplation of the building.

"She must've been a beauty, back in the day," he mused.

"Look at the brick arches, over the doorways." Gera pointed out the details. "That was an interior wall, I suppose, with the grand entrance on the other side."

"Yes, I think so."

"I would love to go inside," she murmured in a wistful tone. "See what is behind those inner doorways. The rooms aren't deep. Were they storage, do you think? Offices?"

Grant looked around, making certain no one was near enough to hear his offer. "I could take you inside," he said, voice low.

She turned to him in surprise. "You could?"

With a trench coat and hat, he could've passed for a spy, offering to exchange highly confidential information. He kept his eyes straight ahead, speaking out of the side of his mouth. "It's against the rules. Insurance, you know. No unauthorized personnel allowed. But I have a key."

Gera wondered what the secrecy was about. He was president of the Chamber. Surely he could grant her temporary authorization, without all this cloak-and-dagger effect. She saw a few heavy-duty extension cords scattered about, proof the building wasn't entirely off limits. But she would play along. She kept her eyes straight ahead and whispered back, "I would love to go inside."

"Meet me here this evening, before dark. Most people will be on their way home from work or school, and won't pay us a lot of attention. The shops will be closing then, too, so there will be fewer tourists."

"Shall I wear a disguise?" she asked in an exaggerated whisper.

Grant looked at her sharply, and laughter burst from her lips. "I'm sorry," she said. "You just sounded so serious, like we were plotting to rob that vault over there."

His grin was a bit sheepish. "I guess I'm not accustomed to breaking and entering, simply to impress a beautiful woman."

He leaned in and added, less modestly, "I normally don't have to work so hard at it."

Maybe meeting him tonight wasn't such a good idea, after all. But she really wanted inside these gates…

"It's not breaking and entering if you have a key," Gera pointed out, overlooking his personal innuendos.

"But it is breaking the rules, so perhaps we should keep our little date to ourselves, eh?"

Gera bit her lip. "Date?"

"Poor choice of words," he assured her. "Appointment."

She nodded and glanced down at her watch. "Oops, I've gotta go. Can't keep the detective waiting."

He seemed surprised. "You're meeting with Detective Chao a second time?" In response to her unspoken question, he offered, "The other day in the café, remember? Mike Cooper mentioned your appointment with Chao."

"Oh yes, that's right," she remembered.

He hinted for her to elaborate. "Didn't get in all your questions the first time, I suppose?"

"Something like that."

The moment turned awkward. Gera clearly didn't intend to discuss the matter with him.

"So, we'll meet back here this evening?" he finally asked.

"Definitely."

As Gera departed from the railings, she realized what today was. One week ago tonight, Grant had discovered Abe's body. Oddly enough, they were meeting here, at the scene, around the same time of day he made the discovery. Would it bother the banker, she wondered, being there again so soon? Would it bring back unwanted memories of the traumatic event? There had to have been blood there that night, and he had already mentioned the unnatural pose of his body. Perhaps she should offer to reschedule their tour.

Gera turned around to call to him, but Grant was already halfway down the sidewalk. He really was a striking man, she acknowledged, tall and athletic, and in excellent physical condition. He had a nice walk, too.

Not that it did anything for her, not sexually, but she did appreciate the graceful carriage in his stride, much as she might appreciate the grace of a tiger.

Tigers, however, were dangerous.

And Grant? Well, Grant believed in a ghost named Mac, and in convoluted theories about a whole town sliding off a mountain.

No offense to her friend, but Grant wasn't dangerous; he was simply nuts.

The problem with arranging a meeting with an overworked police detective, Gera discovered, was that he could be called away on emergency at any moment. Turns out, a murder-suicide trumped scheduled appointments, every time.

Gera had no more taken a seat at the man's desk when the call came in. A domestic dispute turned deadly in one of the city's better neighborhoods. Obsession knew no economic boundaries, it would appear.

With time to kill before her dusk meeting with Grant, and with the internet and cell service still iffy up on the mountain, Gera went to the library. She could do some research the old-fashioned way, thumbing through volumes of out-of-print books and out-of-date history. Sometimes, the very best sources hid in plain sight, right on the shelf of the local library.

On a whim, she decided to look up the legend of the hidden gold in Sycamore Canyon. All of Minnie's tales about gold were entertaining, if not interesting, but she still questioned their validity. However, after only an hour of digging through old records and musty tomes, she found information on all three.

Spanish expeditions into the canyon were well documented, with names, dates, and details of each foray into the wilderness. And disturbingly enough, the story about the government confiscating all the gold was absolutely correct. With the swipe of a pen, the president had robbed citizens of their privately owned stash of gold. It was no wonder the newer legend of hidden gold had sprung to life. There were hints in several publications about a new hoard of precious metal concealed from the prying eyes of government, but Gera found only a single book that explored the conspiracy in detail.

According to the author, people all over the country found creative ways to sidestep the law. A man in California stuffed his golden nuggets—most of them mined right there on the property and passed down from his grandfather—inside the mount of a grizzly bear, also harvested from the property. A footnote documented how that very bear had taken the old miner's life and how his vindictive grandson tolled out justice.

A bachelor in Virginia had buried his stash in a shallow grave and marked it with an engraved tombstone, claiming it was the remains of his dear wife. A woman in Kentucky reportedly had caps of pure gold on all her teeth. A jeweler in Utah cast excess gold into seemingly everyday objects. It was rumored even his dog had a collar inlaid with the precious metals. The story continued in the final paragraph of the page. It was noted that in Jerome, Arizona, a—

Gera quickly moved to the top of the next page, but the passage made no sense. She went back and reread, but still it skipped to a new topic. That was when she noticed the fine ragged edge of a missing page, ripped from the spine of the book. A glance at page numbers confirmed it. The book went from page 132 to page 135.

She snapped a photo of the opened book, documenting the missing page and the name of the book. *The Great Gold Conspiracy of Executive Order 6102.*

The name jogged a memory. She dug into her notebook, until she found the small slip of paper that had fallen free of Miles Anderson's files. It had only one scribbled, ambiguous notation upon it—TGGCOEO6102, p. 133.

Until now, she had no idea what it meant.

Gera pushed from the table and hurried up to the librarian's desk. Sometimes libraries kept logs of visitors to the library, particularly to reference sections such as this, and of those patrons who asked for copy services. Gera bet that Anderson, like his deputy, still did things old school. It would never occur to either man to snap a digital photo with their cell phone, not when they could fire up the old copy machine and kill another tree.

Sure enough, Miles Anderson visited the library on several occasions, and had, in fact, requested copies made. The last visits were recorded almost a year ago. Long before Abe's death and the investigation into its motive. Long before the rash of petty crimes that seemed to point to only one suspect.

But far enough in advance to plot such a scheme.

23

S he wouldn't be long, she promised, in response to Jake's offer to grill steaks for the evening. Just long enough to get an inside look at the old hotel-turned-bank-turned-more. Not long enough to draw attention.

She smirked as she trudged up the sidewalk to the skeletal building. Grant acted as if it was such a big deal, allowing her a clandestine peek into the property. It was on the corner lot of Main Street, smack dab in the middle of town. There were no outer walls. People would see them, no matter.

So Gera was surprised when she reached the railed structure and found no tourists taking pictures of the abandoned bank vault, no townspeople milling about the sidewalk. Cars moved along the street out front, but none turned on First Avenue. Most of the businesses along the street were closing now, but one was just getting primed. An unusual string of vehicles fringed the perimeters of the *Cactus Bar*.

Ah, Tuesday night poker, she remembered.

She was also surprised to reach the locked gate and discover it not locked.

Seeing as she had arrived before Grant, Gera peered through the rails in anticipation. What lay behind the wooden doors? She would soon know. She put a hand on an iron bar and leaned forward, startled when it actually gave way. She jerked as the gate crept slowly inward. The movement felt awkward, as if the gates designed to swing outward had a mind of their own. Her clumsy jerk caused the padlock to clatter to the ground.

Scooping down to pick up the lock, she called out to her host. "Grant? Are you already here?" She kept her voice low, mindful of their cloak-and-dagger game.

She attempted to replace the lock without looking at her hand movements, her eyes already sweeping through the gathering shadows of the interior. Apparently, Grant had gone in without her. When the lock fell to the ground a second time, she impatiently stuffed it inside her pocket and slipped through the gate.

Gera felt a thrill of excitement as she approached the weathered doors. She was stepping into a piece of history. More than that, she was stepping into a crime scene. Anticipation skittered along her nerves, sharpening her senses.

As if she trespassed onto hallowed ground, the hinges protested with a long, painful screech.

"Grant?" she called again. "You in here?"

When she heard no answer, she ventured forward. It was the area she originally pegged as a stage, the first along the narrow corridor of tiny rooms. The strip, defined by brick walls on either side, was the only part of the old structure that still had a roof of any sort, and was a place where shadows gathered deep, like secrets from the past.

Gera still wasn't certain what this first room was other than an entry, but it no longer offered forward progress. A rickety wall and an opening with bars made certain of that. More bars stood between her and the crumbling staircase to her right. Her only choice was to go left, to the steps where Abe was murdered.

However, that wasn't entirely accurate, she realized. Now that she was inside, she saw the dark stain of blood. Abe was stabbed here inside the unidentified room, then fell—or was pushed—down the steps.

She snapped a few pictures to document the area.

It was that time of day, she realized, when the light was quickly fading, casting murky shadows and that air of mystique, even in the open areas. Gera discovered that—when inside a forbidden old building, no matter how airy it might be, and when that building was the scene of a recent crime, and when she stood in that odd, shuddered light looking at the dried remains of a man's blood—twilight could take on an eerie and ominous glow.

For some reason, it occurred to Gera at that moment that she was undetectable from Main Street. Even someone at the park across Main couldn't see her here, at sub-level. A person would have to be traveling along First Avenue, or peering down from the sidewalk on this side of Main, to notice activity below.

That, she realized now, explained part of how Abe's murder was undetected.

And she was certain that time of day played a part in the secrecy. Now, like one week ago, time suspended into a lull as people wound up their workday, more focused on getting home than paying attention to the goings on around them. Unless it stood between them and the dinner table, most people were unconcerned with the happenings in town. The day was over, the evening not yet started. This was no time to have their attentions tangled elsewhere.

And light, Gera thought, as she moved down the steps. Lighting would have been a crucial element in order for a murder to take place, unwitnessed, in the middle of town. The streetlights, few and dim though they were, had yet to kick on. Things looked distorted in the low light. Lines shifted, shadows moved.

She thought a shadow moved now, catching the movement out of the corner of her eye. "Grant?" she called again, her voice stronger this time.

An uneasy feeling tickled her scalp. Danced along the fine hairs of her arms.

She moved further into the open area, where the light was better. She was quickly losing interest in keeping their tour a secret.

She saw the shadows move again, inside the entryway she had just come from. Gera saw the silhouette of a man, but it wasn't the banker who had invited her. Not unless he had taken to wearing a long-tailed coat and stovepipe hat.

Gera immediately saw the folly of stepping into the lower level. The man posing as Mac stood between her and the only exit.

She was effectively trapped.

And staying here, in the open, wasn't an option.

Moving forward would leave her far below street level. She could never jump high enough to catch anyone's attention.

And not enough traffic traveled the one-way path of First to see her flagging for help.

The only place that wasn't out in the wide open was behind the inner brick wall, and in those tiny rooms filled with shadows. Earlier today, she had wondered if those might be closets, offices, or even bathrooms. She was about to find out.

Gera dashed into the first of the narrow doorways. Mac's lookalike was just on the other side of the rickety wall. The barred opening protected her, kept him from coming forward. She wasn't sure the same could be said for the thin, rotting wall. It looked as if a strong gust of wind could push it over.

"Gera?" he called softly, his tone taunting. "Come out, come out, wherever you are."

The man clung to the shadows of the first room, most likely to remain unseen, should a passerby wander near. Gera scanned the sidewalks in hope, but to no avail.

She pressed against the wall farthest from her stalker. That voice was familiar, but she couldn't make it sound like Miles Anderson. Not salty enough.

Squeezing around a small sapling that sprouted inside the cubicle, Gera slipped into the adjoining space, the next of the unexplained rooms along the corridor. This one was a bit larger, but more cluttered and more overgrown. Not as badly as the last room, though.

With another wall in front of her, Gera was running out of options, and fast.

"Why did you do it, Gera? Why did you insist on following this story? I told you to leave it well enough alone."

Gera searched for a way out. Well above her head was a pathetic excuse for a sub-ceiling, and above that, some sort of flat roof. She could see patches of sky between the broken and warped wood of the roof, with the biggest gap in the far corner. She doubted any of the weathered sticks would support her weight, even if she found a way to reach them.

The bottom portion of the wall still sported plaster, perhaps even brick. She quietly kicked at it. Yep, brick. The upper half was more of the slatted wood, with so many gaps she could easily make out the old staircase on the other side. Perhaps she could break through the flimsy wood and get to the other side.

And what? she asked herself. The gates on that archway remained locked, as well. She quickly decided the slim patches of sky were her best option.

Gera swallowed hard. She should think of this as an adventure, a head-on thrill. A wall to scale, much like at an amusement park.

She found the first foothold along the plaster. She lost her footing as she looked over her shoulder, checking her stalker's progress. Darkness gathered close, the sky now filled with more night than twilight. He would no longer be so worried about being seen.

She had to move fast, before he did.

She found another foothold, and then another. Gera boosted herself higher, using a combination of support from the saplings, the slats on the wall, and sheer determination. Luckily for her, the horizontal slats above the plaster were spaced wide apart, offering enough room for her feet to wedge sideways. More bow legged than any Old West cowboy, Gera scrambled up the wall.

"I liked you, Gera. I didn't want it to come to this, but you're leaving me no choice."

Her foot found a rotted board.

The ancient timber cracked and gave way.

She almost fell.

She searched for another board and pushed off, inching ever higher. She needed to reach the top, before he reached this room.

Gera could hear murmuring below. Anderson was talking to himself, she supposed, but she dared not look down. She was literally climbing a wall, some ten feet off the ground by now, and losing what little daylight there was.

After a series of bumps and a rustling of feet, her stalker spoke.

"We've worked too hard to let you ruin it for us now."

Us? Miles Anderson has a partner? She had never considered that angle.

She could use a partner right about now. Without warning, the slats became closer, too narrowly spaced to fit her fingers between, much less her feet.

What now?

She could fall at any given moment. Her muscles had seen enough abuse Sunday, without adding the strain of clinging precariously to a wall. She couldn't last much longer.

Gera peered through the shadows, spotting a pipe that dropped down out of the ceiling. Her eyes strained to follow its path as it disappeared into the brick wall.

If the brick was strong enough to hold the pipe, she was in luck.

"The townspeople were convinced, Gera." Anger moved into his voice. "All it took was a few Mac sightings, a few manipulated witnesses, and everyone was convinced that Mac had turned on them."

Did she dare try the pipe?

"It was the perfect crime, Gera. We set it up with so much care. Had it all planned out. And then *you* came to town!" He spat the last out with such hatred, such malice, that Gera knew she had to do it.

She leaned outward, stretching her body until her fingers brushed against metal. Closing her hand around the pipe, she gave a hearty yank. When it didn't fall from the ceiling, she took a leap of faith. Literally.

Gera jumped, throwing herself off the wall and toward the pipe. For one awful moment, as both hands grasped the pipe and she suspended there in space, she felt the line sag. She thought the old cast iron would give at any moment, and she would go crashing onto the floor.

She held her breath, as if emptying her lungs of air could make the difference in her weight, which dangled there in its entirety from the old plumbing. She shouldn't have eaten those pancakes this morning. Or that barbecue sandwich last night. Too many carbs. Carbs added weight.

She was forced to take in a sip of air, bracing herself for the worst.

Nothing happened. The air made her no heavier! She greedily swallowed down another gulp, then another. As her lungs filled with oxygen, her mind filled with hope. This might work yet.

Now that she had a close-up and personal view, she realized it wasn't a roof overhead, but what little remained from the flooring of the first story. The boards there were wide and looked sturdy, so, theoretically, if she could make it up there, she could hide.

Gera began making her way across the ceiling, hand over hand, inching along the pipe. She tried to grab for wood when she could, but twice the boards came off in her hand. One fell noisily to the ground.

"Where are you, Gera?" he called in singsong. "We're coming after you."

Gera picked up the pace. Just a few more feet, and she would be at the opening. *Just like monkey bars, Gera girl,* she told herself. *Only these have splinters.*

Another broken board and Gera fell, catching her full body weight with her bandaged arm. She gasped aloud from the pain, biting back a cry as her legs grappled with dead air, trying to find a current that would push her back up. Using more strength than she knew she possessed, she pulled her body up and managed to grab the pipe again. She was almost there.

It was fully dark now. She could no longer see the ground beneath her, but she knew she was at a disadvantage. What little light coming into the space came by way of the broken bits of floor just above her head. The moment Anderson or his partner stepped into the room, they would see her, dangling there in the spotlight.

By now, Gera was certain her shoulders pulled from their sockets, yanked out by the roots, but she had finally reached the corner. She had to figure out a way to get through the slats, over the floor joists, and up on top of the boards. Piece of cake.

Gera never considered herself particularly athletic, but she was impressed with her prowess this night. In a matter of minutes, she had scaled a wall, crossed a ceiling while hanging from a pipe, and was now wiggling her way through an itty-bitty gap in the ceiling. It was amazing what one could do when stalked by a madman.

Make that by two. She could hear them both now, closing in on her.

"Damn it, Billy Boy, where did she go!"

Billy Boy? *That* was his partner?

Gera knew it would be noisy, but there was no other choice. She had to pull away a rotted board. She might even need to push away a bit of crumbling brick, here at the very top of the wall. She had come too far to let a little thing like her hips keep her from freedom.

Gera squeezed her shoulders through the small gap. The fresh night air hit her full in the face, the sweetest thing she had ever tasted. She wiggled some more and felt her shirt catch on a nail and tear, and suspected that her skin may have torn, as well. She felt blood trickle down her back. She pulled at another board. Okay, so maybe her hips weren't so little. But, damn it, she had to get out of here!

Pushing and clawing and kicking when necessary, finally Gera pulled herself free. A brick broke off and skittered to the ground, falling into the open plaza of the lower level. It took a bounce toward the bank vault.

"I think she's out here!" Billy Boy said. Gera heard the scuffle of feet as they hurried forward.

Exhausted, Gera lay down upon one of the boards, careful to avoid the cracks. Sooner or later, they could come back in. Sooner or later, they would think to look up. She had to be extremely quiet and extremely careful.

Every muscle in her body ached. It was all she could do not to whimper. She lay there long enough to catch her breath. Long enough to hear the men shuffle back inside the space below. Their voices were angry.

"Where the hell did she go?" Billy Boy stormed.

"How should I know?"

"You were the one to screw this up. You should've stopped her to begin with!"

"Don't get smart with me, young man."

"Just because you're my old man, doesn't mean you can tell me what to do."

Gera stopped her silent moaning and turned her head so she could hear better. This bit of news surprised her. Billy Boy was Miles Anderson's son? She thought he was impotent.

"I own you, boy," his father said harshly. "I can tell you what to do because I'm the only thing standing between you and a jail cell. I've paid off so many of your debts and pulled you out of so many scrapes, you'll never be able to repay me."

"I killed the old man for you. That ought to be enough."

"Well it's not. It won't ever be enough, until I get what I want. And I want all three pieces of property." His vicious tone left no doubt. He would do whatever it took to get what he wanted. "Don't just stand here, you nitwit. Look for her! Find her!"

"She's not here!" Billy Boy insisted.

"You're as worthless as your mother," he snarled. Gera heard a resounding smack; no doubt, Billy Boy now sported a red mark on his cheek. "Keep looking. I'll go out to the street, make sure she didn't somehow make it out."

"There's no way out," the younger man insisted, but she heard banging and shuffling below. He must be moving everything that wasn't nailed down, trying to find her.

Gera tried to think. What did she do now? What three pieces of property did Miles Anderson want? And why did his voice still sound so odd, not at all like him? Had his gruff, Old West demeanor all been a ruse? His voice sounded smoother tonight. At least, when it wasn't spiked with hatred.

She should text Jake, she thought. And Grant. He might be able to save her. Where was the banker, anyway? He was supposed to meet her here a good fifteen minutes ago.

What if Miles had hurt him? Gera chewed on her lip as the new worry occurred to her.

"Dude, get in here," she heard Billy Boy hiss.

His father came quickly. "Did you find her?"

"No, but something just dropped on my head."

Gera couldn't see, but she imagined Billy Boy pointing upward. Her shirt was soaked through now, from the ragged scrape on her back. Had a single drop of blood made its way down to drop on his head? Did it take a path down his tattooed arm, following the twist and turn of the inked-on snakes he favored? Or perhaps it was a drop of sweat. She was wringing wet from exertion.

Gera thought she felt the burn of their eyes, searing her back through the wooden floor.

"It's no use, Gera," the lawman called out, in his not-like-himself voice. "We know you're up there. It's the only place you could be."

Billy Boy laughed. "That's okay, she'll be down soon. The place is crawling with snakes up there."

In spite of herself, Gera jerked. Forgetting to be quiet, she whimpered as she looked around in panic, searching for slithering, slimy guests.

His ruse worked. "She's up there all right," Billy Boy laughed.

"Might as well save us the effort and come on down," his father called. "It's getting cold out here. I feel the chill. It must be really cold up there."

Gera frowned. What was he doing, trying to use the power of suggestion on her? The night was downright balmy. Perfect for sitting on the patio with Jake and eating steaks. If she had chills working her skin like an active ant pile, it wasn't because of the cold.

His voice grew exasperated. "Will you really make Billy Boy come up there after you?"

"Me?" the other man sulked. "Why me? You climb up there and get her."

"Do as I say, boy."

"How?"

"Do I have to do all the thinking for the both of us? Can't you ever have an original thought in your head?"

"It was my idea to put the snakes in her car," his son boasted. "And to put the snake in the old woman's yard. I'm the one who rigged all the lasers, so people would be sure and see Mac around town."

"After I told you to do it."

"But that's the point. You bark out orders, and I do all the dirty work. I'm the one who has to go around in this freaking coat and hat all the time. You try wearing this garb."

"I did," his father reminded him harshly. "When your brilliant snake idea went bust, I had to clean up your mess, as always."

"Yeah, well, your idea went bust, too. So much for choking her. I guess you just don't have the stomach for the hard stuff." Billy Boy's voice was derisive, and filled with loathing.

"I've killed too, you know." It was obvious it rankled him, having his own son doubt him. Having to prove himself, after all he had done for the boy.

"Big deal. You pushed an old woman down a couple of flights of stairs, like ten years ago. Smothered her neighbor, also old, in his sleep. You've gone soft, old man," Billy Boy taunted him.

Gera gasped. The police chief had killed Minerva Cody! He had pushed her, just as Jake suspected someone had done.

"This could've all been over, eight years ago, if Leo hadn't turned their books around," the madman ranted. "I went to all the trouble of befriending the old broad, convincing her to take out a loan and update her hotel. Then I got her out of the way, so I could repossess *The Dove* and search for the hidden gold. But those two turned the hotel around, made it profitable again. Paid the whole thing off, before I could call in the loan."

Wait a minute, Gera thought. *Why had the police chief held the mortgage on the hotel?*

Then it hit her. That wasn't Miles Anderson down there.

It was Grant.

Her mind balked at the thought. *Grant?* Grant, the man she had befriended? The man she had defended to both Loretta and Jake? *Look who's nuts now!* her mind jeered.

Well, obviously, it was still him. Crazy was more like it.

But Grant? her mind continued to scream. Billy Boy Macandie was Grant's son? How had *that* happened?

She knew *how* it happened, of course. Thinking about it, she recalled Chief Anderson's comment, about suspecting Grant still carried on with Tiffany, even after their marriage. Just because she eventually married Macandie didn't mean he was the biological father of her son.

But still, *Grant?* Her mind had trouble wrapping around it. Grant was so suave and smooth. And Billy Boy was so... not.

"None of this would've mattered," Grant continued to rage, "if I had gotten that hotel!"

She heard another angry slap.

"Ow! What did you do that for?"

"Because you're still standing here! Get to climbing, and bring that girl down. She knows too much."

"Fine," Billy Boy huffed. "But we'll have to flip for which of us gets to kill this one."

While Billy Boy attempted to find a way up, Grant started up a conversation with Gera, as if they met over pancakes again.

"I tried to give you another story," he said. He chided her with a tsk-tsk. "What kind of reporter are you, Gera? Who wouldn't jump on a story like the one I gave you, of a town poised to slide off a mountain?"

She finally spoke. Might as well. They knew where she was. "It was too fanatical. Just like you."

"Ah, but it would've worked, if you hadn't butted in," he said softly, his voice filled with regret. "I had the townspeople eating out of my hand. I encouraged them to believe it was Mac, and they did. All I had to do was get a few witnesses to confirm they had seen the ghost, doing a handful of dirty deeds. It's amazing what people are willing to do when you hold the lien on their homes, or on their businesses." He laughed, but the sound held more lunacy than humor. "They're willing to perjure themselves, to change county records, to lie in a deposition, or in a courtroom, if need be. Of course, how would there be a court trial, when the guilty party doesn't even exist?"

"So you never believed in the ghost to begin with?"

"How could I, Gera? Ghosts don't exist."

The entire time Grant was speaking, his son tried to scale the wall. But he wasn't as light, nor as graceful, as Gera. His attempts were futile. After a dozen tries, twice as many angry curses, and a handful of splintering slats, he turned around to yell at his father, "This isn't working!"

"Because you're a clumsy moron. And keep your voice down, you fool." There was a long pause. Gera couldn't see what was happening below, but she could hear them. "Here," Grant eventually said, "we'll pull you up."

"That's an extension cord," Billy Boy protested. "What are you going to do? Light up the place so everyone can see?"

"No, you idiot, I'm going to throw it around that ceiling joist and use it like a pulley to hoist you up."

"It's not long enough."

"Then get that other one and tie them together. Pull them tight, so they can't come apart."

Gera heard them working on the plan. After a few minutes, she heard a familiar slap against wood, as Grant attempted to hit his mark.

They knew she was here. She had nothing to lose. She pulled out her phone and sent a text to Jake.

SOS. We were wrong. It's Grant. Top of old hotel. Hurry.

Below, Grant still hadn't made the throw.

"I thought you were some hotshot basketball star," Billy Boy sneered.

"It's not as easy as you think, you moron. That's a long way up there, and these cords aren't cooperating."

If the situation hadn't been so serious, it might have been comical. They sounded like a couple of actors from a slapstick western, but Gera knew that wasn't the case. These men were deadly. If they ever found a way to execute Grant's plan and Billy Boy made it up here, she was dead.

She should distract him, she realized. Throw off Grant's concentration.

"Why did you do it, Grant?" she called down to the banker. She might as well move around now, look for a way off this strip of leftover floor.

Gera carefully stood, balancing herself on the warped plank of lumber. Her shirt was sticky with blood, and clung to her back. She eyed the roof of the adjacent building, but it was too high to scale. The brick wall beside her stretched just as high, all the way to the top of the one-time roof. No one on the street could ever see her.

"Why?" Grant answered. "Because there is hidden gold here in Jerome, Gera."

"Legend, Grant. Nothing but legend."

Perhaps she could pick her way forward toward First Avenue, and somehow jump to freedom. It was worth the risk.

She stepped onto the next piece of wood and felt it give beneath her foot. She moved over, stepping gingerly onto another plank. This one felt solid.

"That's where you're wrong," Grant said. "I have it on good authority that not all the gold was turned in, back when Roosevelt confiscated our country's gold. Did you know about that, Gera? Did you know FDR took gold from the people of the United States?"

"Yes, Grant. I know that."

Careful. Another rotted board.

"But some of the people outsmarted him. Some people hid their gold. People like Richard Luna, and Eli Cunningham, and Cecil Thurman. All three were executives at the mines, and all three lived way up high on Cleopatra Hill, all in a row."

Gera carefully maneuvered her way forward. This plank wasn't rotten, it was flat-out missing. She held her arms out from her sides, balancing on a ceiling joist beam.

In the dark, it was slow progress. One misstep and she would go tumbling below.

"I've been working on this for a very long time," Grant informed her coldly. "Why do you think I agreed to come back here, to this God-forsaken town? Do you know there is a clause in my trust fund? I have to live here on this mountain to retain ownership of the bank." His voice shook with fury.

Good, she thought with satisfaction. *He'll be too shook up to make a good throw.*

"I could've been somebody, Gera! Somebody important, somebody powerful! I was on my way up in the financial world. And then I was called back home, to fulfill my duties as heir to the throne." He spat the words out, his voice filled with hatred.

Billy Boy broke it with a snide, "Hey, Dad, does that mean I'm next in line?"

"Shut up. Get ready, I've almost got it now."

She couldn't allow him to concentrate. "So you heard about the hidden hoards of gold and decided to find them for yourself. How's that going for you, Grant?" she goaded. The more flustered he became, the less accurate he would be.

Or not.

On the next try, she heard his triumphant gloat. "See? Your old man's still got it," he told his son.

"Yeah, yeah, just hoist me up."

"You see, Gera," Grant continued, "if you want to make a plan work, you have to be committed to it. Dedication is the key to success. I've been working on this for the better part of a decade. The gold is my way off this mountain. When I get my hands on the gold, I won't need my trust any longer, or the bank. I will be free to go back to the life I deserve."

"To hell, in other words," she said sardonically.

He took no offense at her words. He merely gave a flat laugh. "Ah, but that's where I've been, my dear, for the past ten years."

Gera's foot found another rotted board. This time, she wasn't quick enough to save herself. Her leg plunged through the soft spot in the wood, sinking her all the way to her knee. She struggled to free herself. She looked back over her shoulder, just as Billy Boy Macandie pushed through the opening from below.

Stovepipe hat and all, he burst through with flailing arms, splintering the pieces of wood all around him as if they were nothing more than matchsticks.

For one crazy moment, Gera watched in something oddly akin to admiration. *He makes it look so easy,* she thought in awe. *Took me twice as long and a dozen splinters in my hands to break less than half as much away.*

She quickly shook the thoughts away. She had no right to admire him, not when he was here to kill her. She was still trapped, caught here like a sitting duck.

Not only was Billy Boy not as light nor as graceful as Gera, but it was also not as smart. He paid no heed to rotting boards or weakened floor joists. He barreled forward, intent on getting his hands around her neck.

Maybe he wouldn't wait for a coin toss. Maybe he would kill her himself, right here, before his father ever had the chance. Gera caught a flash of moonlight on that despicable ring as Macandie's tongue darted in and out like a snake, saw the evil glimmer in his eyes, just as she felt the first tremor.

At first, she thought it was just her, shivering with fright.

Then she felt the shift.

Felt the boards around her list to one side.

Saw Billy Boy's eyes widen.

First in surprise, then in realization.

But it was too late. The added weight of his body with hers was too much for the old floor to support. There was a great groan from the floor joists, and then, with no other warning, the floor began to fall, folding in upon itself.

What happened next was hard to explain. Later, Gera wouldn't be able to say exactly how it happened. Even what happened.

Her leg was trapped. She was on her way down, a horrific fall of at least twenty feet. By some cruel twist of fate, the floor tilted her way, spilling Billy Boy right upon her. If he didn't strangle her with his grappling hands or the tails of his long coat which somehow whipped around her throat, his weight might very well smother her.

She was destined to die, tangled up like a snake with this vile man.

And yet, she didn't.

She didn't die. And she didn't get tangled up with him.

She didn't even fall.

From out of nowhere, Gera saw a shadow. It was tall and lean, and wore a steep hat.

From out of nowhere, gentle hands freed her leg, and delivered her safely to the floor below.

Not the broken, rotted heap that was once the second story floor. Not the twist and tangle of boards and pipe and sharp, rusted nails. Not the whole of the mess, which plunged straight toward an unsuspecting Grant Young.

Gera was delivered, instead, to the plaza floor. She felt the press of cold coins into her skin, as she was settled with great care upon the floor of the would-be wishing well.

There was no explanation for it. No *reasonable* explanation.

She looked up, dazed, in time to see another inexplicable sight. Billy Boy Macandie fell through the air, riding a rotted board to his death. He unceremoniously flapped his arms and grabbed for something, anything, that might stop this terrible fate from happening. The tails of his long coat flew in the wind behind him, the stovepipe hat lifted from his lopsided haircut and came back down again with an undignified plop.

The shadow appeared again, almost a mirror image of the man falling through empty space. The shadow, however, had a certain grace about him, even with his stovepipe hat sitting at a distinct angle.

The shadow rammed itself into Macandie, with enough force to knock the man back up through the air, and with enough force to slam him against the brick wall. The brick wall studded with the sharp, jagged edges of broken pipes and splintered iron and thick, pointed spikes.

Gera didn't see the gory details of how it happened, but she knew. She knew that Billy Boy Macandie was dead, pierced against the wall by a shadow that had saved her life.

She heard Grant moan from beneath the rubble, calling for help, at the same time that she heard Jake's voice. The walls were still crumbling, falling like dominoes in slow motion, stirring up a hundred years' worth of dust and dirt. Jake ran through the gritty filth of history destroyed, frantically calling her name.

Her own Superman to the rescue.

"Here, Jake," she called weakly. She lifted her hand, blood running down her arm, as she waved to him. "Out here. I'm safe."

Jake swooped her into his arms. Miles Anderson was fast on his heels, with Mike Cooper not far behind.

They all bombarded her with questions, all at the same time.

"Are you all right? Babe, you're bleeding!"

"What's this about? Where's Young?"

"Did he hurt you? Is he armed?"

She answered in reverse order, answering Cooper's question first. "I—I don't think he's armed, but he is dangerous. He and Billy Boy Macandie were in on this together. They posed as Mac and committed the string of crimes, to set up the perfect murder. They killed Abe, and—and others, too." She couldn't break it to Jake this way, not here, telling him that his beloved grandmother had died at the hands of the madman. She touched his face, inadvertently smearing a bit of blood onto his cheek. "Yes, I'm fine. It's just a little blood. It washes off."

"Help me!" Grant called from behind the brick wall. His voice was stronger now, and filled with more outrage than pain. "My leg is trapped! I think it may be crushed."

"Won't matter, Young, not where you're going," the police chief said in a matter-of-fact voice. He seemed in no particular hurry as he and his deputy ambled toward the destruction.

"Jake—"

"Shh, babe, don't talk. Just tell me again that you're okay. There's blood all over your back, and your arm, and your fingers." He touched each one carefully, cataloging her injuries.

"I am. I'm okay, Jake."

It didn't take long to pull the banker from the rotten heap. He came out limping heavily, his normally meticulous outfit now filthy and torn, his shaved head ringed with dust and splintered wood. He leaned heavily into the men on either side of him, holding him up, but he played out his innocence, right to the end. He had no qualms of turning on his biological child.

"It was Macandie! That derelict kid did all this! He killed Abe, and tried to kill me. Hit poor Gera there on the head. She's been babbling out of her mind. You should call her an ambulance." Quite the actor, he shot her a look of concern, even after everything that had happened.

"He's lying," Gera said. "There's some legend about hidden gold, here on the mountain. He wanted to own as much of Cleopatra Hill as he could, especially Abe Cunningham's place, *The Dove*, and that old house in between."

"I know all about the legend of the hidden gold. I grew up here, you know. Done a little research on it, myself," Anderson said smoothly. "And we know he's lying. Young, you should be more careful with your cell phone. Turns out, you left a very long and detailed message on my answering machine. A taped confession, before I even get the pleasure of arresting you."

"That—That's impossible!" Grant insisted, but his face lost all color. "My cell phone was off. I made certain of it."

Miles Anderson shrugged. "Well, somehow it turned itself on and dialed my number. Somehow it recorded your conversation, starting with you saying how cold it was." The chief swiped the back of his hand against his brow, slinging away a fine sheen of sweat. He stared at the injured man, one side of his handlebar mustache lifting in a sneer. "If I didn't know better, I'd say a ghost may have turned your phone on."

In spite of herself, Gera made a bit of a strangling noise. The men looked at her in concern, but she waved away their worry.

"By the way, where is Macandie? Did he get away?" Cooper asked.

Gera shook her head. She didn't need to see it again. The image would be burned into her mind for months to come. She pointed her hand in the general direction, and buried her face in Jake's neck.

"It's over now, babe," he whispered, rocking her slowly back and forth. "It's okay. Let's get you home."

24

I t had been three days, two visits to the police station, and one trip to the emergency room since the ordeal at *The Bartlett.*

Gera had finally slept.

She thought that a full night's sleep would do her good. Thought it would clear the cobwebs from her mind. That it would explain the shadows that lingered in her head and distorted the details from that night.

She hadn't told Jake yet, not about the shadow she thought she had seen that night. How could she? How could she explain it to someone else, when she couldn't explain it to herself?

There had to be a logical explanation for what happened, for what she saw, but Gera hadn't found it yet.

The official police report listed Billy Boy Macandie's death as a freak accident, the unfortunate result of being caught in a collapsing structure. Force of gravity somehow slung his body against the wall, resulting in impalement. The same gravity that killed one person delivered another safely to the ground, unscathed in the fall. The theory wouldn't hold up under close scrutiny—most notably, the impalement was vertical, not horizontal—but who would question it? The only person to mourn Billy Boy's death was his mother, and she was hardly surprised to hear of his untimely end.

As for what Gera saw that night? It had been an optical illusion. A play on light and shadow, causing an unexplained mirror image of Billy Boy's silhouette as he masqueraded as Mac's ghost. Heightened, of course, by nerves and an intense fear for her own personal safety.

It was the only explanation she could accept, for the alternative was impossible.

Gera didn't believe in ghosts.

And while she appreciated Jake's unwavering support, he had hovered over her the past three days, stifling her with his constant concern. Was she comfortable? Did she need another pillow? Could he rub her back, or her feet, or draw her a hot, soaking bath? His intentions were good, his administrations sweet and noble, but she needed space to breathe. Space to put things into perspective.

The best place to think, to breathe, was the mountainside terrace. She had been cooped up long enough.

It was a glorious day, beautiful and sunny, and the view from here was always incredible. Gera found her favorite table among the flowering gardens and sat down with her morning coffee.

Gera mulled the facts of that night over in her head, but it always came down to one thing.

I don't believe in ghosts.
No, seriously, I don't.

She ignored the waver in her own convictions, no matter how insubstantial it might be.

It was quite some time later when she heard Minnie's voice and knew her friend had once again sneaked into the garden without her even knowing it.

"Hello, dear."

No longer surprised by the old woman's appearance, Gera smiled. "How do you do that? I never even hear you come up."

"You were deep in thought," Minnie explained. Her pale face wrinkled in concern, and her intensely blue eyes zeroed in on Gera's face. "I understand you've had quite the ordeal of late."

Gera released a mighty sigh. "You could say that."

"But you got your story, dear. And what a fantastic one it was!"

"You were right, Minnie, about the hidden hoards of gold, or at least the rumor thereof. Publicly, all the police are saying is that Grant had a scheme to own prime property here upon the mountain."

"But he was really after the hidden hoards." It was a statement, not a question.

"That won't be mentioned in my article," she assured her friend. "Don't worry, I remember what you told me, about there being more at stake than just selling an article. That whole lives, and family legacies, could be destroyed if the rumors were encouraged to spread. And you were right."

Gera heaved another sigh. "Did you know he started by killing the man next door? He started this whole crazy, evil scheme almost ten years ago, by smothering the poor man in his sleep. The bank got the title to the house and he started digging up the yard, looking for the gold. And then he pushed the owner of this very hotel to her death, thinking he could do the same here. Honestly, I don't know how Abe and Ruth managed to escape the death toll until now. Did you know them, by the way? The man next door and Minerva Cody?"

"Oh, quite well, my dear," Minnie replied.

"Her grandson runs the hotel now. We're... involved." Gera stared off into the distance, studying the magnificent canyons along the valley floor. She confided in the old woman, as much as she admitted to her own self, "I could fancy myself in love with him, but... how? I've known him barely over a week."

"Ah, Jake is a good man. Handsome, too, like his father, and his father before him. There is something quite special about those Cody men. They're men of integrity. You would be lucky to have a man like that in your life, Gera dear."

"I know, but... he would want to stay here, on this mountain, keeping his family legacy for perpetuity. I have a career. Out there." She waved her arm to the wide expanse of space beyond Mingus Mountain.

"You make it sound as if they're two separate worlds. You're a writer. You already travel as it is," Minnie pointed out. "You use Ogle and that fancy web engine thing to do your work. Those things work up here, just like they do out there. All that would change is your home base." When Gera looked at her, the old woman added, "And whether or not you had someone to share it with."

Hope tiptoed its way into Gera's heart. A light of possibility crept into her eyes. Skittered away. Edged its way back in again. Dared to stay.

"Maybe," she allowed.

"You would be good for him."

They fell silent, each lost to their own musings. After a long moment, Minnie spoke.

"He was looking in the wrong places, you know." A confidential tone wrapped her quiet words.

"Who?"

"Grant Young. He was looking for buried treasure, hidden out of sight, when in actuality, it was right here for all the world to see."

Normally, Gera wasn't philosophical. The girl who punched bullies in the nose and never backed away from a story preferred to work with facts, not the abstract. But Minnie's earlier words stirred something within her. It made her think of her father, and the way he still loved her mother, even to this day. It made her think of family, and Jake's commitment to his family's legacy. Made her think of the way he still felt a spiritual connection to his grandmother. And it made her think of her own dear Grams.

"Yes," Gera agreed softly. "Love and family are the greatest treasures of all."

"So true," Minnie smiled, her eyes indulgent, "but that isn't what I meant."

"Oh?" She waited for her friend to elaborate.

"You know, Gera, sometimes all that glitters truly is gold."

Gera's forehead creased in confusion. Before she could decipher the cryptic words, a commotion from the opposite direction drew her attention. Gera turned to see Lucy waddling up the staggered steps of the patio, huffing and jiggling her way toward them. Her black face split into a pleased smile.

"There you are, pretty girl! And Nerva, too!" She stopped at the top step to rest and catch her wind. "I'll call for tea. We can have ourselves a nice little visit, just the three of us."

"Wait. Nerva?" Gera asked, the crease growing deeper. "But that's what you call Jake's grandmother."

"Yes, Missy, that's right."

"But… this is Minnie," Gera said, motioning to her garden companion.

Minnie was the one to answer. "Yes."

Gera stared at her pale, wispy friend. The one who sat beneath the glint of sunlight, her white curls glowing around her head like a halo. The one whose skin was so puffy and paper-thin it was practically see through. The one who came and went without making a noise. The one who told stories of the past as if she had been there to witness them herself.

"She called you Nerva," she whispered.

"Yes, dear."

"But that's what she called Minerva Cody."

"Yes."

Both women watched as the color faded from Gera's face. As the wheels began to turn in her mind. As realization flooded over her.

"What's wrong, Gera girl?" Lucy boomed, her massive bosom jiggling with laughter. "You look like you've just seen a ghost!"

"Lucy, don't tease the girl," Minnie chided softly. "Give her time to adjust."

"But—But…" It was all Gera could say. All her mind could formulate. She finally managed a strangled, "But Jake's grandmother died eight years ago."

This time when her friend answered, there was a great sadness in her voice. "Yes."

"This—This can't be happening," Gera whispered. "This can't be real." Her voice rose with accusation. "*You* can't be real."

"Well, now, there's the problem, isn't it?" Minnie gave her that smile again, the one where she looked like a child with her hand caught in the cookie jar.

"But… I can see you! Lucy sees you. She talks with you, has tea with you." Gera looked at the old black woman for confirmation, daring her to contradict the claim.

"Well, mostly it's just me having the tea," Lucy chuckled. She pulled out a chair and lowered her hefty body into it. "I eat all the cookies, too," she confessed.

Panic set in. Gera placed her hands over her mouth as she practiced deep-breathing techniques. Slow and steady. One breath in, one breath out. One breath in, one crazy thought pushed out. Another breath in, another impossible notion out.

These women asked her to believe the impossible. To not only believe it, but to embrace it.

"Jake has turned into a fine young man," Minnie continued. Her pale face glowed with pride. "I'm so proud of him. Sometimes I can't help but put my arms around him and just give him a great big old hug." She put her arms around her own shoulders and mimicked the motion, a dreamy expression upon her face. The look clouded as she lamented, "I just wish he could feel it."

"He does," Gera mumbled, in somewhat of a trance. "He gets a warm feeling wash over him, and for no reason at all, he thinks of his grandmother."

A delighted smile touched the old woman's face. "He always called me MiniMa."

"Yes." But Gera shook her head, still trying to process it all. "How can this be?" she cried.

"Haven't you ever wondered, dear, how I can appear and disappear, almost out of the blue?"

"I—I just…" She broke off, finishing with an honest, "Yes."

"I can't always control my energy levels, or my energy sources. When I feel myself fading, I have to make a hasty exit."

"Her feet start tingling," Lucy offered. "Course, mine do too, but the doctors say that's the diabetes."

Ever the one for analytical explanation, Gera studied Minnie's position upon the bench. The old woman always sat directly beneath the sun's beam. "The metal bench is a conductor of energy," Gera realized.

"Yes. And the warmth feels divine." That dreamy expression flooded Minnie's eyes again. "That's one of the things I miss the most about life, you know. Warmth."

"That's why no one else ever saw you," Gera continued. Her voice was still dazed. "I asked about you, but no one ever knew who I was talking about. Lucy is the only one who can see you."

"Lucy believes."

"Then… then why can *I* see you?" Gera asked. "I'm not a believer."

"Really, dear?" Minnie challenged softly. "After all that has happened, you still don't believe?"

She shook her head. "I—I can't. It's not…" Her voice fell to a whisper. "I just can't."

"Remember what I told you, Gera, that not everything in life can be explained. Can you explain to me, for instance, what it is you feel for my grandson?"

She would try, if it meant proving her point. "I guess I feel like he completes me. He doesn't change me, or take away from me, but he makes me a better person as a whole."

"That's *why* you feel the way you do. But how do you *feel?*"

"I—I can't explain it. I just know it, here." She put a hand over her gut.

"So you just *know*, without logical reason, that you're in love with my grandson."

"Yes," Gera admitted weakly, defeated on so many levels.

The two old women cackled with glee. Lucy's bosom jiggled again. Minnie clasped her bent fingers together, but Gera noticed her hands didn't quite meet. They actually seemed to pass through one another, but that was impossible, of course.

Wasn't it?

"That day in the hall," Gera said suddenly. "Why did you push me?"

"Push you? I would never—" Minnie broke off with a frown. "Penelope," she huffed. "She promised me she would behave. I swear, sometimes that woman is more difficult to deal with than the children! I'll speak with her, dear, so this sort of thing never happens again."

"The children?" Gera whispered. "The babies are real?"

Lucy bobbed her head, causing her great bosom to shimmy. "We told Jake, the crying wasn't our doings. Poor Nerva here plumb lost her voice one night, soothing those poor babies with song."

Realization dawned in Gera's gray eyes. "The morning you couldn't quite 'pull yourself together,'" she mumbled.

Minnie's smile was apologetic. "It takes quite a bit of energy, you know, to make oneself visible. That morning, I was so tuckered out I simply couldn't do it."

Gera massaged her temples. "None of this makes any sense!" she wailed. "I must be dreaming. I'm dreaming, right? I just think I'm here in the garden, talking to a ghost. I'll wake up and be back in Jake's bed, safe and *sane*."

Lucy reached out a beefy hand and gave Gera a solid thump on her arm.

"Ouch! What did you do that for?"

"This ain't no dream, pretty girl. Now pay attention. There are things Nerva needs to tell you."

"It's true," Minnie said. "I don't know how much longer I'll have, and there are things you must know."

"You—You're leaving?" Gera was strangely distraught at the thought.

"I'm not sure, dear. My death has been avenged. I no longer have to worry about my grandson, living his life here alone on the mountain and never knowing true love. My unfinished business is almost done."

Minnie glanced up at the sun. She shifted slightly, so that she remained beneath the direct beam of her energy source. Folding her curled fingers upon her lap, she continued. "Now, where were we? Oh yes, keeping our family's legacy intact. You and Jake are a fine match, my dear. You'll do just fine."

The old woman's candid assumptions unnerved Gera. She had difficulty articulating a response. "We're not... we haven't talked about the future, not really. I don't even know if he... I mean, I didn't even know *I* did, until just now."

"If he loves you? Of course he does! As for the future, *The Dove* will be handed down through a trust, so that it will always remain in our family. It is very important, you know, that the hotel stay intact. Our legacy is in the very fabric of the hotel itself. Do you remember the story I told you, dear, of the ashes and the metal?"

Gera recoiled. "Please don't tell me—"

"No, dear, not in the way you're thinking. But did I ever tell you the story of my father, the metalsmith? Did you know that once upon a time, Richard Luna, Eli Cunningham, and Cecil Thurman commissioned him to create great works of art for them?"

"No, I don't think so," she murmured. But the names were familiar. She had heard them that night at *The Bartlett*, during Grant Young's tyrannical rant. *All three were executives at the mines, and all three lived way up high on Cleopatra Hill, all in a row.* According to Grant's version of the legend, they were the men responsible for burying the hoard of gold. Gold that was but a by-product when mining for copper.

She felt overwhelmed again. Her mind felt as if it might explode.

While Gera resumed her breathing exercises, Minnie watched anxiously from the bench. Lucy offered support by way of an encouraging pat.

Jake's voice floated out to the terrace, concern lacing his words. "Gera? Babe, you out here?"

"I must go," Minnie said. A new urgency moved into her voice. "Remember the things we've talked about. Remember to keep the family legacy intact."

"But—"

"Gera?" Jake called again, this time louder.

Minnie's smile was tender as she watched her grandson step from the doorway. "Ah, such a handsome man, my Jake. He looks so much like his father."

Gera followed the other woman's gaze. He was, indeed, handsome. Sudden emotion clogged her throat. "Up here, Jake," she replied.

She turned back to speak to her friend, but only Lucy's smiling face shone back at her. Minnie was already gone.

25

They had dinner on Jake's private balcony. He grilled fish that was tender and flaky, and topped it with a sauce that was, he told her, his MiniMa's recipe. Gera microwaved potatoes that were neither wrinkled nor crusty. It was the height of her culinary skills. Her head-on approach to cooking was to eat out as often as possible.

"Feeling better after your nap this afternoon?" Jake wanted to know.

Without telling a direct lie, she gave the impression of answering in the affirmative. "Your bed is very comfortable."

The truth was that her mind had churned too fast and too tumultuously to allow her even a wink of sleep. On the upside, for the first time in three days, she had closed her eyes without seeing that fateful night replaying in her head. On the downside, it was now Minnie's face that haunted her.

Haunted. The word whispered through her mind.

Jake was still concerned. "When I walked into the garden, you looked unusually pale."

"It's been an unusual past few days."

"Are all the stories you report this crazy?"

"Hardly! If they were, I'd be looking for another profession."

"Has that ever occurred to you? Looking for another profession, I mean."

"It's all I've ever wanted to be," she answered honestly. "What about you? I know you worked security in Vegas before you came back here, but did you ever have dreams of becoming something other than a hotel mogul?"

He laughed at her choice of words. "I'd hardly call myself a mogul. And yeah, I thought about doing other things, but it turned out I was good at security, so that's what I did. But it was only to fill the time. With my father dying so young, I knew I would end up here, sooner rather than later, running *The Dove*. It is my family's legacy, after all."

Yes, Minnie spoke all about that legacy.

Gera's drama teacher would be very proud. She managed now to sound quite casual, even as her heart rate kicked up a notch. "You know," Gera said, "I realized today that I've never seen a picture of your grandparents. Why isn't there a portrait of them here at the hotel, like there is of Richard and Cordelia Luna?"

"Actually, their portrait is being restored at the moment. It normally hangs above the dining room fireplace, between those fancy copper sconces."

"Do you have any pictures of them? I'd like to see them."

If he wondered about her sudden curiosity in his family, he said nothing. "Sure. I have a family album in the living room."

Jake returned with a thick photo album and two bowls, filled with dessert.

"You cheated," Gera accused, recognizing the bread pudding from the hotel restaurant. Her eyes crinkled in the corners. "Did I ever tell you I liked that in a man, particularly when it comes to matters of dessert?"

"I'll keep that in mind," he laughed. He sat beside her and opened the book. "These are my grandparents, Minerva and Jacob Thomas Cody. Or, as they called each other, Minnie and JT."

The breath caught in Gera's lungs. Until now, she had clung to the stubborn notion that it had all been a dream. Despite Lucy's thump and the newest bruise upon her arm, she convinced herself that none of it was real. With one photograph, Jake had just destroyed her delusional claims.

That was definitely her friend Minnie, standing beside a man handsome enough to be Jake's double. She was much younger in the picture, but there was no mistaking that smile or the twinkle in her vivid blue eyes. Eyes that looked, Gera realized belatedly, a great deal like Jake's.

There were more photos, many of which Jake appeared in, first as an infant, then as a toddler, and eventually, at his college graduation. Minnie aged in the photos as well, her hair growing whiter and her body more bent and frail, until by the last of the album, she looked exactly like the woman Gera knew from the garden. Funny, but she hadn't aged a day since then.

But then, she wouldn't, would she? Gera reasoned.

Perhaps *reasoned* wasn't the right word. Nothing about this was reasonable or rational or even remotely sane.

"Is that why you called her MiniMa, because your grandfather called her Minnie?" she guessed.

"Yes, exactly."

Gera continued scouring the album. These were photos of when the couple first opened for business. Hairstyles had definitely changed through the years. There was Minnie presenting a tray of baked delights, and Jacob greeting a guest. This one showed both of Jake's grandparents and the custom-built check-in counter. Jacob smiled from behind the desk, while Minnie stood in front, fanning her hands in presentation. The shiny copper inlay glittered in the camera's flash, winking back as if it knew a grand secret.

It hit her with staggering force.

Pieces of the puzzle swirled in Gera's head. Scattered conversations. Random bits of knowledge. Flashes of intuition. The pieces fell smartly into place, locking into a nice, tight pattern.

This house has more than its share of secrets.

I learned from an early age that there are some things in The Dove that can never be discarded.

Our legacy is in the very fabric of the hotel itself.

The Great Gold Conspiracy of Executive Order 6102.

There is more at stake here than merely selling an article.

Knowledge is power.

Did I ever tell you the story of my father the metalsmith?

He was looking for buried treasure, hidden out of sight, when in actuality, it was right there for all the world to see.

Gera gasped as the realization hit her.

You know, Gera, sometimes all that glitters truly is gold.

"Gera?" Jake's voice was warm with concern. "Babe? Are you okay?"

"I—uhm, yes. I—I'm fine."

"No offense, but you don't look fine. You look like you've seen a ghost."

Funny you should say that, her mind smirked.

She shook away the distraction. Her voice came out on a squeak. "You said your great-grandfather made this piece on the front desk?"

"Yes, that's right. For Richard Luna, back in the day."

"It's very intricate. I noticed it matches some of the other pieces around the hotel. The scrollwork around the front door, the carvings in the elevator. The sconces by the fireplace."

"They say he was a very talented metalsmith," Jake agreed, but his eyes skittered away from hers.

"I notice they're quite shiny, too."

"We hand buff them."

Something about his casual tone was just a bit too casual.

"It's true!" Her whispered words were slightly incredulous.

A long second ticked between them. Jake glanced at her intelligent eyes. Glanced away, just as quickly. "What's true?"

She kept her words whispered. They were outside, after all, no matter how high they were from the rest of the world. "The legend. Executive Order 6102."

"That was no legend. That truly happened."

"It's okay, Jake," she assured him, slipping her hand into his. "Your secret is safe with me. I would never tell."

This time, when his eyes met hers, they clung. "How did you figure it out?" he asked softly.

"Sometimes, all that glitters really *is* gold." She repeated Minnie's words softly, a smile playing on her lips as she fully understood them.

"Funny, that's exactly what MiniMa said to me when I was just a kid. It took me several years to figure out what she was talking about." He noticed how pale she had become. "Gera?"

"I—I'm okay."

"You're exhausted." His voice turned firm. "Why don't you go to bed? I'll clean all this up."

"No, I can help."

"I got this. You go up and get ready for bed."

"You'll come soon?"

"Yes, but don't wait for me. You need your rest."

As Gera climbed the spiral staircase to his bedroom, she noted that her muscles were loosening at last. It no longer hurt to raise her arms above her head or to bend her knees. Her scrapes and cuts had scabbed over, and her bruises were in various stages of fading. The place on her neck was gone. The scars on her memory were all that remained.

Gera dressed for bed, but she didn't crawl into it. Instead, she turned out the lights and curled up on the couch, staring out at the dark valley below.

"Gera? What are you doing, babe? Can't sleep?"

"Just thinking."

"I don't have a penny, but I can give you a raincheck," Jake offered with a smile. "Is this seat taken?"

She moved her feet aside so that he could sit. She leaned into him, breathing in his scent.

"What's bothering you tonight, babe?"

He already knew her so well.

Her smile was bittersweet. "When I came here ten days ago, I thought this was the strangest town I had ever seen. Buildings stacked against the mountain, everything built on a grade, everything in layers. And then to learn that most everyone here believed in ghosts, or at least in the possibility of a tangible spirit, staying behind after death." Her snort was nothing if not honest. "I thought everyone in this town was crazy, and I couldn't wait to leave."

She turned her face so that she could look at him. "I hadn't wanted to come, and I couldn't wait to leave. Now here it is ten days later, and in spite of everything that has transpired, I don't want to go."

"Then don't."

Her reply was sad. "I have to."

"Why?"

"Because—" She suddenly couldn't think of a single logical reason.

"Before you say anything, there are two things I want to tell you."

"I'm listening."

"You know that old Hermann building, the one that wore a cute little red Mazda cap for a couple of days?"

She wrinkled her nose at him. "I know the one."

"It houses the local newspaper. You know, the one that comes out once a week and provides vital information to the town, like what movie is playing down in Cottonwood and what vegetables and flowers grow best in dry, arid soil that clings to the side of a mountain?"

Another wrinkle. He referred to a conversation in which she had poked fun at the local rag. "I read a copy once, front to back," she said airily. She bumped her shoulder into his, unable to resist a playful barb. "Took me all of four minutes, and that's because I stopped to do the crossword puzzle."

"Well, it turns out the current owner of the paper is ready to retire, and his kids don't want it. He's thinking of putting the whole thing up for sale, including the building. The car on the roof was the final straw. Said he didn't need the aggravation and would rather spend his days on a golf course."

"Oops."

"He mentioned a very reasonable price, given the circulation the paper has. Did you know he has readers all over the world? He says that when people come to visit our sleepy little town, they want to take a remembrance back with them, or keep up with our calendar of events. That often includes a subscription to the local paper. Digital subscriptions have soared in the last five years, but he says he's getting too old to keep up with the changing technology."

The breath stalled in her lungs. "What—What are you saying, Jake?" she asked breathlessly.

"I know you have your heart set on the front cover of a magazine, but what if you could see your words on the front cover of a newspaper, every single week? A newspaper with worldwide readership, where you were able to pick and choose—and write—whatever you wanted?"

"It would be a reporter's dream," she murmured.

"I have a little money set aside, Gera. I've been looking for a solid investment. But the thing is, I don't know the first thing about running a newspaper. Or about writing for one. I couldn't sink that kind of money into something, without knowing I had a partner to run things on that end. So, I was wondering... do you know anyone who might be interested?"

Gera looked into his hopeful face, noting the brightest of his blue eyes. "I might know someone," she said, keeping her expression solemn. She blinked a time or two, but his gaze remained steady. A smile teased the corners of her mouth. "So, you're into investments, huh? Did I ever tell you I like that in a man, too?"

"No, but it bears noting." He kept his tone light, but the look in his eyes deepened.

That look stole Gera's breath away. Robbed it right from her lungs and held it hostage.

She wanted to know what inspired the look. Head on, Gera bluntly asked, "The other thing you wanted to tell me?"

"I know this may sound a little out there, since we've only known each other ten days. But sometimes you just know when it's right. And I've always considered myself a good judge of character."

"So did I," Gera muttered derisively, rolling her eyes, "until this whole Grant Young debacle."

"Stay with me here, Gera. I'm trying to tell you something very important."

She was already smiling. "Then say it, already."

"I think I'm in love with you."

"You *think*?" she challenged in mock insult.

With a firm finger, Jake pushed his glasses up on his nose and corrected himself. "I love you, Gera."

"Good. Because I love you too, SuperClark."

"Should we seal it with a kiss or something?"

"Or something," she agreed, winding her arms around his neck.

Later, after they had sealed their declaration of love with exhausting and exhilarating thoroughness, Gera lay content in his arms, gazing out the window at the vast valley far, far below. She wouldn't have to leave it behind, after all, except for short periods at a time.

Odd, how much pleasure that thought brought to her.

"Jake?" she murmured softly.

"Yeah?" He was almost asleep.

"She loved you so much, you know. And she is so proud of the man you've become."

"You mean MiniMa?"

"Yes. There's something else I want to tell you, too, but it can wait. Remind me one day to tell you."

"I'll try," he mumbled. "What's it about?"

"Oh, just something I learned today in the garden."

"Sure, babe," he said groggily. "Love you."

Gera smiled, snuggling down into his arms.

Just ten short days ago, she didn't believe in ghosts. Dead, after all, was dead.

Maybe she still didn't believe. Maybe she was beginning to. Maybe, just maybe, she did believe now. But it didn't matter, because Gera now knew something else.

Dead was dead, except when it came to love. And love alone had the power to outlast death.

It was a hauntingly beautiful sentiment to carry with her as she drifted off to sleep, tucked safely upon the staggered heights of Cleopatra Hill, and its sleeping village of ghosts.

Thank you for reading! I hope you've enjoyed my tale.

If so, I would appreciate you leaving a brief review on Amazon. It may seem insignificant to you, but for authors, reviews are an invaluable asset. Reviews give our work merit, visibility, and better placement on Amazon pages. Reviews help other readers know if a story is right for them, and help authors know what worked and what didn't.

You may contact me directly at beckiwillis.ccp@gmail.com, follow me on Facebook and Twitter, and read about my other works by visiting www.beckiwillis.com.

Again, thank you so much for spending this time with me in Jerome. Happy Reading, everyone!

Thanks!,

Becki

Made in the USA
San Bernardino, CA
13 May 2017